Carl Weber Presents

Curtis Duncan, Bounty Hunter

Carl Weber Presents

Curtis Duncan, Bounty Hunter

Ben Stephens and La Jill Hunt

URBAN
BOOKS

www.urbanbooks.net

Urban Books, LLC
300 Farmingdale Road, N.Y.-Route 109
Farmingdale, NY 11735

Carl Weber Presents: Curtis Duncan, Bounty Hunter

Based on characters from the Family Business series by Carl Weber

ISBN 13: 978-1-64556-778-3
EBOOK ISBN: 978-1-64556-779-0

First Trade Paperback Printing January 2026
Printed in the United States of America

10 9 8 7 6 5 4 3 2 1

Distributed by Kensington Publishing Corp.
Submit Orders to:
Customer Service
400 Hahn Road
Westminster, MD 21157-4627
Phone: 1-800-733-3000
Fax: 1-800-659-2436

The authorized representative in the EU for product safety and
compliance
Is eucomply OU, Parnu mnt 139b-14, Apt 123
Tallinn, Berlin 11317, hello@eucompliancepartner.com

Carl Weber Presents

Curtis Duncan, Bounty Hunter

by:

Ben Stephens and La Jill Hunt

Prologue

Curtis

The bass inside the Sanctuary nightclub in the ATL hit differently. It didn't just vibrate through the speakers. The music pulsed through my chest, syncing with my heartbeat, letting me know I was alive. Neon lights—electric blue, fiery red, neon green, and bright yellow LED beams—bounced off the polished dance floor, casting vibrant colors across the crowd. I sat in the back, tucked away at a table, sipping a glass of my favorite drink: 1868 Uncle Nearest premium whiskey. The taste was smooth and strong, just like me. Unlike the other clubgoers, I wasn't there to party. I was there to hunt.

To the rest of the club, I was just another guy taking in the scene, but my eyes were scanning every face that passed by. I was not there for the music, the women, or the overpriced bottle service. I was there for one reason: Carlos Garcia. Carlos was a ghost. The FBI's Top 10 kind of ghost. A smooth-talking, security-system-hacking, alias-switching son of a bitch who made millions robbing the world's most luxurious jewelry stores from Fifth Avenue in New York City to boutique shops on Rodeo Drive in Beverly Hills. Every time the feds thought they had him, he disappeared without a trace. But tonight would be different. I could feel it in my soul.

Spotting him in this crowd was like finding a needle in a haystack, but unlike most bounty hunters, I wouldn't miss. I sat still, ignoring all the sexy-ass women throwing glances my way, and remained patient. That's the thing about being a hunter: you wait, watch, and strike when the time is right. Then, I saw him, standing over the top balcony in the VIP section, holding a bottle of Moët with a couple of honey dips by his side. Fresh cut, designer Versace outfit with about $50,000 worth of ice that draped his neck and wrist. I've never been a hater, so I had to give him his props. He was moving like a Duncan— but he had no idea that the designer shit he had on was about to be replaced with an orange jumpsuit.

I slowly stood to my feet, crouching like a black panther, making sure my moves were smooth and deliberate. I slipped into the crowd behind him, close enough to watch, but far enough so as not to alarm him. One thing I hate are runners, and I was not about to let this bastard take off on me. But just as I was closing in, our eyes locked, and it was a wrap. A flash of recognition lit up his face, and then it turned to fear. He bolted.

"Fuck!" Cursing under my breath, I took off after him. The club became a blur of bodies, light, and heat as I chased him through the packed dance floor. The reggaeton blasting from the speakers faded into background noise.

Carlos crashed through the back doors and into the alley behind the club. The scenery instantly shifted from flashing lights to the gritty, dark street and sirens howling in the distance. I spotted him trying to blend in with a group of partygoers outside, but I was already on him. When he turned to run again, it was too late. With one clean shot, I punched him in the jaw. The punch landed so hard, I swear Mike Tyson would've been proud. Carlos dropped like a sack of bricks, his body folding into the pavement with a groan. He was down, and while the party inside Sanctuary continued, nobody had a clue what had just gone down outside in the alley. A feeling of quiet satisfaction settled into my chest. My job was done. Another name crossed off the list, another bounty captured.

Ten minutes later, red and blue lights painted the night as cruisers pulled up to the scene. The sound of reggaeton still drifted faintly from the club, clashing with the static of police scanners. I was standing in the midst of it, calm, my heartbeat finally easing back to normal, when Detective Marcia Mitchell walked over with her smooth, brown cinnamon skin and dark eyes that could read you like scripture. She was a beauty who made men trip over their tongues. Her badge gleamed under the streetlight, and even though she was all business, the fire between us was simmering.

"Thanks for your help. You really saved my ass tonight," she said, her voice low and steady.

I shrugged. "Just doing my job."

A slow, flirtatious smile crept across her face. "You know, I could use a skilled bounty hunter like you more often."

"We make a good team," I told her, spotting exactly what I was looking for: the spark, the sexual tension that was right there in front of me, lingering in the air.

She stepped closer, eyes locked on mine, her smile bright enough to cut through a heavy cloud of fog. "We do indeed," she said. Then, she whispered softly so only I could hear, "But for now, let's keep it professional."

My disappointment flickered for a second, then I replied with a cool demeanor, "I respect that. I'm always a professional, Detective."

She slowly turned and walked back toward the crime scene, her silhouette glowing like a goddess under the flashing lights. I watched her go, my eyes taking in every curve of her body, knowing that our time was coming.

Being Curtis Duncan, "America's Baddest Bounty Hunter," came with weight. My name carried respect and fear in the streets. I never backed down. Not from danger. Not from threats. Not from anybody. My father, Larry Duncan, made sure I understood one thing growing up in Waycross, Georgia: Duncans don't run from shit. That mindset was instilled in me from damn near birth, and I live by that code to this day.

Chapter 1

Senator Richard Winbush

Café Milano always smelled like money and secrets. It was one of the few places in Georgetown where folks like me could talk without worrying about who was at the next table. The lighting was just dim enough to hide both wrinkles and wrongdoing, and the soft jazz floating through the air wasn't ambience. It was a cover that drowned out all the dirty little confessions whispered over crab cakes and champagne.

I sat in my usual corner booth, posture perfect like always. To the world, I was every bit the polished politician they'd elected year after year. Charcoal suit tailored sharp enough to cut glass, tie straight, and pocket square just right. Every morning, I dressed for success. I knew the look mattered, especially in D.C., where your image walks into a room ten seconds before you do. My smile never faltered. My handshake always hit with just the right amount of pressure, and it always instilled confidence. People trusted me, believed in me. Hell, half of them would take a bullet for me. To the world, I was the definition of integrity. But none of that had anything to do with who I really was.

Some of my opponents called me greedy. Others said I would do anything to hold onto power. They weren't wrong. But where they saw desperation, I saw discipline.

I'd survived because I don't let idealism get in the way of execution. I knew the game, and I played it better than most. That's why I surrounded myself with men like Scott Bowens. Strong men. Men who understood the cost of power.

"This place always makes me nervous," Bowens muttered, stirring sugar into his espresso like it was laced with explosives. "Too many ears. Too many eyes."

"That's exactly why I picked it," I said with a smile, leaning back in the booth. "People only hear what they want to believe in a place like this."

He looked like he wanted to argue, but he didn't. Scott was a dangerous man, but so was I.

Bowens wasn't sitting across from me because of his résumé. He got where he was by moving like a ghost in a warzone: quiet, deadly, and never leaving fingerprints. He looked like a public servant on the outside, but behind the scenes, the man was straight-up lethal. Half his rise came from secret deals and pressure applied in just the right places. The other half, from people mysteriously losing their careers—or their lives—when they crossed him.

A waitress in pearls and red lipstick brought over a basket of warm bread and kept it moving. No name tag. No small talk. Another reason I loved this place. Discretion was the house special. We didn't say anything until she disappeared.

"He's getting sloppy," Bowens said, voice low and tight.

"Sloppy don't even begin to cover it." I leaned in, resting my elbows on the white linen table. "He's out here moving like he's bulletproof. Flashy cars. Big parties. Talking loose to people who don't even have clearance to know his damn name."

"He thinks he's untouchable."

"And that," I said, lifting my wine glass just a little, "makes him a problem."

We didn't say Johnny Boy's name out loud. Not here. That name carried weight, and in D.C., walls have ears and favors come with high price tags. Jonathan Boykins, known in certain circles as Johnny Boy, was a Haitian kingpin who'd built an empire off drugs, blackmail, money laundering, and pure intimidation. He was dangerous, no doubt. He was also profitable. For a while, he'd made both of us a whole lot of money. But now, he was a threat to everything we'd built.

"Tomorrow's hearing," Bowens said, barely moving his lips, "we've got everything in place. Judge is solid. Prosecutor's ready. Media's been fed."

"All we need is the fall," I added.

We both knew what "fall" really meant. Johnny Boy was walking into that courtroom thinking we had his back. What he didn't know was that we were the ones pulling the rug out from under him. The moment that verdict dropped, he was either going behind bars for life or dying before he ever made it to his cell.

The waitress came back, refilled our water glasses. I flashed her a smile that could win an election and then watched her walk away.

Bowens shifted in his seat. "You ever feel bad, Rich?"

"Bad about what?"

"About setting up a man we did business with? Made money with?"

I didn't blink. "You ever see a lion apologize to the gazelle?"

He laughed, not because it was funny, but because that's what we did. We laughed to keep the truth from tasting too bitter.

"The second that verdict hits," I said, lowering my voice, "he's done. Expendable. Just another body in the dirt."

We didn't mention the real goal, not out loud. That wasn't for today's discussion. That was the end game.

"Tomorrow," I said, raising my glass.

Bowens clinked his lightly. "To power."

I smiled. "To survival."

In this town, they were one and the same. Johnny Boy was done. He just didn't know it yet. And when the dust cleared, everything he built would belong to us. That's how it works in Washington. You build empires and burn bridges. And if you're lucky, you live long enough to collect what's owed. But luck runs out. Tomorrow, Johnny Boy's would, too.

Chapter 2

Detective Marcia Mitchell

I never show up unannounced. Not at work or in life. I'm a planner by nature: steady, disciplined, precise. But with Curtis, all that structure goes out the window. I stood at his door, my pulse throbbing slowly in my ears. My fingers hovered for a beat before I knocked, two firm taps. While waiting quietly, I could hear the subtle click of movement. I knew that sound. Curtis never opened his door without checking the peephole first, never without his gun within reach. Years of bounty hunting had taught him to keep his instincts sharp and his trust minimal. In that way, we were very much alike.

I heard the low slide of a lock, and then the deadbolt disengaged. The door creaked open just slightly at first. Our eyes met, and the familiar sense of recognition melted away the tension that had been building in my chest as I waited at the door. He looked me over slowly, deliberately, his gaze like a hand sliding across every inch of me. His gray sweats hung from his hips like temptation itself. Standing in the doorway, barefoot and shirtless, the man looked like he was carved from stone, and I hated how easy it was for me to lose my control with him.

"Detective Mitchell," he said, his lips curving into a lazy grin. "This a social call?"

"Something like that."

I didn't wait for an invitation. Instead, I stepped inside, welcomed by the warmth of his penthouse. His place always impressed me, no matter how many times I'd been there. Marble floors that gleamed like glass, curated art pieces along the walls, and those massive floor-to-ceiling windows that showed off the Atlanta skyline like it was his own personal painting. Every inch of the space reflected who he was: refined, elegant, and quietly powerful.

Curtis closed the door behind me as I reached for the belt of my black Tom Ford trench coat, unknotting it slowly, letting the silk slide apart. His eyes focused on the newly exposed lingerie I wore: a deep wine-red lace that clung to every curve and dipped just low enough to leave no room for imagination. His stare was wide and hungry.

"You always know how to make an entrance," he murmured.

"I do my best," I whispered back.

The coat slipped from my shoulders in one fluid motion, falling to my feet. I stepped toward him, purposeful, one hand pressing lightly against his bare chest as I leaned in. My lips made their way to the tender spot just beneath his jaw. His skin was warm and smooth, the kind of skin you don't just touch, you memorize.

"I've been thinking about you all day," I whispered.

I felt his hardness against me. His eyes were now shut, confirming that my words had landed exactly how I wanted them to. Then came the moment we both knew was inevitable. Our mouths met in a kiss that was slow at first, exploratory, like we were reminding ourselves of one another. But it didn't last long. Passion emerged between us. He pulled me backward, guiding me further into the living room, his hands caressing my body as we made our way to the center of the room. Our connection always started like this: slow, tender, then fast and familiar. His lips moved to my neck, sucking and biting softly at the same time, causing even more heat between us.

Then, he lifted me effortlessly as I wrapped my legs around him. As he carried me toward the bedroom, the city skyline provided all the light we needed. All I could focus on was him: his scent, his grip, the way his heartbeat synced in rhythm with mine. When we made it into his room, he laid me down like I was precious and rare, but the hunger in his eyes said something else entirely. Gentle was the last thing he was going to be. His fingers ran their way from my collarbone to my chest, making my already hardened nipples even more erect. In one motion, he ripped off the lace garment I was wearing, leaving me butt-ass naked, minus the Guiseppe heels on my feet, an overpriced birthday gift to myself purchased for moments like this.

"Mmmmm." I moaned, enjoying the teasing of his tongue while his hands softly caressed between my legs. My warm wetness welcomed his fingers.

"That didn't take long." He smiled, teasing me with both his handsome smile and talented fingertips.

Before I knew it, he was on his knees, his tongue replacing his fingers. The man had an oral skillset like no one else, and it didn't take long before my cat was purring. I pulled him back onto the bed, straddling him, watching the smirk vanish as I leaned down to kiss him again. It was my turn to reciprocate, and I loved making him feel as good as he made me. Then, the journey became one of mutual satisfaction. Every move we made, every touch, was a language only we understood, a rhythm only we knew.

Curtis's hands roamed across my body, memorizing me all over again, and my fingertips slid along the ridges of muscle in his back. His strength was overwhelming, but so was his gentleness. That contradiction, that duality, was what drew me in every time, and even though I knew better, I let myself fall once again.

"Cum for me," Curtis whispered, sensing that I was on the verge of no return.

"Not yet," I whimpered, enjoying the pulsating rhythm of his thick manhood inside of me.

"Fine, I'll make you." He moaned, then pushed my legs even wider and rubbed my clit.

"Noooooo," I cried out as my body gave in to the orgasm I'd been fighting to hold onto. I opened my eyes to see the playful-ass grin on his face, a sign that once again, he'd won. But it didn't take long for him to arrive at the same destination.

"Oh, shit." He shuddered and groaned, his climax turning me on all over again.

The hours passed in a blur of tangled sheets and whispered names—moans swallowed by kisses. Skin on skin, we devoured each other, and when it was over, our bodies lay still, and the fire between us dulled to a slow burn.

I curled up against his chest, tracing lazy circles over his skin. This was the part that always got to me: the quiet aftermath. He held me like I was his and there was no one else, kissing my forehead like he cared. Like maybe I mattered more than I let myself believe. But I knew better. For two years, we'd been caught in this pattern, this push and pull of desire and denial. It started professionally. My department had hired Curtis to help bring in the worst of the worst, fugitives nobody else could catch. He always delivered. He was ruthless when necessary, but efficient and focused; sexy, bold, and aggressive in an appealing way—all the things I enjoyed in a man but rarely found. They were things that should've been red flags to stay the fuck away from him, but our chemistry was undeniable from day one. The first time we crossed paths, it was supposed to be all business, but by the third time we worked together, that line got blurred and then shattered as we crossed it, falling into bed like we'd been made for one another. But it never turned into anything more. Not officially.

I knew I wasn't the only woman in his life. I wasn't naive enough to not know that women surrounded Curtis like planets to the moon. But, when I was with him and it was just us, he made me feel like I was the only one that mattered, and sometimes I allowed myself to believe it, knowing that I shouldn't. The facts were that I was accomplished, respected, and worked hard for everything I'd earned in Atlanta PD. My reputation was one built on integrity, and my record was clean. I fought harder and smarter than most of the men I worked with. But, when it came to Curtis Duncan, I was as weak as they come. I hated the fact that I wanted more from him than what I was able to have.

As I pressed my face against his chest, inhaling his scent, something just felt like home, though I knew it wasn't. He didn't speak. He never did afterward. He just kissed the top of my head, holding me like it meant something. I wasn't sure if it did, or if it was just routine for us. And in that quiet, floating space between sleep and reality, I told myself what I always do.

I'm okay with this. I'm not catching feelings. Being friends with benefits is enough.

Deep down, I hated that I wanted him, not just for the night but for mornings, conversations, PDA in public. I wanted a future with him, and I wasn't sure if that was something he'd ever give me. So, I settled for being held in his arms while falling asleep, dreaming about the what-ifs that would never be.

Chapter 3

Curtis

I lay sprawled across my king-sized bed, the morning sun beaming through the blinds, casting tiger-like stripes across my chest. The scent of Marcia's perfume lingered on the pillow beside me, a tantalizing reminder of the night before. My muscles ached pleasantly, a testament to our shared passion.

The digital clock on the nightstand blinked 6:12 AM. For most, it was early; for me, it was practically midday. Yet, I wasn't in a rush. The room bore the aftermath of our rendezvous: clothes strewn about, the air thick with the remnants of desire. Marcia cuddled beside me, her long, dark hair cascading over the pillow like a waterfall. The sheet had slipped down, revealing the smooth curve of her back. I reached out, tracing a finger along her spine. Coming out of her sleep, she started to get up to begin her day.

"Where you think you're going?" I murmured, my voice husky with sleep as I flirtatiously pulled her back down.

She turned to face me, a playful smile tugging at her lips. "Some of us have real jobs with real hours, Mr. Duncan."

I chuckled, pulling her closer. "The Atlanta PD can survive without their star detective for another hour."

She laughed, and the sound was like music to my ears. "Must've missed that memo."

We lay in comfortable silence, the world outside forgotten. But then, she shifted, propping herself up on one elbow, her face now serious.

"Actually," she began, "I've been meaning to talk to you about something."

I raised an eyebrow, sensing the shift in mood. "Talk? Sounds deep for 6:18 in the morning."

She smiled, but it didn't reach her eyes. "Maybe it is deep."

I sighed, sitting up. "Can't we wait until after coffee? You know I'm not a talker before my caffeine fix."

She shook her head. "It's been almost two years, Curtis. I think it's time we define what this is."

I frowned. "We've got a good thing going, don't we? Great chemistry, dope convo, no drama, amazing sex. Why mess with a good thing?"

She looked at me, her gaze piercing. "That's exactly what I'm saying."

I tilted my head, saying, "What?"

"The way you summed us up, like we're a tight operation, smooth and no strings attached. You handle relationships like your bounties, Curtis. You scope it out, plan your moves, make the catch, and then . . . you bounce before it gets real."

I opened my mouth to protest, but she held up a hand. "You're slick at what you do because you see patterns. But do you ever notice your own? How you keep women at just the right distance, close enough to vibe, but too far for them to really reach you?"

Her words hit harder than any punch I'd ever taken. I looked away, unable to meet her stare.

"I've watched you for two years now," she continued. "You're charming, handsome, attentive, got skills in bed. But as soon as someone talks about locking it down, you start plotting your escape. It's like commitment gives you hives, like you are allergic to it."

I swallowed hard. "So what are you saying? You want something more?"

She sighed, sitting up. "I do, but I know this works for us, especially if I want to keep seeing you. I get you, Curtis. I'm not expecting you to turn into some dude dreaming of a family and white picket fences. Honestly, my career is important to me right now, and I like having someone who doesn't ask for more than I can give, but one day, I would like to spend the rest of my life with someone special."

Relief washed over me but I was a little confused about where this conversation was going. "Then what's the deal?" I asked.

"The deal is you're selling yourself short." Her eyes softened. "You keep women at arm's length because you're scared of what might happen if you let them in. And I get it. In your line of work, getting attached is risky. But life ain't a bounty, Curtis. If you want something real, you're going to eventually have to change your ways."

I tried to argue, but she silenced me with a look. "I'm not trying to hurt you," she said gently. "I just want you to see what I see: a man who has way more to offer than he realizes."

I looked at her, truly looked at her, and saw the sincerity in her eyes. She believed in my ability to love someone fully, even when I didn't believe it myself.

"And what makes you think I can offer more?" I asked, my voice barely above a whisper.

"Because I've seen how you are with your family. The way you talk about your mother, how protective you are of your sister. That's not a man incapable of deep connection. That's a man who knows exactly how powerful love can be, and it terrifies you."

Her words hung in the air between us, heavy with truth. I had always compartmentalized my life: family in one box, work in another, women in a third. It made situations neat, manageable, and most of all, safe.

After a moment, she spoke again, her voice softer. "There's someone at work who's been asking me out. Works in IT, smart guy, he also runs a blog about international travel."

The little jealousy that flared within me was unexpected and unwelcome. "And?"

"And I've been thinking about saying yes." She watched my reaction carefully. "We've never promised each other exclusivity, Curtis. That was your preference, remember?"

Not only did I remember, but I had insisted on it, in fact. That no-strings-attached setup was my idea, my rule, and one I stood on like gospel. But hearing her talk about another dude—smart, polished, international traveling type—had me feeling some type of way.

"So that's what this morning sermon's about?" I asked, sitting up straighter, a bitter taste in my heart after hearing the news. The crazy thing is, I didn't want her, but I didn't want anyone else to have her either. "You tryna let me down easy? Say your goodbyes before homie from the IT department takes my spot?"

Marcia turned back toward me. As we lay in bed, she wrapped her right arm around my midsection, the way women do when they're about to drop a truth bomb you can't dodge. "No," she said slowly. "This ain't a breakup speech. This is a mirror, Curtis. You can keep doing your thing, keep ducking from real feelings like you duck bullets. But just know that eventually, all that running? It catches up to you."

I ran a hand down my face and sighed so deeply it felt like it came from my soul. "And you think I can just . . . flip the switch? Change overnight?"

She shifted closer, beautiful and bold like a goddess sent to humble me. Then she kissed me softly, slow enough for me to feel it, quick enough for me to miss it when it was gone.

"I think you've been chasing everybody else your whole life," she whispered, "when the one person you need to face is looking back at you in the mirror every morning."

Damn.

She didn't raise her voice or cry. She didn't pull a dramatic exit. But her words cut deeper than a butcher knife.

Marcia moved to the edge of the bed, slipping into her panties and reaching for her bra. I watched her in silence, unsure of what to say. Everything in me wanted to pull her back under the covers—not for sex or even comfort, but to stop her from walking away with my pride still sitting on her lips like lip gloss.

She turned one last time before heading to the bathroom. "For what it's worth," she said, eyes as soft as her voice, "I believe you're capable of a love that doesn't come with an escape clause." She gave me a look—one of those deep, soul-snagging stares that feel like they strip you bare. "Maybe one day," she said, "you'll believe it too."

Then she disappeared into the bathroom, and the sound of the shower starting up was the only thing keeping me grounded. I lay back, staring at the ceiling like it held all the answers. And maybe it did, because something about what she said kept bouncing around in my head like an echo I couldn't escape. I'd made my name tracking down fugitives, people who thought they could outrun fate, but the one man I hadn't caught was me. I was the one ducking feelings, ghosting anything that looked like forever, keeping women at arm's length like love was a loaded gun pointed at my chest. I'd been living life like a mission: objective in sight, get in, get out, no attachments, no liabilities. But Marcia, she saw through the armor, always had, and that scared the hell outta me.

The sound of the shower cut off. Minutes later, she stepped out, wrapped in one of my towels like she owned the place. And truthfully, in that moment, she kinda did. I sat up and watched her move around the room, pulling on her clothes. I finally spoke up.

"Yo," I said, rubbing the back of my neck. "You serious about that dude at work?"

She paused, not turning around.

"I'm serious about myself," she said. "That's what I'm choosing. Whoever fits into that? We'll see."

I nodded slowly. It was the type of answer that made you think twice about all the games you thought you were winning.

"I ain't ready," I admitted. "But . . . that don't mean I ain't tryin'."

Marcia turned around, one eyebrow raised. "You trying?" she asked. "Or you just scared I'ma beat you to the finish line with somebody who ain't afraid to love me out loud?"

That woman knew how to hit a man right in the ego and the heart at the same damn time.

"Maybe both," I muttered with a crooked smile.

She laughed. "Well, let's see if you can keep up."

Marcia walked over, kissed me once more—on the cheek this time, which somehow stung more than a goodbye. "I gotta go," she said. "But don't be surprised if one day you wake up and realize you don't wanna be the last man standing."

And with that, she grabbed her purse, her badge, and walked out, leaving me with nothing but my thoughts, my bare chest, and the scent of her lingering in the air. I leaned back again, letting out a low whistle. She wasn't bluffing, and she wasn't waiting, either. The woman had a plan, and it didn't involve dragging a man behind her who couldn't figure out whether he wanted to run toward her or keep running from himself.

I sat there for a long minute before swinging my legs out of the bed. It was time to shower, shake it off, and handle the day. But something about this morning felt different. She'd planted a seed, and for the first time in a long time, I was wondering if it was time to stop being the hunter and finally let somebody catch me.

Chapter 4

Johnny Boy

The steps of the federal courthouse in Washington, D.C., had never looked more dramatic than they did today, lined with armed officers and flashing cameras. The atmosphere buzzed with nervous energy. Press swarmed like a pack of aggravating mosquitoes, shouting, snapping photos, scrambling over each other for the perfect angle. My face would be splashed across every screen before noon, but I didn't mind. I welcomed the attention. I had built my empire from the dust of the Haitian streets to this moment, on this stage, and I knew exactly how to perform. Escorted by two armed guards dressed in charcoal suits and designer shades, I adjusted the cuff of my midnight-blue Brioni suit and buttoned the jacket with deliberate elegance. Each step I took echoed power, control, and swagger.

"Mr. Boykins, do you have anything to say before the verdict?"

"Will you appeal if the verdict doesn't go your way?"

I didn't answer. Instead, in response, I just offered a calm, knowing, unapologetic smile, followed by a slow glance toward the camera. I wanted them to see me unbothered, composed. This wasn't the end of my story. It was only the beginning.

Inside, the courthouse air shifted as if a cold wind blew through, the chaos from outside now gone, replaced by silence and tension. The long hallway stretched in front of me with bright overhead lights and floors so polished I could see my reflection. My footsteps echoed as I passed the stone walls of the secured space.

As I approached the courtroom, I gave a subtle wink to Santana Baptiste, my right-hand man and top lieutenant in the Gede Gang, a Haitian-born crime syndicate I had built from the ground up. He was dressed like any ordinary security guard as he leaned against the far wall, watching everything with the same sharp eyes that had helped me rise from nothing. Santana never smiled, but his presence meant the plan was already in motion.

The courtroom itself was damn near clinical with its pale-yellow walls and hardwood benches. The audience was smaller than expected, consisting of federal agents, two rows of legal assistants, and the nine-person jury, all of whom were afraid to make eye contact. I continued to survey the courtroom, my eyes scanning the empty rows, but I didn't see my two associates, Senator Richard Winbush and Attorney General Scott Bowens, who was always a commanding presence in his meticulously tailored suit. I felt certain they would be here to cheer me on, as they had been my secret supporters throughout this ordeal. They had assured me that this was an open-and-shut case, that I would be acquitted of all charges and back to my usual life in no time. A surge of disappointment tugged at me as I realized their familiar faces were absent from the courtroom.

Chains clinked lightly around my wrists and ankles as I took my seat. I sat straight, confident, and composed, signaling to whoever was watching that although my body was cuffed, my mind wasn't. Judge Horace Williams entered the room, and everyone stood to their feet. He didn't look at the prosecutor. He didn't look at my attorney. He looked directly at me.

"Mr. Boykins," he began. "In the matter of United States v. Jonathan Boykins . . ."

He was immediately interrupted by the sharp hiss of silenced gunfire, each suppressed shot cutting through the air like a ghost's breath. For a second, the courtroom stood frozen in confusion. The tension was suffocating, pressing down like a quiet storm.

"Dear God!" the white-haired clerk screamed as she dove to the floor.

My eyes darted from her then back to the judge, standing on his feet, looking around instead of ducking for cover.

This is just the beginning, Your Honor. If only you knew.

Shots rang out. Judge Williams never had a chance. The first bullet caught him in the chest. He stumbled back, gurgling as he collapsed behind the bench. Panic erupted. While some people dove to the floor, others screamed, stumbling over benches and each other in a desperate rush toward any exit they could find.

I stayed seated and, unlike everyone else around me, remained calm. Everything was going exactly as planned. Simeon Lamothe's genius had rewired the courtroom's entire surveillance system two nights ago. While most eyes were watching me, Simeon had turned ordinary dome cameras into remote-activated weapons: silent, wireless, and undetectable until it was too late. When he triggered the command from a remote location just outside the courthouse, they fired in perfect synchronicity, taking out only those who mattered.

This wasn't an ordinary escape. Through the smoke, five figures in black tactical gear moved with chilling precision: Gede Gang soldiers. My soldiers. They appeared from all corners of the courtroom, timing their entrance with the rigor of a military procession. At the center was Santana. Without saying a word, he moved through the chaos, his gloved hand slipping a tiny bolt cutter from his boot. Within seconds, my wrist chains fell. In another, the leg restraints followed. He moved like a ghost.

"Ready when you are, boss," he said.

I stood, rolling my shoulders as if we were just leaving an extended boardroom meeting. "Let's finish the transaction."

We moved as one, the Gede Gang forming a protective circle around me. I glanced back to see the damage.

We exited the side door as smoke floated behind us. Simeon's hacking loop kept the building security cameras running false footage of an empty courtroom, untouched. No trace of us. Outside, a matte black bulletproof Escalade waited in the alley. Santana opened the door, and I slid inside. The moment the door shut, silence wrapped itself around me again.

"Make sure our friends in high places understand the consequences of betrayal," I said coldly, watching the chaos continue to unfold in the rearview mirror. My voice didn't rise. It never had to. The tone was enough.

Santana nodded once. "Message received."

The Escalade peeled off, tires screeching as we cut through the alley and vanished into the streets, the smoke behind us rising like a warning signal. In the mirror, I saw bodies stumbling from the building: people crying. reporters scrambling to find out what had happened, agents shouting.

"Good." I whispered to myself. "They wanted a fucking show. Now they got one."

As we sped into the city, my head rested back against the leather seat, and I closed my eyes for a moment, not in relief, but in calculation. This wasn't victory yet. It was the start of a new game, and every move from here forward had to be strategic. They had tried to play me, and now the game board had shifted. What these politicians didn't understand was that I wouldn't fold under pressure. I would evolve and rebuild. Failure may be a luxury for other men, but not for Johnny Boy.

Chapter 5

Scott Bowens

The courthouse was no longer a sanctuary of justice. It was a crime scene. The hallway air felt dense, and echoes of screaming still lingered. Blue uniforms filled the space, officers barking orders into radios and arguing in low, panicked voices. FBI agents huddled in corners, their faces furrowed and their grips tight on clipboards. Reporters crowded the exits, blocked by security guards unwilling to answer the questions being shouted at them.

Everywhere I looked, all I saw were pieces of the aftermath. The overhead fluorescent lights seemed to spotlight everything: the shattered glass, smears of blood, and the chaos that spilled out of the courtroom and into the hall. Even the waiting room chairs were misaligned during the aftermath, as if the force of the chaos had shoved them.

I calmly moved through it all, detached from the emotions of the devastation in order to remain focused on how to fix this instead of what caused it.

I tucked my hands into the pockets of my long wool coat and walked at a steady pace, giving myself time to process everything that had gone wrong. My eyes bounced from officer to officer, past a woman trembling as she rocked back and forth, mascara streaking down her cheeks, and her arms wrapped around herself like a straitjacket. Instinctively, I wanted to pause and comfort her, offer some words of comfort, but I didn't stop.

Inside the courtroom, it was worse. What was once a room created for civilized arguments now looked like a scene from a horror movie. The smell of smoke and blood was thicker there, mixed with the metallic scent of gunfire. Broken glass was shattered across the floor, and white chalk outlined where the bodies had landed: six men and three women. Most had just come for jury duty, fulfilling their civic duty, and now were deceased. They didn't deserve this.

I stared at tipped-over chairs, papers strewn across the floor, and legal pads now soaked with blood. And the mastermind behind it all—gone. Johnny Boy had turned the courtroom into a goddamn opera house of destruction. A man who should've been wearing chains and catching a life sentence was out in the wind, gone like a magician's final act, leaving behind blood and disbelief.

I turned slowly and spotted Winbush tucked away in the far corner, half hidden in the shadows and away from everybody. For the first time since I'd met him, Senator Richard Winbush didn't look in control. He looked hollow and pale, like somebody had drained the life right out of him. I walked across the room toward him. Our eyes locked. I didn't say a word. Neither did he, but the message between us was very clear: Somebody fucked up.

He doesn't have the stomach for this, I thought. *Never did.*

He didn't rise to greet me or offer his hand. He just exhaled and motioned to the empty seat beside him.

"You look like hell," I said.

"So do you," he replied, voice hoarse, barely audible.

We sat in silence, just two powerful men surrounded by their own pretension, knee-deep in the shit they caused.

"This wasn't supposed to happen," he finally muttered. "We were supposed to win today."

"This was supposed to be his final day savoring the freedom of the open air. Once he was locked away in the cell, we had a plan in place, with someone ready to ensure he would never draw another breath again." I added bitterly. "Not a damn action movie with him riding off into the sunset."

Winbush rubbed his face with both hands. "I don't understand how he pulled this off. Security was tight. We had the judge, the media, the narrative. We had it all."

"'That's exactly why he made a move," I said. "How did he know we were closing in? You think one of our players tipped him off?"

Winbush's eyes snapped toward me. "You think it was internal?"

"I don't think, Richard. I know. He had intel, real-time movement, and a fucking coordinated diversion. There were wireless weapons hidden in plain sight. That courtroom was hacked: literally and figuratively."

Winbush leaned forward, elbows on his knees, hands clasped together like he was praying. "We need to talk."

"Yeah," I said. "We do."

"My office in one hour. No phones. Just us. Clear your schedule and get to my office ASAP."

I stood, glancing around the room at the chalk outlines, the scorched wood, the dried blood. This was supposed to be the end of Johnny Boy, his funeral in cuffs and a clean extraction of a dangerous asset. Instead, it was a massacre.

Now, we had to come up with a new mission. *Meet Winbush. Cancel all meetings. Make a new plan.*

I pulled out my phone, ignoring the plethora of missed calls and text messages. I caught my reflection in a darkened courtroom window. I didn't see the Attorney General of the United States. Instead, I saw a man at the edge of collapse. But collapsing was never an option, so

I recalibrated. This wasn't the end of my career, and it damn sure wasn't the end of our plan. It was just a pivot.

As long as Johnny Boy was still breathing, we had leverage. We knew the man's weaknesses, his habits, his history, and his past crimes, which were buried deeper than the ones the court had ever seen. And most importantly, we had insurance. Lots of it.

As I sat beside Senator Winbush, I took another look at the courthouse and shook my head. Johnny Boy had thrown the first punch, and it landed, but the next move would be mine. And I wasn't going to miss.

Chapter 6

Mya

The yellow caution tape brushed against my sleeve as I ducked beneath it. At this point in my career, sneaking under crime scene tape felt more like part of my job description than the press badge clipped to my coat.

The marble floors inside the D.C. Courthouse, usually pristine and shimmering, were a mess of bloody footprints, toppled chairs, shattered glass, and chaos. Everywhere I looked, people moved with purpose—police officers, forensic techs, federal agents. Meanwhile, my heart sank as I took in the scene—because I knew that scent in the air. It wasn't just chaos. It reeked of a major story, the kind that blows up headlines and takes careers down with it. The kind of story that could set the city on fire and have people whispering my name in newsrooms from here to L.A.

I worked on the fourth-floor investigative unit at the *Washington Post*, one of only three Black women and the only one who steadfastly refused to be relegated to "community interest" features simply due to the color of my skin. I was not just *anybody* in that newsroom. I was an award-winning investigative journalist. Not that it mattered to some of my editors, but it sure as hell mattered to the people I wrote for, the ones who don't have lobbyists or PR firms cleaning up their names. The ones buried by the system and forgotten.

I won the Ida B. Wells Award for courage in journalism. That one mattered the most because Ida never wrote to please. She wrote to expose, to awaken, to survive—like me. I took home the Simeon Booker Prize for Emerging Journalists after breaking a story on gentrification-by-eminent-domain that made it to the Senate floor. Of course, the bill didn't pass, but it made a few people sweat. And sometimes, that's enough to know you're getting close. I was also a finalist for the National Association of Black Journalists (NABJ) Journalist of the Year, the youngest on the list. The award ended up going to someone at a network, but I didn't mind. I wasn't in this for hits and clicks. I was in it for the justice. I received the Salute to Excellence Award from NABJ for a three-part series I did on Black maternal health in Southeast D.C., a story they told me was "too niche" for the front page—until it went viral.

That's the thing about truth. You can try to bury it, but it has a way of clawing its way out. I wasn't here to ease anyone's discomfort. My purpose was to dig deep and bring to light the stories that were filled with intensity, the ones those in power preferred to keep buried and hidden away in the shadows. Every pin was a lead; every length of red tape a connection I'd chased through D.C.'s corridors and back alleys, sometimes only to have the tape cut just before I could tie them into something real. One by one, my exposés were dying quiet, surgical deaths by people who wanted to keep secrets.

I knew to keep it cute and casual. I didn't shove my press badge in anyone's face, but I made sure it was visible. That was how to get in deeper than the average reporter: just enough authority to let them know you belong, just enough charm to make them forget they should probably be escorting you out. The main hall resembled the aftermath of a riot and a war zone simultaneously.

My heels clicked softly as I moved through the chaos, eyes sharp. I wasn't taking notes yet. I learned early on that it was a rookie mistake. The good stuff always sticks to memory.

I slowed near the judge's chambers, where a forensic team was working with surgical precision. I watched them long enough to notice they were avoiding a specific part of the floor. Bingo. Whatever was over there was big enough to need special handling. Probably bio evidence, maybe trace, maybe something else entirely. My lips turned up into a smile.

"You're seeing patterns again," I murmured to myself, the way I always did when the dots started connecting in my mind. I'd been talking to myself like that since I was a little girl in Waycross, Georgia, trying to make sense of a world that rarely explained itself. "Question is... what kind of pattern is this?"

A voice behind me made me roll my eyes before I even turned around.

"Mya Wynn. Please don't tell me you've found another conspiracy."

Dan Harris's voice was gruff as usual, but I could hear the smile underneath. Eighteen years on the force and somehow still not jaded enough to hate my guts.

I turned to face him. "Detective Harris," I said, smoothing my expression into one of mock innocence. "Conspiracy? Me? Never. I'm just a concerned citizen with a front row seat to history."

He groaned, stepping in front of me just enough to block my view without making it obvious. We'd done this dance before: me pushing for answers, him playing gatekeeper. It was our thing.

"You shouldn't be in here, and you know it," he said, adjusting his stance. "Press briefing's in an hour. Couldn't wait for the watered-down version?"

"Come on, Dan. We both know an hour is long enough for someone to edit the truth into fiction," I said, raising one brow at him. "You want me quoting a sanitized press release, or would you prefer I report what actually happened?"

He exhaled slowly. "Every time you show up, I get a migraine."

"And yet, here we are." I smirked. "You secretly like the excitement."

"You're exhausting."

"You're welcome."

He sighed again, rubbing the back of his neck. "Look, I don't have all the details yet. But whatever went down in there, it was bad, real bad."

I looked past him at the chambers again. "How many casualties?"

"Enough." His eyes darkened. "Federal agents are crawling up everyone's ass. Local PD's been sidelined. Somebody important got spooked."

It was the last sentence that got my full attention.

"Spooked?" I repeated. "As in rattled? As in shaken, not stirred?"

Before he could respond, the energy in the room shifted. The atmosphere became stiff as if someone powerful had entered the space. Everyone snapped to high alert. Conversations dipped, postures straightened, phones lowered, and all eyes turned toward the entrance. I followed the shift, and sure enough, there they were. Senator Richard Winbush and Attorney General Scott Bowens, side by side, dressed in charcoal custom suits, decided to get up and leave from the corner of the court-room where they had been sitting out of sight. Bowens had that usual calculated cool about him, but Winbush was clearly on edge. His jaw was tight, his shoulders were too stiff, and he scanned the room like he was looking for someone specific.

Oh, this is better than I thought.

"Now, that's interesting," I commented, already reaching for my phone's voice recorder.

Dan groaned. "Mya, please don't."

"Too late," I said, already weaving my way through the crowd.

I raised my voice just enough to cut through the noise. "Senator Winbush! Attorney General Bowens! Mya Wynn, *Washington Post.* Can you comment on what brings you both here personally?"

Winbush didn't blink. He looked at me like I was a speck of dust on a crisp white shirt and kept walking. There was always something about Senator Winbush that made me uneasy—like he'd sell out the very people who elected him if it served his own interests. I never saw him as a man of integrity, let alone someone fit to hold public office. Bowens, however, paused. For a moment, his eyes looked toward me, and in that split second, I saw the crack in his expression. His mouth tightened, and so did his grip on the leather folio he carried. It was gone as fast as it came, but I saw it.

"No comment at this time, Ms. Wynn," he said smoothly, like the practiced politician he was. "There will be a full briefing shortly."

"Is this connected to the Boykins hearing?" I asked quickly, stepping in. "Or to the sealed federal indictments rumored this week?"

His gaze flickered again briefly before he turned away. I didn't chase him. There was no need because I already had what I came for.

"Mya." Dan was at my side again, looking like he needed two aspirin and a nap. "You've got that look."

I turned to him, eyes still on the retreating figures. "Bowens looked rattled."

"He always looks like that. You sure it wasn't your imagination?"

"Please. That man is built for pressure. I've seen him walk into a congressional hearing grinning like it was brunch. Whatever happened today? It got under his skin."

Dan shifted uneasily. "All I know is there was a breach. High-level. Coordinated. That's all I'm gonna say."

"But enough to bring out the AG and the Judiciary Committee chair?" I tilted my head. "Come on, Dan. This isn't a robbery. This is chess."

His hesitation told me everything.

"You're gonna run with this no matter what I say, aren't you?" he asked.

I grinned. "Now you're catching on."

"Just be careful. These aren't some low-level scammers you're poking at."

"They never are," I said, my voice lower. "That's what makes it worth it."

He looked at me for a long moment. "You ever think about writing something lighter? Lifestyle pieces? Fashion columns? Recipes?"

"I don't do fluff," I said, turning back toward the scene. "I do truth."

Satisfied with what I'd gathered, I slipped my phone into my bag, ducked back under the tape, and walked away. My mind was already firing off angles, headlines, calls to make. I didn't know the full story yet, but I knew enough to follow the trail. Whatever was happening here wasn't over. One thing I'd learned about powerful men: the more they try to hide something, the bigger the story when it explodes.

Chapter 7

Attorney General Scott Bowens

When I left the courtroom, I decided to walk back to my office to clear my mind. The walk wasn't far, just a couple of short blocks. Something is humbling about walking down Pennsylvania Avenue, knowing damn near every building on the block holds secrets you helped bury. I moved with the kind of confidence people expect from the Attorney General of the United States: shoulders back, suit sharp, gait steady. But truth be told, my insides were a damn mess. My brain felt like it was caught in a spin cycle, replaying the courthouse massacre over and over like a bad episode of *Scandal*. Only, this wasn't TV. This was real life.

I had just left the scene after three straight hours trying to figure out what the hell had happened. My head pounded, shoulders ached, and my jaw was clenched so tight I was surprised I hadn't cracked a molar. As I walked through the quiet side streets, I pulled out my phone and typed a quick message to Winbush.

Richard, if we don't handle this now, it could cause problems later. The media story needs quick attention. I'll meet you at your office in 30 minutes.

I stared at the screen for a second. Too soft. I needed him to move like this was life or death, because it was.

Critical timing issue. Confirm receipt.

I hit send and listened to that little whoosh like it was the sound of my dignity being vacuumed into the digital void. Slipping the phone back into my jacket, I kept walking, trying to ignore the eerie quiet around me. Usually, D.C. buzzes during this time. But today, the streets were damn near empty, as if the city was holding its breath. Ironically, so was I. My thoughts started spiraling again with unanswered questions.

How the hell did Johnny Boy pull it off? Who in our camp tipped him off? How deep does this betrayal go?

I passed a bakery storefront with mirrored glass and caught my reflection to confirm that I was still crisp and clean, but the closer I looked, the more I noticed the cracks. There was sweat at my collar. My eyes, which were usually hard and unreadable, now looked scared.

Damn. Am I that obvious?

I turned away, only vaguely realizing the sound of footsteps behind me. I told myself that it was probably just someone jogging past. I didn't really pay it any attention until I felt the grip latched onto my arm just above the elbow like a vice. It wasn't a tap or a warning. This was a strong, unforgiving, full-bodied sign that I was no longer in control.

"What the—" I started, but I never got the rest out. I was yanked back with force. My Italian loafers scraped the pavement, and for the first time in a long damn time, I panicked.

"Don't speak." The voice was calm and measured as if they were reciting an instruction manual.

Then a sleek, black car pulled up with windows tinted so dark, you'd think they were painted. I hadn't seen it before that moment and had no idea where it came from.

"You can't . . . I'm the Attorney General."

"We know exactly who you are," the voice answered in such a way that I immediately shut the hell up.

The rear door of the car opened on cue, and before I could brace myself, I was shoved inside so hard that my knee slammed into something metal. I grunted as my shoulder twisted, but that was the least of my concerns. The door slammed behind me with the finality of a casket lid.

I was in the back seat of a car with no door handles and no way out. The engine purred like a panther, and a moment later, we took off like the damn Batmobile. My breathing became shallow. This wasn't some bluff. This was a kidnapping, premeditated and precise.

My thoughts were scattered as I tried to make sense of it all, but instead of strategy or protocol, my mind jumped to home, to my wife, Veronica. She'd made sweet potato waffles for breakfast, the kind she knew I shouldn't be eating, but she whipped them up anyway, saying I looked like I needed some comfort. Hell, she wasn't wrong. I'd sat at our kitchen table in a half-buttoned dress shirt, tie slung around my neck, trying to glance over court memos while she moved around the kitchen in her robe and slippers like it was Sunday morning. No makeup, no filters, just real, natural, grown-woman beauty.

"You're going to make yourself late," she said, setting a glass of fresh juice down beside me.

I grinned. "I'm already late. I run the damn calendar."

She gave me that look, the one she usually reserved for when I was being slick but stupid. The same look she gave me when I said we should buy that brownstone in Adams Morgan we never furnished. Her eyes narrowed just enough to say, "Boy, don't test me."

"You've been walking around here looking like death and debt had a baby," she said, sipping her peppermint tea. "What's really going on?"

I kept chewing and played it cool. "Just the usual. Politics. People pretending to care about justice when they only care about control."

She tilted her head. "This about the Boykins case?"

I paused. That name on her lips sent a chill down my spine. "I can't talk about that."

She leaned back and raised her mug like it was a gavel. "Can't, or won't?"

"Both," I said quietly.

Veronica didn't argue. She didn't have to. She'd been with me through every promotion, every scandal, every backroom deal I swore was for the "greater good." She had seen me twist the truth into strategy so many times that she could taste the lies before I said a word.

"Whatever it is," she said, "just make sure you come home clean, Scott. I can live with ambition. I can live with secrets. But don't come home with blood on your soul. I ain't got the strength to wash that off."

I looked up from my plate, really looked at her, and for a second, I almost told her everything about Winbush and what we had planned for Johnny Boy. But I didn't because deep down, I knew if I said it out loud, I'd never be able to take it back.

"I love you," I told her instead.

Her face softened. "I know you do. But make sure that love isn't the cost of your conscience."

That stayed with me. Now, here I was, in the back of a speeding car, stripped of power and options, and all I could think about was her: her voice, her warnings, and her strength.

The car took a hard turn. I snapped back to the present, pressing a palm to the cool leather beside me. There were no handles or window switches and no exit. I sat up and straightened my tie like I still had control of the narrative, even though I knew damn well I didn't. I didn't know who was waiting on the other side of that door, but I knew who I needed to get back to. And this time, I wasn't just trying to save face. I was trying to save everything that still made me a man.

I reached for my phone, but it was gone. I leaned forward, squinting into the dark partition, trying to see who was up front, but I couldn't see anything.

"Where are you taking me?" I demanded, trying to channel the same tone I'd used to intimidate gang leaders, crooked mayors, and entire press rooms. No one answered. I took a slow and deliberate breath and tried again. "You don't know who you're messing with. This is a federal crime. You're talking life in prison."

Again, no one answered, and the silence was worse than shouting. My mind started doing what it did best: calculating. This wasn't about ransom. It couldn't be. I was rich, but not kidnap-a-government-official rich. This was political and strategic, maybe even personal. Then, it hit me: Johnny Boy, the courthouse, the devastation and chaos. The panic on Winbush's face. It all made sense. Somebody, maybe Johnny himself, was sending a message.

The city blurred by. The monuments I used to admire now looked like tombstones in a power graveyard. The car moved with purpose, swerving through side streets, avoiding traffic cameras. This was planned and executed flawlessly.

Eventually, the car slowed, and my stomach dropped as we turned into my neighborhood.

The same block where my wife and I slept. Where I kept my secrets buried under imported tiles and designer furniture. As the car turned into my driveway, I damn near threw up. The engine shut off, and my hands were shaking so badly that I couldn't move. The door opened, and that's when I heard the familiar voice.

"Attorney General Bowens," it said. "Welcome. We have so much to talk about."

I turned my head slowly, heart thudding in my chest like it wanted out. I knew the voice and the face behind it.

It wasn't some goon, or junkie, or even a hired gun. The figure stepped back, motioning for me to get out, and I shakily obliged. My legs wobbled, and my spine felt like it was lined with ice. I was the Attorney General, and I was about to be taken into my own damn home by someone who knew more about me than they should. I thought about the meeting with Winbush, knowing that it wasn't happening. This was the real meeting, and suddenly, every deal I'd ever made, every file I'd ever buried, every lie I'd ever told, were all coming due.

Chapter 8

Curtis

I turned off my black Lamborghini, listening as its sound faded and mixed with the distant sirens. The car's butterfly doors eased open, and the Atlanta heat slapped me like an insult I was too tired to return. I looked at the old strip mall that housed On the Run Bail Bondsman. Paint peeled from the siding, the neon sign blinked like it was gasping its last breath, and the parking lot was stained with generations of spilled oil, blood, and regret. Yet, it felt more familiar than the penthouse I paid too damn much for across town.

I stepped out, wearing designer jeans and expensive Italian shoes, and stood on the cracked pavement. The afternoon sun reflected off my black diamond watch as I adjusted my leather jacket, a habit more than a need to look good. In this part of Atlanta, nobody cared about your clothes, just what you had with you and if you'd use it.

Two teenagers standing by a convenience store across the street stopped talking to watch me. I looked back at them calmly, acknowledging their presence. Then I gave them the kind of nod that said: *I see you. And you see me.* They nodded back and turned away, respect understood. I didn't need to show off here. My reputation flowed through these streets, unseen but known.

The bail bondsman's office door creaked loudly as I pushed it open. Inside, the air felt heavy with trapped heat, a slight smell of burnt coffee, and the unmistakable scent of desperation that filled places where people went when they had nowhere else to go. A tired ceiling fan whirled overhead, moving the still air but doing nothing to cool it down.

"Thought that was you pulling up." Jax's gravel voice was deep and dry like he'd been smoking Marlboros since 1973. He sat behind a desk that looked like it had seen many battles, none of them won, stacked with manila folders and sadness. "Who else drives a million-dollar whip to the block?" he added with a smirk, barely looking up.

"Somebody with worse priorities than me," I shot back, sliding into a chair that had more duct tape than cushion.

Jax, nearing sixty, had a face that told stories even without him saying a word. Stories of hard decisions, violent scenes, and a kind of justice that rarely matched the stories in books. His shirt strained against his broad chest and his arms, marked with faded tattoos from his younger days.

"Business that slow you looking out in the parking lot?" I asked.

"Slow enough that I know when my favorite bounty hunter pulls up," Jax replied. "You must be looking for something to chase."

I chuckled. Jax had a way with words. Always had. He'd been in this game longer than I'd been alive—one of the last old-school hustlers who'd traded shootouts for paperwork.

"Always." I leaned forward, resting my forearms on my knees. "Got anything worth my time?"

Jax's mood shifted. He leaned forward, elbows on the desk, eyes tightened in a way I recognized all too well:

the look of a man who didn't have the news you wanted but wished he did.

"Nothing that would interest you." He tapped his fingers on a manila folder. "There's a guy who skipped a DUI and another who did petty theft. The bail wouldn't even cover the gas for that monster car you drive."

I didn't hide my disappointment. "You talkin' pocket change, Jax. I'm lookin' for somethin' with teeth. Nothing bigger coming up?"

"Not right now. It's been quiet." Jax leaned back, his chair creaking. "Maybe try Bucky? He might have something street-level that pays better."

I felt a familiar restlessness stir inside me. It wasn't just about the money, though that was important. It was about the chase. The precise hunt for someone who didn't want to be found, when a trail of clues led to a door and behind it, a fugitive who thought they had escaped.

"Yeah, I might do that." I stood up and adjusted my jacket. "Let me know if you think something may catch my interest."

Jax nodded. "Always will. But, Curtis." He let out a long sigh, then paused, rubbing his temple as he spoke. "You ever thought about taking a break? When's the last time you weren't chasing someone?"

I gave a tight smile. "When I was in the womb, still swimmin' in my mama's stomach. And even then, I came out two weeks early."

Jax gave a tight chuckle, but his eyes never lost that edge of concern. "You keep runnin' like this, one day you gon' catch somethin' you ain't ready for."

"I'm always ready," I said, standing. "But I'll swing through again. Don't keep no good ones to yourself."

"You'll be my first call," he said, but he didn't look convinced.

As I turned to leave, I sensed Jax's worry follow me. It wasn't the first time he'd suggested I slow down, and it wouldn't be the last. But Jax didn't understand. The hunt wasn't just something I did; it was who I was. The chase filled a void that nothing else could. On the surface, I lived large—fast cars, beautiful women, designer clothes—but underneath the bravado, there was a restlessness I couldn't shake. The chase—tracking down dangerous fugitives—gave me a sense of purpose, control, and clarity that my everyday life didn't provide.

Outside, the heat hit me like a quick left hook from Muhammad Ali. I slid into the driver's seat, feeling the familiar leather wrap around me. The engine roared to life, drawing curious looks from people passing by.

As I drove away from the curb, I felt an emptiness grow inside me. Every capture was a quick high that faded fast, leaving me always hunting for the next thrill. The streets of Atlanta blurred past my windows as I sped off, searching for something that always felt just out of reach. I drove with one hand on the wheel and the other tapping an impatient rhythm on the door panel. The Duncan family motto wasn't printed on any coat of arms or hung on any wall, but it lived in my blood: never stop moving, never stop hustling.

"Stillness is the first sign of dying," my father used to say, usually while dragging me and my little brother out of bed before dawn for his latest scheme to put food on the table.

Even though my sleek Lamborghini felt a world away from the rusty pickup trucks and old sedans of my Waycross childhood, the hunger that drove me was still the same. Duncans were never meant for idleness. Every generation had fought hard, inch by painful inch, against the pull of rural poverty.

Waycross, Georgia, now felt like a forgotten page in America's story. The railroad had once made it important, but that had slowly faded over the years. The endless pine forests offered seasonal work for those willing to work hard, while the hospital hired the educated, the railroad hired the connected, and everyone else had to make do with whatever was left. I had seen too many childhood friends vanish into that quicksand. First their dreams, then their ambitions, and finally their hope. Some turned to bottles or needles, others to small-town crime before ending up behind bars. The lucky ones just survived, doing jobs they hated to support families they rarely saw, their eyes dimming a little more each year.

My family had broken the usual pattern. My father, Larry, was particularly good at spotting opportunities in murky situations. My uncles, LC, Levi, and Lou, each had their own skills that helped in the family business. They were masters of that blurred line between legal and lethal. One minute they were hosting a fish fry, the next they were moving weight under cover at night.

They knew about taking risks long before I ever did.

I remember when I was twelve, helping my father and Uncle LC move unmarked boxes from one storage unit to another in the middle of the night. When I asked what was inside, my father simply said, "College tuition." It was years later before I found out it was drugs. My family taught me to walk the line and to earn money by any means necessary. Those lessons stuck with me. I eventually chose a different path. Bounty hunting kept me on the right side of the law, but still gave me the rush I craved. I didn't choose this life for glory—I chose it because jail was never an option. I had a family to protect. My mom and younger siblings needed someone to hold the line, especially with my father gone—locked away in a place called Fresh Meadows, a psychiatric ward that sounded more like a country club than a cage for fractured minds. With him gone, I had to make sure I was here for my family.

I drove into the parking lot of a plain strip mall in East Atlanta. Between a tax office and a discount furniture store was a small storefront with tinted windows and a sign that read: B&B ENTERPRISES. It was hidden well, just as planned.

Inside, the AC was struggling, and the place smelled like microwaved noodles and old printer ink. Bucky sat surrounded by monitors, his thin frame hunched over like a praying mantis and fingers moving like a hacker in a Netflix movie. His glasses sat crooked on his face, one lens always smudged. His typing paused when I cleared my throat.

"Curtis," he said without turning around. "Hold on a second."

I waited, arms crossed, looking at the back of Bucky's head. His hair was cut very short, and a small tattoo, a tribal design from fifteen years ago, peeked above his collar. He tapped away for another thirty seconds before finally turning around in his chair.

His face was sharp and hollow, with eyes that seemed a bit too big behind his wire-rimmed glasses that kept sliding down his nose. He did not look like someone who handled information about some of Atlanta's most dangerous fugitives, which might be why he was still alive.

"You look bored as hell," he said, grinning.

"You got anything?" I asked.

"Not unless you wanna track down some dude who skipped court over a weed ticket."

I didn't respond.

"Didn't think so," Bucky added. "It's dry out here. Even the dumb ones are gettin' smarter. Bad timing, man."

I felt the tightness in my jaw. "Nothing?"

Bucky adjusted his glasses with one finger. "You don't get paid unless it's at least twenty-five grand. All I have are three-thousand-dollar jobs that the regular guys are fighting over."

"I've been hearing that a lot lately," I said, my frustration clear.

Bucky shrugged, his shoulders set beneath a worn t-shirt. "Market forces, man. The economy is okay, which means fewer desperate people doing dumb things. The cops are doing their jobs better. And summer makes even criminals lazy because of the heat."

I ran a hand down my face. "That's two dry runs in a row."

"You mad 'cause the streets are peaceful?" he joked. "How messed up is that?"

"It ain't about peace," I muttered. "It's about purpose."

I understood his point, but I needed action. I had built my reputation on taking high-value, high-risk cases that most others avoided: the dangerous ones that required more than just a phone call or a knock on a door. But those cases were not constant.

"Keep me in mind," I said as I turned to leave.

"Always do. You're my first call when something interesting comes in." Bucky returned his attention to his screens and his digital tasks.

I stood for a moment by my car, feeling sweat collect on my forehead. There were two leads, both of which had come to dead ends. The city suddenly felt empty of promise, like a big playground with nothing to do.

I sat in my parked Lamborghini, watching the city move by like a silent movie through my tinted windows. The lack of work bothered me, not because of missing paychecks—my bank account could handle a few dry years—but because I missed the thrill of the hunt. Money was never the true reward for me. It was just a way to keep score in a game that only I seemed to play. The financial rewards were good, without a doubt. My penthouse, my car, my jewelry, and my clothes were all signs of success in a profession most people only saw on reality TV shows that got everything wrong.

I started the engine, and the Lamborghini roared to life with extra power. Moving was better than staying still, and action was better than just thinking. I pulled away from the curb, merging into Atlanta traffic as I headed home.

Chapter 9

Johnny Boy

"Every king remembers the day his crown was stolen."
The TV cast a cold blue light across my face, the bourbon in my glass catching it just right, almost like it was spotlighting the moment. I leaned back on the Italian leather, legs crossed, one arm draped like royalty, the other slowly swirling ice in my drink—smooth and chill, just like me.

"Authorities are still investigating how Boykins managed to escape federal custody," Roland Martin continued, his expression appropriately grave for prime time. "Sources close to the investigation suggest possible corruption within law enforcement, though no arrests have been made."

To the world, I was Jonathan Boykins, but where I was from, back in Port-au-Prince, they call me Ti Wa: Little King. I was a long way from the dirt roads in Miragoâne to Georgetown's finest neighborhoods. But I was still a problem, a storm wrapped in a silk suit. Today proved that. The fact that the media was trying to act surprised about my "escape" was an insult. That wasn't a miracle. It was pure precision and mathematical planning, requiring a level of brilliance that only I had.

I let out a little laugh. The TV switched to some blurry footage of a black SUV tearing away from the courthouse, chaos frozen in a snapshot. Martin popped back on screen, standing at the courthouse steps, mic in hand. "We caught up with Attorney General Scott Bowens earlier today," the broadcast continued, showing Bowens with his silver-streaked hair shining as he spoke with passion. "He promised quick action and a deep dive into what he's calling 'a catastrophic security failure.'"

"We won't leave any stone unturned," Bowens vowed, looking all determined. "Jonathan Boykins is a serious danger to the public, and we're throwing everything we got at getting him back."

I hit mute, the ice in my glass shifting as I finished my bourbon. The irony was thick. Bowens talking tough about catching a guy who would soon be sitting in the same room with him, a guy who, if he captured me, would give him a political boost. But that's politics for you: shady deals and temporary friendships. Betrayal was just a matter of when, not if.

"Enjoying the show, boss?" Santana asked, his big frame filling the doorway, hands calmly folded. Six-four and built like someone on the cover of *Muscle & Fitness* magazine, he was loyal like a pitbull that only listens to one voice: his master's.

"Bowens got good media training," I muttered, standing up and straightening my cufflinks. "Makes betrayal sound like civic duty."

"Want me to prep the car?" Santana asked.

I cut my eyes at him. "Prep the house."

He nodded once and stepped back. It was time to visit a ghost while he was still breathing.

The Bowens' brownstone was Georgetown-perfect: columned, quiet, the kind of house that screamed "old money" and whispered "secrets." I'd studied the layout six months ago when the betrayal hit my radar. I never moved off emotion. I always waited and planned, and when it was time to strike, my victims never saw it coming. They would just feel the cold and realize that their time was up.

We walked straight in, Santana and three of the Gede boys behind me, all dressed in black, faces calm, movements smoother than a surgeon's scalpcl. Simeon, the technical guru of the crew, had jammed the neighborhood security grid. There would be no calls, no cameras, and no warnings.

Inside, I found Scott exactly where I wanted him, sweating in his own damn leather chair, those silk ties of his finally doing some real work around his wrists and ankles. Across from him, his wife, Veronica, looked like she'd aged ten years in ten minutes. Her robe wasn't even tied right, and her makeup was smeared down her cheeks. I stood between them like a conductor in front of an orchestra, amused by the fear in their eyes.

"Nice place," I said, walking around slowly, brushing my fingers over the framed photos on the bookshelf. "Fake smiles. Family beach trip. Bowtie at a fundraiser. You always was good at pretendin', Scott."

He squirmed. "Jonathan, this is . . . this is a mistake. We can work something—"

"Nah," I cut him off, pulling out a small recorder. "We past 'mistakes.' We at receipts now. Technology is wild these days. These gadgets catch everything: calls, private whispers, even those low-key talks in supposed 'secure' government spots."

I hit play, and just like that, the room filled with his voice:

"Winbush wants Boykins locked up for good. The evidence is shaky, but we can make it stick. The Haitian issue needs to vanish before the election."

I didn't say a word. Just let it marinate.

Scott's mouth fell open. His color drained like I'd sucked the blood out of him. "That . . . that was taken out of context."

"Context?" I repeated, chuckling. "You talkin' 'bout context when you framed me? When you and that puppet-ass senator sold me out?"

"You don't get the kind of pressure—"

I lifted my hand, and Scott stopped talking, his instincts kicking in like a dog trained to sit.

"Pressure? Oh, I get it, Scott. The grind of hustling from nothing. Keeping order when chaos pays the bills. Trusting dudes who smile in your face while they got a blade ready to stab you in the back." I moved around the chair slowly. "What I don't get is betrayal."

"Please." Bowens' voice cracked, his professional composure fracturing like thin ice. "We can work something out. I have access to case files, evidence that can be . . . misplaced. I can help you."

I smiled. "You already helped me, Scott. You helped me see exactly how Washington works. Loyalty lasts only until the next election cycle or the next headline. You helped me understand that men like you only respect one thing."

My eyes went to Santana, who gave a subtle nod.

I stepped closer to Scott, my voice steady. "You gave up a Black man from Haiti like it was nothing. Thought I'd just rot in prison while you took my land. My name. My future."

He started babbling. "Please . . . my wife, my grandkids . . . we can offer you money, documents. I have access to the files. I can make it all disappear."

"You already disappeared me once," I snapped. "I won't let you do it again."

His wife Veronica jumped in. "We have money! Three million dollars, untraceable, in an offshore account. Please, just take it and leave."

I crouched in front of her, voice soft but razor-sharp. "Ma'am, I ain't here for your husband's dirty money. If I were, I'd have taken it already. I'm here because I believe in balance. Y'all call it revenge. I call it correction. This isn't a negotiation. It's a consequence."

Her sobbing intensified, shoulders shaking under her silk blouse. "We have children . . . grandchildren. For God's sake, we're people, not just—"

"So was I." I cut her off. "When your husband here and his friend Winbush decided I was better used as a scapegoat than a business partner, I was a person too. When they fabricated evidence and threatened my family, I was a person too." My voice remained level, and she shivered as if my words sent a chill down her spine. "But they didn't see a person. They saw a convenient solution to their political problem."

Scott licked his dry lips, eyes shifting from me and the door as if he were calculating impossible odds. "Jonathan, listen to reason. Killing us won't solve anything. It will bring heat, federal heat, down on you and your operation. Everything you've built will collapse."

I laughed, but there was no humor in it. "You still don't understand. Everything I built already collapsed the day you betrayed me. This isn't about preserving my business, Scott. This is about justice. The kind that doesn't happen in your courtrooms."

I nodded to Santana, who stepped forward from the shadows. The enforcer moved with surprising grace for a man his size, each step deliberate as he produced a silenced 9mm pistol from beneath his jacket. The weapon looked almost dainty in his massive hands, like a child's toy.

Scott's eyes widened as reality set in. "No, wait! Please, I can fix this! Winbush was the one who pushed for your prosecution. He's the one you want!"

"Don't worry." I leaned closer, my voice almost gentle. "The senator is next on my list. But hierarchy matters, Scott. As attorney general, you get the privilege of going first."

Santana positioned himself behind Scott, the silencer hovering inches from the back of his head. Scott's breathing came in rapid, shallow gasps, as if he were a drowning man far from water.

"Look at me," I commanded, and Scott's terrified eyes locked with mine. "I want you to understand something. This isn't personal. It's structural. You're not dying because I hate you. You're dying because you're part of a system that decided I was disposable."

Veronica started to scream, but no sound came out as Santana pulled the trigger and the silencer released a single bullet. Scott's body jerked forward, then slumped, head falling at an unnatural angle. A dark stain appeared on the leather chair beneath him, blood seeping.

The room fell silent except for Veronica's whimpering. She stared at her husband's body, shock temporarily overriding her terror. When she finally spoke, her voice came out broken and small. "Why? Why both of us? I never hurt you. I never even met you before tonight."

I straightened my cuffs, a nervous habit developed as a way of maintaining composure in chaotic situations. "Mrs. Bowens, you benefited from every deal your husband made, enjoyed the fruits of every betrayal. The house we're standing in, the jewelry around your neck, the vacations in photos on your walls, all purchased with blood money and broken promises." I nodded to Santana. "Besides, I don't believe in loose ends."

She looked at me, trembling. "Please . . . I didn't do anything."

"That's the thing," I said, backing up. "You didn't stop anything either."

"No, pleas—" Her final plea died with her, another soft thump from Santana's weapon cutting her words short. Her body crumpled inward, collapsing like a puppet whose strings had been cut.

I surveyed the scene, noting the minimal blood spatter. Santana's work was always clean. The bodies slumped in their chairs might have been sleeping if not for the unnatural angles and growing dark stains. I felt no triumph, no euphoria, just the cool satisfaction of a debt partially settled.

"Have Simeon and Michel remove any traces of our presence," I instructed. "No fingerprints, no DNA, nothing that connects back to us."

I took one last look at Scott Bowens, the man who'd stood before cameras promising justice while dealing in corruption. Death had stripped away his authority, leaving only an empty vessel in an expensive suit.

"Time to go," I said, straightening my jacket. "We have more appointments to set up."

We moved through the house with precise efficiency, leaving nothing disturbed except the two bodies in the study. Outside, the cool night air carried the scent of cherry blossoms in bloom. A black sedan eased up to the curb, its engine humming low. We kept the exit quiet—no fuss, no flash. Just the way we wanted it. We didn't want to make a scene. I slid into the back seat of the lead car, Santana folding his large frame in beside me. As we pulled away from the curb, the brownstone faded into the distance, its dignified exterior masking the deadly truth it now concealed.

We'd traveled six blocks when a phone buzzed. It wasn't my personal cell phone, but Bowens' mobile that I'd pocketed earlier. I examined the screen, a smile spreading across my lips as Senator Richard Winbush's name appeared.

"Perfect timing," I murmured, sliding my finger across the screen to accept the call, putting it on speaker.

"Scott, where the hell have you been?" Winbush's voice boomed through the car's quiet interior, impatience evident in every syllable. "I've been trying to reach you for hours. We need to coordinate our response to this Boykins situation before—"

"Hello, Senator," I interrupted, my voice deceptively pleasant. "I'm afraid Attorney General Bowens can't come to the phone right now."

The silence that followed stretched for five full seconds. An eternity in conversation, time enough for understanding to take place.

"Who is this?" Winbush finally asked, the tremor in his voice suggesting that he already knew.

"I think you know exactly who this is, Richard." I let the familiarity hang in the air, a reminder of connections that happened before our current adversarial relationship. "Your friend Scott and I just had a very productive meeting. Well, productive for me."

There was another stretch of silence before Winbush responded. "Where's Scott?"

"Getting cold," I replied simply. "As is Mrs. Bowens. You should be more concerned about where I am, Senator. Or rather, where I'm going to be."

Winbush's breathing became louder, quick and shallow. "Listen to me, Boykins. Whatever grievance you think you have—"

"Save your speeches for your constituents, Richard. They might still believe them." My tone remained conversational, almost friendly. "I just wanted to let you know that I received your message: the one you sent through the federal prosecutor and the judge you bought. I'm now hand-delivering my response."

"This is insanity," Winbush hissed. "You can't possibly think you'll get away with this. Do you know who I am? The resources I can—"

"I know exactly who you are." I cut him off. "A man with many resources but very little time. Spend what's left of it wisely, Senator. Maybe with your family. Maybe making peace with whatever god you pretend to worship during campaign seasons." I let the silence hang, giving the weight of my words time to land. "You chose the wrong man to sacrifice, Richard. I'll see you soon."

The call ended before Winbush could respond, and I held the phone for a moment between my fingers as if weighing it. With methodical precision, I used my handkerchief to wipe the device clean of prints, then lowered the window. The cool night air rushed in as I tossed the phone into the darkness of Rock Creek Park, where it would become just another piece of urban debris, stripped of meaning and connection.

"To the Sanderling Hotel," I instructed my driver, settling back against the leather seat. "The senator will be making some frantic calls to his security team. I want to know who responds and how quickly."

Santana nodded, already texting instructions to our surveillance team positioned near Winbush's residence. I closed my eyes briefly, mentally checking off the first name on my list of traitors. The Bowens matter was concluded. Winbush would come next.

The car glided through Washington's streets, passing monuments illuminated against the sky, stone sentinels to a justice system I no longer recognized as legitimate. I'd created my own justice now, administering it with the precision and finality that the courts had failed to provide.

My hands were steady, my breathing calm. Where guilt might have lived in another man's chest, I felt only the cool certainty of purpose, the next step in a plan months in the making, now finally in motion. Washington taught me an important lesson about power and its application. It was a lesson I would now teach back to my former instructors, one bullet at a time.

Chapter 10

U.S. Marshal Deputy Raynard Bradford

They say the truth will set you free, but that's a damn lie. The truth will trap you just as fast as a bullet to the back, especially when the truth has a name like Jonathan Boykins. The shadows in my home office grew longer as the night dragged on, spilling across the floor like fingers pointing blame. The desk lamp threw a faint glow over the folders, photos, and the greasy-ass Chinese food carton I hadn't touched in hours. The bourbon in my glass had turned warm, and the coffee in my cup was long gone. My eyes were on fire from too much reading, but I couldn't tear myself away from the messy papers, each a piece of the puzzle that was Jonathan Boykins. Not when Johnny Boy was still out there in the streets.

I grabbed my empty coffee mug for the third time that night. The kitchen felt like it was a world away, and I didn't have the energy to spare from my deep dive into this case. My badge was tossed aside on a stack of bank statements, its authority taking a back seat in this unofficial chase that had been eating up my nights ever since Johnny Boy's escape.

"Where are you, sick bastard?" I mumbled, rubbing the bridge of my nose. Fifteen years with the Marshals

Service had taught me plenty of patience, but Johnny Boy was pushing my limits hard. I'd been in the game long enough to know that when the bad guy don't run, it means he's already won.

I leaned back in my comfy-ass work chair, staring at the wall of photos I'd taped up like some TV detective— red strings, sticky notes, maps. And right in the center was that smug bastard, Johnny Boy. The file in front of me was packed with the usual stats—height, weight, those little marks everybody's got—but none of that dry stuff came close to describing the dude who built an empire from scratch. This Haitian-American cat moved smoothly between the gritty criminal underworld and the slick halls of Washington power. Surveillance pics caught Boykins in those sharp, tailored suits, his smile cold and calculated, shaking hands with guys whose faces were all over the news and election posters. He was slicker than a greased eel, built like a street general with the smile of a congressman. The kind of man who'd make you laugh at dinner and disappear you by dessert.

My fingers lingered on one photo in particular: Boykins chilling at the RNC with his arm casually slung around Attorney General Scott Bowens' shoulder. The photographer snapped something in Boykins' look: not friendship, but like he owned the dude.

The pile of evidence spread out on my desk told a wild tale, with witnesses suddenly forgetting everything whenever Johnny Boy's name came up. Connections ran deep, from street thugs to the big shots in D.C., weaving a web with Boykins dead center, untouchable as a spider that never has to get its hands dirty. Something seemed strange, but I couldn't put my finger on it.

My shoulders were killing me from bending over those damn files. I stretched, and my back popped like gunfire echoing in the quiet room. Exhaustion had dug in deep

hours ago, a constant shadow whispering defeat whenever I felt weak. This wasn't just any case; it had hit home,
a challenge to see if justice could break through the walls
of power these folks had built around themselves. Johnny
damn sure wasn't just another fugitive. The bodies were
stacking up. Good men, honest agents, and now whispers
that Bowens, the damn attorney general, had gone ghost
too. I hadn't seen confirmation, but my gut was already
holding a eulogy.

The file screamed CONFIDENTIAL: GEDE GANG OPERATIONS,
laying out a whole network stretching from D.C. to Haiti
and back, a slick operation moving cash, drugs, and
whatever else stacked paper. Johnny Boy had crafted the
Haitian Syndicate with ruthless skill, taking out rivals
and turning officials dirty with precision. The gang's
name, nodding to spirits that walked the line between life
and death in Haitian Vodou, was on point. They played in
that same gray area, dealing out death while living large.
Everything I'd found tied Boykins to a syndicate with
more reach than an octopus on Adderall—drugs, money
laundering, arms, human trafficking, and every now and
then, a government contract or two for good measure.
The worst part was that half the people who should've
been helping me were either silent or suddenly forgetting
how to speak English when his name came up.

My hand hovered over a gruesome crime scene pic,
one I'd seen way too many times but couldn't stop
checking out. The body had been dumped in an alley
just three blocks from Capitol Hill, a mid-tier aide who'd
supposedly decided to spill the beans for an investigation.
The official story called it a robbery gone sideways. I
knew better: the accuracy of the wounds, the missing
tongue, the message it screamed.

Just as I was about to drift off, the ringing of my phone
yanked me back to reality and sent the papers sliding

off my lap onto the floor. The alert was harsh, cutting through the midnight silence. I paused, eyeing the caller ID—UNKNOWN—before grabbing the receiver.

"Bradford," I answered, my voice all scratchy from lack of use and straight-up exhaustion.

"Thank God you picked up." The voice on the other end was shaky, panic barely contained, but I clocked it instantly. Senator Winbush didn't hit up federal marshals at midnight unless things had gone seriously south.

"Senator? What's up?" I said, already reaching for my notepad, my professional instincts kicking in hard despite the tiredness.

"He's gonna kill me." The words came tumbling out, rushed and frantic. "Johnny Boy . . . he's threatened me and my family. I ain't got time to lay it all out, but I need help. Official channels are blown."

My pen froze mid-scribble. The senator's words cut through my exhaustion like a jolt of pure adrenaline. I'd figured Johnny Boy had his claws in deep with the government, but to threaten a sitting senator so boldly, that took either mad desperation or supreme confidence.

"Take a breath, man. What exactly did he say? When'd he reach out?" My voice remained steady, even though my heart was racing.

"An hour ago. A package was delivered to my home. Inside was . . . Christ, there were photos of my children at school, my wife at her yoga class. He knows where we are, what we're doing, hell, probably what I had for breakfast." The senator's voice cracked. "And he left a message. Said that I was next after Bowens."

My blood went cold. "Bowens? The attorney general?"

"He's dead, Ray. Him and his wife both. It's not public yet, but they were found at their house an hour ago. Made to look like a break-in, but it's him. It's Johnny Boy."

The room seemed to tilt slightly. Attorney General Scott Bowens . . . dead. The same man who'd been photographed smiling with Boykins at the RNC. The implications cascaded through my mind like falling dominoes. If Boykins had reached Bowens, one of the most protected officials in the justice system, then his influence ran even deeper than I feared.

"Where are you now, Senator?" I asked, already calculating security protocols.

"I'm at home, but the place is swarming with Secret Service—and I don't know who I can trust anymore. That's why I called you directly. Your reputation . . . they say you can't be bought."

The compliment landed hollow in my chest. I hadn't been bought, true, but I'd failed to bring Boykins in all the same. The wall of corruption had proven too thick, the evidence too circumstantial, the witnesses too frightened.

"We need someone who can move outside official channels," the senator continued, his voice steadying as he spoke. "Someone who doesn't need warrants or jurisdiction. Someone who can find Johnny Boy before Johnny Boy finds me. Someone like Curtis Duncan." He paused, then asked, "You know him?"

I let the silence hang for a beat before I answered. "Yeah... I know him. Real well. He's like a brother. I'm the one who got him into the bounty hunting game. He passed on being a U.S. Marshal. Said it was too structured. I told him to try bounty hunting instead. Turns out, that was the right call. He's the best there is."

"Good. Then you know what he's capable of," Winbush said.

I asked, "How do *you* know about Curtis?"

There was a faint chuckle in his voice. "I've read about him in numerous national articles."

"The man's a ghost. A ghost that brings bad men to justice." I leaned back in my chair, thinking this wasn't some random choice. If the senator was making late-night calls, bypassing federal agencies, and requesting Curtis by name, it meant this job was high-risk and serious.

"Perfect." The relief in Winbush's voice was noticeable. "That's exactly what we need. Someone Johnny Boy won't see coming through his network of informants."

My fingers drummed against my desk. Curtis wasn't just any bounty hunter. He was the best I'd ever seen, a tactician with military precision and a man who kept his word. More importantly, he was someone I trusted, a rare commodity in Washington's compromised ecosystem. "But I have to be straight with you, Senator. Curtis doesn't operate like law enforcement. He'll bring Johnny Boy in, but I can't guarantee the condition he'll be in when that happens."

There was a pause on the line, the silence heavy with implication.

"I understand," Winbush said finally. "At this point, I don't care how he does it. Just so long as it gets done."

I hesitated. This conversation was already deep in the gray area of legality. Authorizing a bounty hunter to pursue a suspect outside official channels crossed several ethical and legal boundaries. But with Bowens dead and a senator shaking in his boots, the rulebook might as well have been toilet paper.

"There's something else, Ray." The senator's voice dropped lower. "There's a bounty. One million dollars for Johnny Boy . . . dead or alive."

My eyebrows shot up. "A million? Who's putting up that kind of money?"

"Better you don't know. Plausible deniability. But the funds are real, and they'll be transferred the moment Johnny Boy is neutralized."

The word "neutralized" hung in the air like cigarette smoke, acrid and lingering. I understood the implication. He preferred Boykins dead, unable to reveal whatever he knew about whoever was offering the bounty. I exhaled slowly. This was it: the line between justice and revenge was blurred, and the senator was jumping over it with both feet.

"Will Duncan need convincing?" Winbush pressed when I remained silent.

"No," I answered truthfully. "He'll take the job. But he'll want verification of the payment, and he'll have questions I can't answer."

"I'll tell you whatever he needs to know, but don't reveal the source of the bounty. That stays between us."

I pinched the bridge of my nose, feeling the headache building behind my eyes. My hands were numb from hours of sifting through files, but there was a warmth in my chest, an uncomfortable heat that I easily recognized as guilt. This wasn't by-the-book Marshals Service procedure. This was something else entirely.

"I'll contact him," I said finally.

"Good." The senator exhaled loudly. "Time is critical. Johnny Boy knows I've been investigating his connections to certain officials. That's why he's coming after me. I've got protection for now, but he has people everywhere."

"I understand. I'll get Curtis on this immediately."

After exchanging final details about secure contact methods, I hung up and stared at the phone. The conversation replayed in my mind, each word heavily weighted with consequence. The attorney general murdered. A senator threatened. A million-dollar bounty offered in the shadows.

The man had evaded capture for years, building his empire while corrupting the very systems designed to bring him to justice. Regular methods had failed consistently.

Maybe it is time for Curtis Duncan's approach.

I hung up and stared at the phone like it might bite me. I reached for my personal cell phone, not the government-issued one, and scrolled to a contact labeled simply "C.D." My thumb hovered over the call button for a moment as I considered the path I was choosing. Once Curtis was involved, there would be no controlling the outcome, no ensuring the clean resolution that the justice system ideally provided. But ideals crumbled quickly in Washington's reality. I hit the button and dialed Curtis's number before I could talk myself out of it, making the call, committing myself to a course that could save lives or end careers, possibly both.

As the phone began to ring, I gathered the Boykins files into a neat stack. Curtis would need everything I had, every scrap of intelligence, every lead, every known associate. The hunt was about to begin, and God help Jonathan Boykins when Curtis Duncan found his trail.

Chapter 11

Johnny Boy

The leather in the chair damn near swallowed me whole, like it was made to hold kings or monsters—and I knew which one the world saw when they looked at me. I reclined back, the dark brown leather contrasting against my crisp, cream-colored Gucci suit. The cigar I held between my fingers wasn't just smoke and fire; it was patience, it was silence, it was power wrapped in leaves and lit slowly. Smoke drifted up, twisting and turning like it was doing a lazy dance, heading toward the high ceiling all decked out in fancy decor. Hidden away in this exclusive cigar bar, the secret spot displayed a kind of underground luxury: a hidden haven, tucked away from the nosy crowd and the hustle and bustle of the streets.

In this tight hideout that had been hidden in plain sight for years, Santana and Simeon, my top dogs, stood like statues next to me, their faces a slick mix of sharp curiosity and low-key worry. Santana leaned in, eyes blazing with a fierce, almost hunting vibe, locking his steady stare directly at me.

"Johnny, if you knew they were tryna put you away for life, why didn't you flip on them? That would've been the simplest escape," he asked, his voice a low but pressing whisper through the haze of smoke.

I took a slow, intentional pull from my cigar, letting the smoke curl out of my mouth like I had all the time in the world. Because I did. I leaned forward, looking him dead in the eyes, tackling the question with unshakeable determination.

"Number one, I ain't no snitch. Period. I don't fold. Not for nobody. That's not how I operate."

Simeon nodded slowly, arms crossed over his chest like he was waiting on the next line of a sermon. "And number two?" he asked, his tone mixing anticipation with solid determination.

My eyes burned like hot coal and flashed with a spark ignited by the memory of deep-seated betrayals and the promise of unyielding vengeance. Locking eyes directly with Simeon, I continued, "Number two, I didn't want to flip on them because I wanted them dead. They stabbed me in the back, and I wasn't about to let that slide. I waited until the trial at the courthouse to make my move. With the entire place thrown into chaos, security distracted, and everything spiraling out of control, it was the perfect opportunity to strike and slip away."

Santana's lips curled into a cold, calculated smile as he soaked in the bold move. "You played the long game. Well played, boss."

"Checkmate," I said, tapping ash into the tray. "Now, Bowens is food for flies. And Winbush?" My voice dipped lower, the tone transforming into a menacing promise. "He's next. He's just as guilty, and he's gonna pay big time. We'll take him down, and anyone who even dares to stand in our way will suffer the same ruthless fate. And when the dust settles and only the ruins of our enemies remain, we'll vanish from this country. But mark my words. I ain't leaving until that motherfucker is dead."

Santana responded with an evil grin. Cracking his knuckles with a sound that resonated like a solemn death toll in the room, he stated with cold determination, "I'm ready. Just say the word."

Simeon cracked a grin. "You want surveillance?"

"Nah," I said, shaking my head. "We already been watching him. I know his movements better than his own damn wife. What I want now is disruption. Let's break routine. Deliver a message."

Santana leaned forward. "Direct hit?"

"No," I said again, slower this time. "We take the long route. Show him how it feels to be hunted. I want him watching over his shoulder, looking twice before he crosses the street, sleeping lightly."

Simeon hit back with a blunt, powerful declaration. "We're with you, boss. Whatever you need."

I crushed my burning cigar in the ashtray. The dying embers glowed like a faint echo of the violence flickering in my eyes. "Good. We'll hit them hard and fast. No mercy. And when we're done, they'll know without a doubt that we're not to be fucked with."

Heavy silence followed, and we shared a look of deep, unspoken understanding, a bond built in the fires of countless battles and endless bloodshed, unbreakable and absolute. Together, we were a force to be reckoned with, and anyone stupid enough to cross us was doomed.

As the night grew darker, we sat close together, planning our next steps carefully. We each whispered plans and strategies filled with the excitement of upcoming revenge. The danger coursing through me was like a steady drumbeat, both exciting and risky. I was at the top of my game, and my target had already messed up. With my loyal crew beside me, I was ready to bring a wave of revenge on my foes. The challenge had begun, and I was determined to win, no matter what.

"You know what really pisses me off?"

Santana looked at me, eyebrows raised. "What?"

"Them thinkin' they could erase me. Like I was disposable."

The ice clinked in my glass as I downed the last of my drink. I stood, brushing a bit of ash off my slacks. My reflection in the glass wall was sharp, dangerous, and focused.

"You know what to do," I said. "Start the sequence. Winbush's countdown begins tonight."

As I walked out of the lounge, Santana and Simeon fell in behind me like shadows with purpose. The air outside hit me, cool and sticky, and the sounds of D.C. go-go music buzzed in the background like white noise. But all I could hear was the clock ticking for Richard Winbush—and I planned to be the one to stop it.

Chapter 12

Curtis

My penthouse was on the top floor of a glass tower that looked like it floated above Atlanta's skyline. As evening fell, I sank into my leather couch, an expensive piece imported from Italy that held me like a comforting embrace. The overstuffed cushions, filled with a down-cotton blend that cost more than some cars, responded perfectly to my weight. Yet, despite the comfort, an uneasy feeling followed me home, lingering in the climate-controlled air like an unwelcome guest.

Thoughts swirled in my mind like a gathering storm. Restless, I got up from the couch and moved into the kitchen. The kitchen shone with professional-grade stainless steel appliances and marble countertops, much like a high-end restaurant. Cooking was a gift from my mother. She taught me recipes when I was too small to reach the counter without standing on a chair. While my father and uncles taught me the art of war, my mother showed me how simple ingredients could transform into something wonderful.

I opened the refrigerator and looked at its contents with practiced eyes. Without even thinking, my hands reached for bell peppers in bright red, yellow, and green, onions, garlic, andouille sausage, chicken thighs, and rice. Jambalaya—my mother's recipe that I had memorized through repetition. The simple rhythm of preparing the meal soothed me. The knife against the cutting board, the crunch of vegetables yielding to the blade, and the sizzling sound as oil met meat, all offered comfort. Steam rose as each ingredient joined the others in the heavy cast-iron pot that had been my mother's and was now mine, a small piece of home that had traveled with me through every move.

As I stirred the developing dish, the tight knot of anxiety in my chest began to loosen. The questions about life remained, but their urgency faded as I focused on cooking. My shoulders relaxed and my breathing deepened. The kitchen filled with scents that reminded me of family dinners around a worn table, of my mother's gentle guidance during my clumsy childhood, and of holidays when our family set aside busy schedules to be together.

I had just added the bay leaves to the jambalaya when my phone vibrated on the counter, and my mama's face lit up the screen. Seeing her always eased my heart, a familiar comfort. Nee Nee Duncan, with her hair pulled back in a simple bun and smile lines framing her eyes that had experienced both hardship and joy. Even through a digital screen, she radiated the quiet strength that had kept our family together through tough times.

"Hey, Mama," I said, placing the phone on the counter so I could continue to stir.

"I see you cooking," she said warmly. "What's on your mind? You always cook when something is bothering you."

I paused, the wooden spoon hovering above the pot. My mother understood me better than anyone, reading my feelings through the miles and phone lines. Our bond had grown long ago, even before my days as a bounty hunter, and had deepened during the darkest days of my life, after her Stage 3 breast cancer diagnosis when I was a teenager. I was only fifteen then, just beginning to establish myself in high school. I didn't go away to Chi's Finishing School overseas like the rest of my family—because for eight months, I accompanied my mom to treatments, holding her head during the worst of the nausea, and cooking for her when nothing else seemed to work. In that small kitchen, she taught me her favorite recipes, and we communicated through the act of cooking when words were not enough.

"Work is slow," I admitted as I stirred. "I'm thinking about coming home for a while to spend some time with the family."

"Well, that would be wonderful," she replied with a hint of surprise. "It's been a while since you've stayed longer than a weekend. Your old room is still there, even though I've been using the closet for storage."

"How's everyone doing? Is Lauryn still running the world over there?"

My mother began updating me about my younger sister, her voice warm and excited whenever she talked about her children's achievements. Lauryn had always been physical for a girl. We nicknamed her Lil Larry because her energy was so much like our father's. Like the rest of the Duncan women, she attended the Chi's, a prestigious finishing school that specialized in combat and tactical training. My family believed it taught more than just how to fight. It instilled discipline, focus, and a warrior's mindset.

"That girl," she said proudly, "finished at the top of her class. She wants a job that uses all her combat skills, not just the ones that look good on paper."

I added a pinch of cayenne into the pot and asked, "Did she ever mention any interest in what I do?"

"Funny you should ask. Just last Sunday dinner, she said that the corporate security world feels too . . . what did she say? '*Sanitized.*' She mentioned that she might want something with more edge." My mother paused before adding, "Are you thinking about involving her in your business?"

"I don't know," I said, hesitation thick in my voice. "She's got the training and the instincts, but what I do . . . it's extremely dangerous."

"Mmm-hmm," my mother hummed, a sound loaded with meaning. "You've always been a lone wolf, just like your dad. You never wanted anyone slowing you down."

I was about to reply when I noticed my mother's sharp intake of breath. The sudden silence told me something had changed.

"Curtis Duncan," she said, her voice lower and stern in a way that once scared me as a child. "Is that a piece of women's underwear on your living room floor?"

I turned and saw a small scrap of pink lace on the hardwood floor—evidence of an impromptu encounter with . . . Trisha? Tiana? I couldn't remember for sure.

"I—" I began, but my mother interrupted before I could speak.

"I raised you better than to live like a bachelor from one of those reality TV shows," she said, her disappointment clear. "When are you going to settle down with a good woman, Curtis? Start building something that lasts longer than a night."

The echoes of Marcia's questions filled my mind, doubling the sound of all the women's judgment. My mother softened her tone, shifting from anger to concern.

"You're thirty-eight years old, dear. I'm not getting any younger, and I want to see at least one grandchild from you before I go. Not that I'm planning on leaving soon," she added quickly. "But time doesn't stop. You keep chasing after people who run away, but maybe it's time for you to stay. Find someone to build a family with."

"I hear you, Mama," I said at last, turning back to the stove where my jambalaya needed my attention. The image was clear: a dish that needed constant care so it wouldn't burn, much like the relationships in my life.

"Do you? Because I've been telling you this for years, and that fancy apartment of yours still looks like a hotel room. No photos, no mementos, nothing to show you have a past or are planning for a future."

Her words hit me hard, breaking through my usual defenses. She was right. My home, no matter how expensive or luxurious, held nothing lasting. Nothing that couldn't be packed up or replaced in one day. As a bounty hunter, I set up my life for movement and chasing the next thing, not for putting down roots.

Just as she was about to go into another long, passionate rant about me finding purpose in life, my second phone, the one I used for business, rang, interrupting her train of thought.

"Mom, I hear you, but my money phone is ringing." I raised my hand apologetically as I grabbed the other cell phone from the table. The device lit up with bright colors and notifications as I answered, and just for a second, I tuned out my mom's words.

The voice on the other end was sharp, commanding, and yet I recognized it immediately. It was Deputy Raynard Bradford. His booming voice filled my ear. There was that warmth between us—a friendship that made even a phone call feel casual.

"Curtis, it's Ray. I've got a major assignment for you, my friend. It's worth a million dollars," he said.

"A million dollars," I repeated. "Who the hell is the target?"

My heart skipped a beat. Danger and reward were mixed in his words. This was exactly my kind of gig and with one call, I was thrown back into the action. Ray wasted no time.

"Be ready in three hours, Curtis. I'm sending a private jet to pick you up. We'll head to an undisclosed location and go over the target details."

My pulse raced with excitement as I ended the call and told my mother I had to go. There was no time to waste. I had a million-dollar assignment, and I was going all the way.

Three hours later, I was on a private jet roaring through clear skies. Below, rural towns gave way to sprawling cities. Washington, DC, the heart of American politics, was waiting. This was my first mission in the Capital, and I felt a mix of adrenaline and cautious determination. Ray had summoned me here for a reason, and I wasn't about to let him down. The plane descended steadily toward the runway. I saw the city stretch out like a maze of buildings and monuments. With a small bump, the jet touched down smoothly. I gathered my belongings and soon found myself being escorted in a waiting car through busy city streets. Finally, I arrived at a plain building, where Ray was waiting.

"Curt, I'm glad you made it, brother," he said, giving me a warm hug before asking me to take a seat. He got straight to business. "I have some important info for you about Johnny Boy and his organization."

"Johnny Boy? Wait—isn't that the dude who broke outta the courthouse in broad daylight?" I asked, eyebrows raised.

Ray nodded. "Yup. That's him. Real name's Jonathan Boykins, but everyone just calls him Johnny Boy."

"Man, I remember seeing that on the news. Wild."

Ray let out a breath. "His crew's called the Gede Gang. They're into everything— smuggling, laundering, trafficking. You name it."

"Damn. So we're not talking local street thugs."

"Not even close," Ray said, locking eyes with me. "They've got serious international ties. We need to shut them down and capture him fast."

I listened carefully as Ray detailed Johnny Boy's criminal empire. He leaned in, his voice low but steady, like he was unloading something too heavy to carry alone.

"They run drugs up and down the coast. Launder money through fake shell companies. Human trafficking, racketeering . . . it's all on the table. These guys got reach. Offshore accounts, foreign connections. Real organized crime."

I didn't say a word. Just nodded slowly, letting it all sink in. This shit wasn't street-level chaos. This was a whole damn empire.

Chapter 13

Senator Richard Winbush

I'd stood at a lectern under the punishing glare of the chamber lights more times than I could count, my voice echoing across marble floors while protesters outside hurled my name like a curse. I remembered the sound of their chants—metallic, raw—bouncing off the Capitol walls like an anthem of disdain, mocking every word I spoke. I'd felt the sting of boos cutting across live broadcasts, judgment from millions in real time. I'd sat in hearings flanked by rivals, their questions polished like bullets, ready to draw blood. And more nights than I could name, I'd been ambushed beneath flickering lot lamps, reporters lunging with recorders like weapons. But none of it ever rattled me. I ran from nothing—and I wasn't about to start now, not because of some gangster puffed up on street cred. I knew Johnny Boy murdered Attorney General Bowens. I'd read the black-bag briefings—grainy surveillance photos of bodies twisted in car trunks, intercepted calls dripping with cryptic threats. I was not blind. I knew the reach of this man. But fear? Fear never found purchase in me. I was forged in the hollers of West Virginia, raised on the taste of hunger and the sting of a belt. My four brothers and I learned to fight long before we learned to forgive. I still remembered the clink of canned beans over a fire that hissed

more smoke than heat, my stomach curling with every
bite. And I remembered my father's fists. What they did.
What they tried to break. The night I snapped his hand
bone by bone for touching my mother again, blood and
shame soaked into the floorboards like an oath. That
night, I became a man who'd never bow to fists, fear, or
anything in between. So, when my security detail pressed
in, I listened, but I didn't bend.

"Senator, you're a high-priority target."

"Senator, we need you out of the city—today."

"There's a safe house ready in rural Virginia."

They meant well, but they saw a man in a tailored suit
and forgot what lived underneath. The safe house they
pitched was something out of a spy thriller, hidden in
the thick of the Virginia woods, surrounded by pines and
oaks so dense that sunlight barely touched the ground.
From the gravel road, it looked like a forgotten hunting
cabin—wood siding gone soft with moss, tin roof rusting
to the color of dried blood. A crooked mailbox slumped at
the end of the drive like it had given up.

But inside that illusion was a fortress— motion sensors
buried in the brush, infrared cameras perched like birds
in the trees. A silent perimeter alarm ran underfoot,
and reinforced steel doors and ballistic windows faced
nothing but wilderness. Blackout curtains sealed the
world out; leather chairs stared across rooms lined with
weapons, burner phones, and encrypted gear. Beneath
it all, a biometric-secured command center blinked and
buzzed: monitors flickering with satellite feeds, servers
breathing in the dark, and an armory stocked heavier
than some bases I'd visited overseas. It was a marvel
of protection, a place designed to vanish you, and I
hated every inch of it. I wasn't going to disappear. Not
for Johnny. Not for anyone. I'd spent my entire career
walking into the storm—legislation, scandal, protests,

chaos. I wasn't about to retreat into the shadows when the real work needed to be done in the light.

"I'm a senior Senator of the United States," I told them, my voice low but unshakable. "I have work to do. And I'm not trading my office for a hole in the woods."

They looked at me like I'd gone mad. Maybe I had. Maybe there's a razor-thin line between resolve and recklessness. But that was the line I'd always lived on. I didn't claw my way from the dirt just to vanish when the fight got close. I was not some faceless bureaucrat hiding behind glass and security briefings. I was the headline. The decision. The voice in the room when things were burning down. And truth be told, a part of me welcomed the heat. It stirred something ancient in me. That old fire from childhood—the one that taught me survival—wasn't just a skill. It was a promise. Johnny Boy might have ruled the underworld, but I walked the halls of power. He sent fear like a whisper through the streets. I sent bills through Congress that shook the nation. If he wanted to come for me, let him come. But I wouldn't be waiting in a cabin. I'd be here—under the dome, in the spotlight, exactly where I belonged. We would see if he was bold enough to enter my world.

Chapter 14

Curtis

I glanced at my black diamond watch again for the fifth time in just three minutes as I paced the lobby of The Park at 14th. Twenty-two years felt like both a blink and a lifetime, a heartbeat stretched into eternity since our last goodbye. My stomach was knotted, not with that usual pre-hunt adrenaline, but with something raw and real: the excitement of seeing Mya Wynn, my childhood bestie who moved from Waycross when she was just 16 years old. There was always something unspoken between me and Mya, like an unopened letter resting quietly in both our hearts, daring us to delve into its contents but remaining untouched. We weren't just friends; we were each other's constants. I was the wild one—reckless, impulsive, forever chasing some thrill or fleeing from one adventure to the next, living as if tomorrow was a mere possibility. She was the calm in my storm—measured, brilliant, fiercely loyal. She knew exactly how to reel me back when I spiraled out of control, which was more often than not. I, in turn, knew how to coax her out from behind the walls she built when she became too guarded. We fit together seamlessly, without the need to explain how or why. We grew up like that. Tight. Intimate, but not lovers. Playful, yet never crossing the line.

I stopped at the host stand, giving the maître d' a quick nod, even though the guy had already told me twice that my table was reserved. The dude's polite smile got a bit tighter each time I rolled up. I felt like a nervous teenager, just thinking about having lunch with my old friend. If my targets caught a glimpse of me now, my tough-guy rep would melt away like sugar in hot coffee.

"She'll be here," I muttered to myself, rolling my broad shoulders to release the tension. My fingers tapped against my thigh, a rhythm that matched my quickening pulse. I'd gone toe-to-toe with some of the most dangerous and armed fugitives in the world with less apprehension than I felt while waiting for a girl I used to build mud forts with back in the woods of Waycross.

The restaurant buzzed with the vibe of D.C.'s power lunch crowd. Important chatter filled the air, interrupted by the soft clatter of silverware on fancy plates and the occasional controlled laughter. Glasses tapped in subtle toasts as waiters navigated the tables with smooth precision. The place was filled with the scents of sizzling meat, rich sauces, and pricey perfume: a mix that screamed deals going down and connections being built over meals that cost more than some folks make in a day.

I took a deep breath, letting the scene around me keep me grounded. In my line of work, staying sharp was the name of the game, so I instinctively scoped out the exits, checked the angles, and memorized the faces of the other diners: a habit I couldn't drop even in a spot like this. Over in a corner booth, a lady kept fiddling with her ear while chatting low-key with her companion. I clocked it right away. She had an earpiece. Probably some congressional aide getting live updates to her boss who couldn't be bothered to show up.

The familiar process of observation steadied me, but my mind wandered stubbornly back to Waycross, to hot Georgia afternoons when times were simpler. We were ten years old, crouched behind Mrs. Tanner's azalea bushes with mud streaked across our cheeks like war paint. Mya had insisted on the camouflage, despite my protests that it was unnecessary for capturing frogs.

"You don't know nothin' about catching frogs," she'd whispered fiercely, her dark eyes serious beneath the bill of her father's too-large baseball cap. "My daddy says the element of surprise is the most important weapon."

I nodded solemnly, accepting Mya's wisdom as gospel. Her father was a lieutenant in the Army, which gave her automatic authority on all matters of strategy and stealth.

"On three," Mya commanded, her skinny arm extended toward the small pond where our amphibious targets croaked, unsuspecting. "One . . . two . . ."

Before she could say "three," I lunged forward, cupping my hands and capturing not one but two small frogs in a single grab.

"Curtis Duncan!" Mya shouted, jumping to her feet, outrage and admiration battling in her expression. "That's cheating! You went on two!"

I grinned up at her, proud and unapologetic. "Sometimes you gotta break the rules to get results."

She shook her head, but laughter had bubbled up, dissolving her anger. "You're impossible," she declared, dropping to her knees beside me to peer at my prizes.

"That's what my mama says too," I replied, carefully transferring one wriggling frog to Mya's waiting hands.

Our fingers brushed during the exchange, and for a moment, something shy and unfamiliar passed between us, a current more startling than the cool, damp skin of the frog. Then Mya punched my shoulder, breaking the spell, and we returned to the serious business of examining our catch.

The memory dissolved as the restaurant's heavy glass door swung open, and my heart jumped. Twenty-two years fell away in an instant.

Mya Wynn strolled into the lobby, and it was like the whole vibe shifted to welcome her. The girl who used to rock dirt-smudged jeans had leveled up to become a stunningly beautiful woman. Her caramel skin glowed under the chill restaurant lights. Her hair, once wild and free from those rushed braids, now flowed in sleek waves that kissed her shoulders. She was rocking a charcoal blazer over a simple ivory blouse, keeping it professional, but her gold necklace glinted when she moved, just enough flex to show she was confident, not flashy.

But it was her eyes that kept me steady. The same sharp, scrutinizing look that once measured frogs, climbing trees, and later, high school crushes. Those eyes locked onto me instantly, like she knew exactly where I'd be posted up. For a split second, we simply stared at one another across the lobby, all the years between us hanging in the air but not mattering at all. Then, Mya's serious look broke into a big smile that lit up her whole face, and she started striding toward me with determination.

"Curtis Duncan," she called out, her voice dripping with that Southern charm and a hint of Georgia twang that D.C. couldn't quite wash away. "Look at you, always on time."

Before I could say a word, she threw her arms around me with a hug so tight it didn't match her slim figure. I quickly hugged back, caught up in the weird mix of now and then, the new shape of the woman she was now mixed with the memories of the girl I used to know.

I stepped back to get a good look at her. "Didn't wanna chance you bouncing before I got here."

"As if I'd do that." She checked me out closely, her eyes noting how time had done its thing. "You look handsome. A bit more rugged, but it fits you."

"And you look . . ." I waved my hand around, at a loss for words. "Not like the girl who used to snatch snakes barehanded."

Mya laughed, the sound drawing the attention of nearby diners. "Oh, I can still catch them if needed. The snakes in D.C. just wear better suits." She glanced around the restaurant. "Speaking of suits, this place is a far cry from the Dairy Queen parking lot where we used to hang out."

The host approached with visible relief that my companion had finally arrived. "Your table is ready, sir, madam. Please follow me."

We were led to a corner table partially screened by a decorative partition of dark wood and etched glass—private without being isolated. I had requested this specific table when I made the reservation, wanting both discretion and a clear view of the entire restaurant. Old habits.

"Still keeping your back to the wall, huh? Just like you did at lunch back in elementary school. I remember you used to say your dad told you never sit anywhere unless you can see the whole room. Said you never wanted anybody sneaking up on you." Mya remembered as we settled into our seats, proving her own observational skills hadn't dulled.

I smiled. "Some things don't change."

"And some things do," she countered, accepting a menu from the server with a polite nod. "America's Baddest Bounty Hunter? Really, Curtis? That's what the *Post* called you in that profile last year."

I winced. "Not my idea. That was some PR nonsense from the bail bonds company I was working with."

"Hmm," she said, her tone making it clear she didn't entirely believe me. "It's quite the reputation you've built. Tracking down dangerous fugitives, recovering millions in bail jumpers. A long way from Waycross."

"No further than the *Washington Post's* star investigative reporter," I countered. "I read your series on Senate corruption. Pulitzer material."

A pleased flush colored her cheeks. "We'll see. The committee announces next month." She set down her menu. "But you didn't invite me to lunch to talk about my articles, did you?"

"No." I should have known she'd cut straight to the chase. It was what made her such a formidable journalist.

"First off, I owe you a real apology—for not reaching out sooner. I've had a lot of time to think about what happened . . . and what I did. Messing around with your best friend Rochelle? That was low. I ain't even gonna try to justify it. It was foul, and you didn't deserve that. Truth is, I was scared. Scared of messing up the one thing in my life that always felt solid—you. What we had wasn't just some casual friendship. We had a connection that ran deep, way deeper than either of us ever said out loud. From the time we were kids, we just knew each other. And that kind of bond? You don't find that every day. But instead of honoring that, I let fear make decisions for me. I thought if I crossed that line with you and it didn't work out, I'd lose you completely. So, I sabotaged it before it even had a chance. I thought staying in the 'friend zone' would protect us . . . but all I did was crash us anyway. I know I hurt you. Even if we never put a title on what we were, we both knew it was more than just friendship. I hate that I became the reason you had to question what we had. I can't change what I did, but I needed you to hear from me that I was wrong. And I'm so sorry."

Mya reached over the table and grabbed both of my hands and whispered, "Thank you."

I guess time heals all. With my apology out of the way, we sat in silence for a second, then quickly ordered our food. Mya chose the seared scallops, and I got the steak, medium rare. For the next half hour, we traded stories over expertly prepared food. Mya described her brownstone near Catholic University, the challenges of navigating the competitive world of political journalism, and her mother's frequent complaints about her living so far from Georgia. I shared edited versions of my more interesting cases, we talked about my sister Lauryn for a bit and how she'd grown up, and my mom's ongoing campaign to see me "properly settled."

"She still calls me, you know," Mya said, dabbing her lips with her napkin. "Your mother. At least once a year to check on me and remind me that I'm not getting any younger."

I groaned. "That sounds like my mama. Sorry about that."

"Don't be. It's sweet." Mya's expression softened. "She sent me a care package last year—homemade peach preserves and those spicy pecans I used to love."

"The ones with cayenne and brown sugar? She still makes those for Christmas every year."

"Some traditions are worth keeping."

Mya set down her fork and fixed me with a direct gaze. "Now, are you going to tell me why you really wanted to meet? Because while this has been lovely, I know you didn't track me down after all this time only to apologize."

I nodded, shifting into the focused demeanor that had served me well in my professional life. "I need your help, Mya. Your journalist's resources and your connections in the city."

"I'm listening."

"How much do you know about the Gede Gang?"

Mya's eyebrows rose. "The Haitian organization? Enough to be careful. I wrote a feature story on their gang, but for some unknown reason, it was pulled at the last minute, right before it was set to go to print. They've got their fingers in everything from drug trafficking to political extortion. Their leader's name is Jonathan Boykins. Goes by Johnny Boy. He keeps a low profile."

I nodded, impressed. "You've done your homework."

"It's my job to know the power players in this city, legitimate and otherwise." Her eyes narrowed. "Curtis, please tell me you're not going after them."

I didn't answer directly. "I need information. Background on their operations, political connections, territory. The kind of stuff that doesn't make it into police reports."

"The kind of stuff I might have in my files," Mya said slowly. "Curtis, these people are dangerous. Not your typical bail jumper with a history of bad decisions. They're organized, sophisticated, and absolutely ruthless."

"I know exactly what they are," I said, my voice hardening slightly. "That's why I need to be thorough."

Mya said firmly, "I don't share information that might get people killed—even old friends."

Her principled stance didn't surprise me. It was one of the things I'd always respected about her. "I'm not asking you to compromise your ethics, Mya. Just to share what's already in the public record or what you've gathered through legitimate sources."

She leaned back in her chair, assessing me with the critical eye that had likely unnerved numerous interview subjects. "On one condition."

"Name it."

"You keep me in the loop. Whatever you're planning, whatever you find, you don't shut me out. Not only for my peace of mind, but because two brains are better than one. And from what I remember, you could be a bit reckless when you set your mind to something."

I smiled. "Like jumping off the Haversham Creek bridge after you said it couldn't be done?"

"Exactly like that," she said, not returning my smile. "Only this time, it's not just a broken arm at stake."

The seriousness of her concern sobered me. "I'll keep you informed. But, Mya, I need to be clear—I don't want you anywhere near these people physically. Information only."

She nodded, though something in her expression suggested she wasn't making any promises. "I'll email you what I have tonight. And Curtis?"

"Yeah?"

"Be careful. I didn't reconnect with you after twenty-two years just to attend your funeral."

"Always am," I assured her, though we both knew the nature of my work made such promises tenuous at best.

We finished our meal with lighter conversation, but the undercurrent of our agreement flowed beneath our words. When the check came, I insisted on paying despite Mya's protests.

"Next time's on me," she said as we walked together to the exit. "And there will be a next time, preferably before another decade and a half passes."

Outside on the street, the sun cast long shadows between the buildings. We hugged goodbye, and I felt the weight of our shared past and newfound purpose in her embrace.

"I'll call you when I've sent the files," she said, stepping back.

"I appreciate this, Mya. More than I can say."

She smiled, a mix of exasperation and affection. "Just don't make me regret it." With a small wave, she turned and walked toward the Metro station, her confident stride carrying her quickly into the flow of pedestrians.

I watched until she disappeared, then pulled out my phone. My cousin answered on the second ring. Li'l Vegas, real name Nevada Duncan, was my younger cousin and my trusted right-hand man. He handled surveillance, hacking security systems, tracing burner phones, and digging up dirt that even law enforcement couldn't find. Together, we were pretty much unstoppable. Li'l Vegas grew up watching and idolizing me, but now he'd carved out his own lane in the family. He talked fast but thought faster, and he didn't scare easily. He was not a fighter like me, but he'd bring a drone swarm or jam a GPS signal without blinking.

"Li'l Vegas, it's me," I said, already moving toward where I'd parked my car. "I need your help with something big."

There was a pause before he answered. "What's the job?"

I took a deep breath, knowing the gravity of the situation. "Have you heard of a guy named Jonathan Boykins, aka Johnny Boy? He's a dangerous Haitian crime boss."

"Johnny Boy?" Nevada whistled. "Yeah, that's the guy who just escaped from the federal courthouse, right?"

"Yeah. That's him."

"That's some serious heat, Curtis. I know you're the best in the business, but—"

I interrupted him. "The bounty is a million dollars."

"A million dollars? What's the plan?" he asked.

"I need you to dig up everything you can on him: who his parents are, his daily routines. This guy is slippery, and we can't afford any mistakes," I explained.

"You got it, Curtis. I'll start right away. This one's not going to be easy, but if anyone can pull it off, it's you."

Even though he couldn't see me, I nodded. "Thanks, Li'l Vegas. I'm counting on you. We need to be smart and fast."

"Roger that, big cuz. I'll have some intel for you ASAP," he promised.

"Cool. I knew I could count on you," I said with a small smile.

"We'll talk soon. Stay safe out there, Curtis. I love you," he added before the call ended.

I slipped the phone back into my pocket as my mind raced through the next steps. With my team in place, it was time to get to work. Johnny Boy wasn't going to know what hit him.

Chapter 15

Mya

The dead-end alley was narrow, damp, and choked with the smell of rotting trash and fried grease from the carry-out around the corner. It was lit with harsh fluorescent lights that bounced off the stained, cracked concrete like a spotlight on everything grimy and forgotten. I entered first, the heels of my Dior sandals clicking with each step. Following behind me was my larger shadow, Curtis Duncan, his footsteps nearly silent despite his size.

We located Sticky Fingers with help from a guy named Butchy, who smelled like weed, motor oil, and menthols. His left pinky was missing—bit off in a fight outside a pool hall in Southeast. I got to know him during my early days reporting in the field years ago, when I was writing an exposé—which was later buried—on housing fraud in Ward 8. Butchy had been working as a maintenance man in one of the buildings—one of the few people who would actually talk to me. He walked me through how the rental scam worked. I promised to keep his name out of the article, and he never forgot that. Ever since then, he was my trusted street source.

The man we'd come to see stood in the middle of the alley when we arrived, his thin fingers pausing mid-count over a small stack of crumpled bills. Sticky Fingers, a name earned rather than given, looked up with the wary eyes of someone who'd spent a lifetime calculating exits.

"Sticky," I said, sounding more like an around-the-way girl instead of a polished *Washington Post* journalist. I had the ability to switch back and forth like a chameleon. "I'm Mya Wynn. We need to talk."

Recognition came across Sticky's face, followed by confusion. He tucked the bills into one of his many pockets with a slick hand that would impress the head man in charge of security at a casino.

"I know who you are," he said, eyes darting between me and Curtis. "The question is, what are you doing here?" His gaze lingered on Curtis, whose broad shoulders looked like mountains. "This ain't exactly your usual interview setting, Ms. Journalist."

Curtis said nothing, content to let his presence speak. He'd positioned himself between Sticky and the exit of the alley, a fact Sticky clearly noted.

I stepped closer, my eyes locked on him. "I need information about Johnny Boy and the Gede Gang."

Sticky's nervous tap became a quick and sharp beat. "You are asking the wrong questions in the wrong part of town." He flashed a smile that Curtis didn't find funny. "I deal in cash and coins, not suicide missions, you feel me?"

"We heard something different," I said, my tone conversational but firm. "Word is you've got ears everywhere in this city, especially where it concerns the Gede Gang."

Sticky's eyes narrowed, glancing toward the exit again. "Whoever told you that did you no favors."

"But they did you a favor," I continued, "because now instead of Curtis here tracking you down for that warrant in Maryland, you get to have a civil conversation with me."

Tiny beads of sweat formed on Sticky's upper lip. "I don't know what you're talking about."

"Prince George's County." I gave him a pleasant smile. "Grand theft auto, wasn't it? The judge wasn't happy about you skipping that court date."

Sticky swallowed so hard that his Adam's apple bobbed. "Look, what you're asking . . . it's not like swiping a Rolex off some drunk congressman. The Gede Gang, they don't play. Johnny Boy finds out I've been talking, you'll find pieces of me all over the District."

Curtis stepped forward, moving deliberately and with measured steps. The light hit his face just right, throwing shadows that made him look even more serious than he already did. Curtis smirked and cracked his knuckles. "Lemme explain how this works. You can talk now and keep your teeth, or I can rearrange your fuckin face 'til the truth falls. Either way, you're gonna sing. I'm just givin' you the courtesy of choosing the song."

Sticky backed up until his back pressed against the water-stained wall. "You don't understand. These people . . . they've got cops on payroll. They've got eyes everywhere."

"So do I," Curtis responded.

"Not like them," Sticky insisted, his voice rising an octave. "They killed a dude last month just for parking in the wrong spot outside their club. Skinned his face off and left him where his kids would find him. You think I want that kind of attention?"

Curtis's expression didn't change. "I think you want to stay out of a cell in PG County even more."

Sticky laughed nervously. "At least I'd be alive in a cell."

"You assume I'm giving you a choice." Curtis closed the distance between them in two long strides. He reached out, grabbing Sticky's shirt just below the throat, and lifted, not enough to choke, but enough to leave his feet barely scraping the ground. "I'm not."

Fear flashed in Sticky's eyes, the raw, no-filter kind that cut through all the tough talk. His hands flew to Curtis's arm, but it was like grabbing a damn brick wall, solid and unshakable.

"Jesus, man," Sticky wheezed. "This is—this is assault."

"This is a conversation," Curtis corrected, his voice still eerily calm. "The assault comes if I have to ask again."

I watched from a few feet away, forcing myself to remain neutral. This wasn't my preferred method, but I'd known Curtis long enough to know when to let him take the lead. Some folks listened when you talked sense and promised them protection. Others weren't moved by words, only by feeling the heat right then and there.

"Okay, okay," Sticky gasped, his hands now raised in surrender. "Just . . . put me down, man. I'll tell you what I know."

Curtis studied his face for a moment, then slowly lowered him until his feet touched the ground. He didn't immediately release his grip on the shirt.

"Start talking," he said.

Sticky's hands trembled as he straightened his collar. "Could I get some water or something? My throat's—"

"Talk," Curtis repeated, taking half a step back but remaining close enough that his presence felt like a physical weight.

Sticky's eyes darted around the alley once more, as if expecting hidden listeners in the shadows. The fear had seeped into his very posture, hunching his shoulders and making him look smaller than he already was.

"All right," he finally said, his voice barely above a whisper. "The Gede Gang's been moving product through an old warehouse in Landover. Big operation, guns coming in, drugs going out. Johnny Boy doesn't usually show his face there, but word is he's scheduled a big meeting tomorrow night. Something about a new supplier from overseas."

Curtis's expression never changed, but I caught the slight shift in his stance. The information had struck a chord.

"Address," Curtis demanded.

"It's that abandoned furniture factory on Landover Road," Sticky said, words tumbling out faster now. "Big brick building with the busted sign. They've got lookouts a quarter-mile in every direction and security inside that would make the Pentagon jealous." He swallowed hard. "That's all I know, I swear. I've never been inside. I just heard things from people who have."

Curtis finally released his grip on Sticky's shirt, stepping back to give him space. Sticky immediately put distance between them, sliding along the wall until he was closer to me than Curtis.

"If you're lying . . ." Curtis's threat dangled in the air, loud without him saying another word.

"I'm not," Sticky insisted, a desperate edge to his voice. "That's exactly what I heard. Going there is suicide, but that's your business."

I stepped forward, my posture relaxed in contrast to the tension radiating from the two testosterone-filled men.

"Thank you, Sticky. We appreciate the information." I reached into my purse and took out a small envelope. "For your trouble."

Sticky's eyes widened at the sight of the envelope. He reached for it with still-trembling fingers but hesitated just before taking it. "If they find out I talked . . ."

"They won't," I assured him. "Not from us."

Sticky snatched the envelope, flipped through the cash quickly, then slid it into one of his deep pockets as if it were muscle memory. Relief hit his face, but his eyes stayed sharp, like he knew not to get too comfortable.

"Let's go," Curtis said to me, already turning toward the exit of the alley.

I nodded. As we got ready to leave, my eyes caught a quick flash on Sticky's wrist: a familiar black diamond watch with a distinctive emblem partially hidden by his sleeve.

"Curtis," I said.

He turned back, his gaze following mine to Sticky's wrist. Sticky noticed our attention and instinctively tugged his sleeve down, but not before Curtis saw what had caught my eye.

"Seriously?" Curtis asked, his tone more fed up than fired up.

Sticky's face ran through a whole slideshow. First, confusion, then that lightbulb moment, followed by a wild mix of fear and don't-give-a-damn defiance.

"What? I didn't—"

"My black diamond watch," Curtis interrupted. "This shit is custom, man, and it cost me a lot of money."

Sticky's face fell, caught in a lie he couldn't talk his way out of. He slowly pushed up his sleeve, revealing the watch that Curtis had been wearing when he walked in. With smooth, practiced hands, Sticky popped it open and held it out to Curtis like it was nothing.

"Force of habit," he offered weakly. "No disrespect intended."

Curtis took the watch, slipping it back onto his wrist with a practiced motion. Instead of anger, his expression held something closer to professional respect.

"You've got skills," he admitted. "Must have happened when I grabbed your shirt. Didn't even feel it."

Sticky eased up a bit, but you could still see he was low-key on guard. "Best in the District," he said, a hint of pride creeping into his voice. "No offense."

"None taken," Curtis replied. "But if I ever catch you lifting my shit again, I'm going to fuck you up."

The threat still hung in the air as Curtis headed out of the alley. I trailed behind, but after a few steps, I paused and threw one last look back at Sticky.

"Stay safe," I said, my words hitting harder than they looked on the surface.

Sticky nodded, already fading back into the cut like he was part of the shadows.

As we walked out of the alley, Curtis and I locked eyes: no words, just that knowing look that said it all. We knew the risk, we were still in it, and we had each other's backs like always.

"Landover," I said simply.

Curtis nodded like he was already mentally mapping his approach. "Tomorrow night."

We walked toward Curtis's black Lambo parked half a block away. Our strides matched despite the difference in our heights. As we pulled off into the night, for some reason, this just felt right.

Chapter 16

Curtis

My black Lamborghini idled by the curb like a sleek predator lying in wait. The long street stretched before me, and as I turned off the engine, silence wrapped around us like one of my grandmother's old quilts: thick, warm, and full of unspoken dreams. The houses on Mya's block were old and packed in tight, showing their age with no shame. The air smelled like freshly cut grass and somebody's takeout all mixed together.

I glanced at Mya. It had been too long since I'd allowed myself this kind of peace, the kind I didn't need to chase or put in cuffs. Mya stared out the window, eyes soft with admiration. She was soaking in the sights: cozy cafes with outdoor seating, eclectic art pieces in front yards, and vibrant murals on every corner. This was her world now, nestled in an arts district full of galleries and studios. The manicured lawns and tidy houses were a far cry from where we grew up in Waycross, Georgia.

"Why are you looking at me like that?" she asked, a playful smile tugging at her lips.

I hesitated, watching her closely. She wasn't the same girl I grew up with. The tomboy who climbed trees and played basketball with the guys was long gone. Now, she was a confident, stunning woman.

"I don't recognize you," I said, still amazed at seeing her at the restaurant. "I remember you playing with frogs, but now . . . you're this beautiful, incredible woman."

Her cheeks flushed, and a wide, dimpled smile took over her face. "Thanks," she said. "You're not too shabby yourself."

I chuckled a little, warmth blooming in my chest, a feeling I hadn't experienced in a long time. The ease between us was familiar, something that had never quite faded, no matter how much time had passed. She was amused, but there was something fond in it, a spark of our old connection.

"So, do you still cook like you used to?" she asked, recalling my love for food.

"Absolutely," I replied with a hint of pride. "To tell you the truth, if I wasn't a bounty hunter, I'd open my own restaurant. I'd call it Nee-Nee's Kitchen."

Mya's laugh was soft and teasing. "I see you're still a mama's boy, huh?"

I shrugged with a knowing grin. "Guilty as charged. My mom taught me everything I know about cooking."

She looked thoughtful, and I could see the wheels turning in her mind. "Well, if you're such a great cook, when are you going to cook for me?"

I grinned mischievously. "How about tomorrow night?"

"Tomorrow night?" She raised an eyebrow. "Okay, it's a date. And you better not disappoint me."

I took in the full weight of the moment as it settled in the air around us. Mya and I hadn't spoken like this since she left Waycross many years ago. She opened her arms for a hug, and I leaned right in, no hesitation. For a second, everything else faded, just me and her, wrapped up in old feelings and memories. Neither one of us was in a rush to let go.

When we pulled back, we did our old handshake, the one we did as kids when the streetlights came on. Our hands moved in perfect sync, a memory that still felt fresh.

She laughed with delight. "I can't believe we still remember that."

I smiled, feeling a rush of nostalgia. "Some things you just never forget."

I walked around the car and opened the door. I grabbed her hand, and as she climbed out, she said, "All right, Chef Curtis, see you tomorrow at seven p.m. sharp."

We slowly moved up that stone walkway to her brownstone like we were walking through old memories with every step. Each one hit differently; some sweet, some heavy. When we got to her door, I pulled her in for a long hug, holding on a little longer than I probably should have, then finally peeled myself away and headed back to the whip.

As I pulled off, the engine growled, and I hit the gas, flying down streets lined with concrete and dreams waiting to pop off. The city slid by in a soft blur, not as cold as usual, like it was giving me a little hope for once. Whatever tomorrow had in store, I was ready. I gripped the wheel tighter, the way you do when something finally feels like it might actually mean something.

After leaving Mya's brownstone and arriving at the condo I was renting, I realized something about me had shifted. I couldn't sleep. I lay on my back for hours, thinking about every dish I'd ever seen my mama prepare, wondering which ones Mya would love the most. It was weird because I'd never cared this much about cooking for a woman before. But this? This felt different.

By the time the sun peeked through my window blinds, I was already up, scrolling recipes on my phone and pacing the kitchen like a man on a mission. I hit two different exclusive stores before 9 a.m. I purchased a bottle of Screaming Eagle Cabernet Sauvignon, one of the most prestigious and expensive wines from Napa Valley, often priced between $3,000–$10,000+ per bottle. I also purchased fresh herbs and short ribs. If I was gonna cook for Mya, it had to be perfect. I wanted a meal that not only tasted good but also felt special.

Back at the condo, I laid everything out on the counter like I was prepping for battle. But before I fired up a single burner, I tapped my mama's name on FaceTime. If anybody could bless this meal from miles away, it was her. I adjusted the phone angle, waiting for it to connect. Mama never trusted technology. Said it felt like staring into a stranger's eye. Seven rings later, her face popped onto the screen, warm and familiar as ever.

"Sorry, son! I was out in the garden and had to rush in to catch the call," she said, her voice still sweet with that Georgia drawl. "Look at you. Lookin' all rested. Where you goin' tonight?"

I ignored her question. "Hey, Mama. You look good. That's the scarf I sent for your birthday?"

She touched it proudly. "Yes, baby. Your daddy said it brings out my eyes."

I laughed because my dad was always trying to spit game to my mom, but he didn't lie.

She squinted into the screen. "What's got you up calling me before noon on a Saturday? Somebody dead, or you finally decided to give your life to the Lord?"

I grinned. "Nah, Mama. I'm good. Just . . . thinkin' 'bout what to cook later."

She leaned closer to the screen like that would help her read my intentions. "Mm-hm. You buying herbs before breakfast means somebody special coming over. You gon' tell me who, or I gotta guess?"

I scratched the back of my neck with a knowing smile. "It's Mya. Mya Wynn."

The silence hit fast. Then her face lit up like the Fourth of July. "Oh, baby . . . Mya? I been callin' that girl every year, remindin' her she ain't gettin' no younger! I used to tell you she would be a good catch as y'all got older. She comes from a great family."

I laughed. "Don't start."

"Oh, I'm startin'." Her grin turned knowing. "You cookin' for her?"

"It's not like that." I was not trying to get my mom's hopes up, in case this dinner turned out to be nothing. She'd been a fan of Mya's for a long time.

She wasn't buying it. "Boy, please. What you makin'?"

"Your short ribs. The wine-braised ones with the rosemary and thyme. Roasted potatoes and the kale salad with cranberries. The whole spread."

She pressed her hand to her heart. "You makin' my short ribs for her?" Her voice got soft. "Mmm. That house is 'bout to smell like Sunday."

"I hope so. Like I'm right back in your kitchen."

Her smile wavered just a little. "That little girl used to tear through my house barefoot stealin' biscuits." Then she got serious. "Curtis, does she know what you do?"

"She knows, Ma."

Her eyes narrowed, that mama warning flaring up. "Don't bring that girl into your mess. Her people are good folks. Don't have her gettin' caught up in your world."

"I won't," I promised.

She nodded, but her eyes didn't soften. "I already worry enough about you. Just . . . don't give me another reason."

"Okay, Ma. But listen, I gotta go. I'll call you later and let you know how everything went."

"You better," she warned, wagging a finger at the camera. "And I want more than just 'dinner was good.' I want details. Did she eat everything? Did she go back for seconds? Was she dressed nice? How was the vibe?"

I smirked, nodding. "I got you. Full report."

"Good. And you tell Mya I still got them pictures from that sixth-grade play. She know the one where she's wearing the pink tutu."

"Are you serious, Ma?" I laughed.

"Real serious. Love you, baby."

"Love you too."

I ended the call, letting the screen go black as I sat in silence for a second, then smiled, shaking my head. I stood, rolled my shoulders, and went into action. I moved through the penthouse like I was a criminal clearing a crime scene: efficient, focused, precise.

A few hours later, the short ribs that had been slow-cooking filled the space with a deep, savory aroma that hit like a 5-star restaurant. I tasted the rich and velvety sauce, then added just a little more cracked pepper and fresh thyme. The kale was prepped, rinsed, and massaged with olive oil. I tossed in dried cranberries, crushed walnuts, and crumbled feta cheese, mixing it all in a big wooden bowl. I pulled the roasted potatoes from the oven, golden and crispy around the edges. I plated the food like a chef gunning for a Michelin star. The wine was open and breathing, two glasses standing by. Candles flickered softly. The smooth sounds of Maxwell's "Urban Hang Suite" were playing in the background. I even dimmed the lights just enough to cast a warm glow over the whole place. Everything was ready.

I showered and threw on a fitted black Unknown Union long sleeve that featured the muscles in my arms, paired with the black DKNY pants and my signature double roll black-diamond necklace. I wore the fresh, aquatic scent of Acqua di Gioia cologne with a clean taper and a black-diamond watch on my wrist. I had a sharp eye for style, so when I wasn't out chasing bad guys, I cleaned up like a GQ cover model.

At exactly 6:59, the doorbell rang. Mya was right on time. I glanced around the penthouse one more time and headed to the door with that same calm I used when walking into unknown situations. Only this time, the mission was dinner and maybe, just maybe, something real.

Chapter 17

Mya

I stood outside Curtis's door, holding a glass cake dome in one hand and adjusting my blouse with the other. Inside the dome was my signature key lime pound cake, his favorite back in Waycross. I'd added a fresh whipped cream topping, just the way he liked it. I'd been nervous the entire time I was baking it, second-guessing the recipe even though I'd been making it since I was 13 years old. My hands had trembled a little as I packed it. I told myself it was just excitement—that we were just friends. That any feelings I might've had were buried long ago, back when he started dating my best friend, Rochelle. But the truth was harder to ignore. Those feelings weren't gone. They'd just been tucked away, and now they were starting to surface again.

The moment he opened the door, I had to catch my breath. Six-foot-two, caramel brown skin, crisp black shirt clinging to muscles, and black slacks that sat just right on his hips, Curtis looked even better than he had the night before. His curls were fresh, still damp at the edges like he'd just stepped out of the shower, and his scent—fresh, warm, and laced with something dark and masculine—wrapped around me like the ocean before he even touched me.

He stood there with that familiar smile of his, and for a second, I just looked at him. Not the boy I grew up with, but the man he'd become: confident, fine as hell, and dangerous in all the right ways.

"Are you planning to let me in, or should I eat dinner in your hallway?" I teased, keeping my tone light, though my heart was doing flips.

Curtis laughed and stepped aside, letting me in. I walked into the penthouse, surprised by how well he'd pulled it together. It wasn't overly decorated, an obvious rental with neutral tones and a few impersonal touches like generic art and a candle that was trying too hard to smell expensive, but somehow, it still felt warm and lived in. On the dining table, everything was laid out just right. There were candles flickering, two wine glasses waiting, real linen napkins. It felt personal, intentional, and I was flattered that Curtis had put forth so much effort.

"I brought dessert," I said, holding up the covered cake container like it was a gift wrapped in gold. "Your favorite key lime pound cake. And yes, there's whipped cream."

His eyes lit up like I'd just handed him a winning lottery ticket. "You serious? You made the cake?" He stepped closer, grinning wide. "Now I know you came to play."

"I did," I said, unable to stop smiling. "And from the way it smells in here, so did you."

I kicked off my heels near the entryway, stretching my toes into the cool hardwood floors and relaxing instantly. The whole place smelled like rosemary, garlic, and something rich and slow-cooked. And when Curtis smiled at me like that, like he was glad I was there in a way that had nothing to do with the food or the case we were working on, it hit me harder than I expected.

For the first time in a long time, I felt like I was exactly where I was supposed to be.

"If that cake tastes half as good as you look, I might mess around and fall in love."

I rolled my eyes, but I smiled, too. "Keep talking slick, Duncan. Smells amazing in here. What did you whip up for me? "

"You'll see." He moved ahead of me, setting the cake on the kitchen counter. "I been in the kitchen all day, like it's a holiday or something."

As he walked past, he brushed up against me like he had no sense of personal space.

"Uh, watch it," I said, giving him a look as I tilted my head up at him.

"My bad," he said, all smooth. "Didn't realize you were standing that close."

The lie was bold, and so was the way his eyes lingered just a second too long. He looked at me like he was trying to memorize something. It was a familiar gaze, one we both knew well but had never dared to act on.

Then he broke the moment. "You hungry?"

"Starving."

"Let's eat," he said, and led me into the dining room.

He poured two glasses of wine, dark and expensive, not the cheap stuff we used to sneak from his mama's pantry when we were 15 years old. When he handed me my glass, our fingers brushed. The spark wasn't subtle.

"You always had a heavy pour," I said, taking a sip. "Remember that time you got me tipsy sneaking that five-dollar wine from your mama cabinet. Those were the good ole days."

"I always did know how to loosen you up," he said, sitting down across from me at the candlelit table he'd set with real linen napkins and good china. The view of the city twinkled through the windows like it was eavesdropping on our dinner.

"This is . . . not what I expected," I admitted, easing into my seat.

"Yeah? What'd you expect?"

"Takeout. Paper plates. You in a tank top."

Curtis smirked. "Don't disrespect me like that. I got range now."

He brought out the food. I took one bite and closed my eyes. "Oh my God. This is your mama's recipe, isn't it?"

"Straight from Nee Nee's kitchen," he said proudly. "She says hey, by the way."

"She told you to tell me that?"

"She did. And she said she still got pictures of you in a pink tutu from the sixth-grade play."

I nearly dropped my fork. "Curtis!"

"That's what she said."

I shook my head. "Remind me to delete her number."

We ate slowly, letting the conversation stretch. We talked about our hometown, his sister, my brother. Who from Waycross was married, who was divorced, who was on their second round of baby mamas. We talked about my job at the *Washington Post*, his work chasing fugitives.

"Curtis Duncan, you've been strategizing since middle school," I said with a grin, thinking back to when he hijacked our history class in eighth grade. "You didn't just take over the lesson. You had Mr. Chambers sitting there learning like one of the students."

"You knew back then I'd end up doing something wild?" he asked.

"I knew back then you'd never be average," I said.

He didn't say anything for a moment. Just looked at me across the candlelight.

"I missed this, just being able to talk to you."

"Me too."

After dinner, he pulled out the cake, sliced us both big pieces, and topped mine with an extra swirl of whipped cream like he remembered I liked it.

"This," he said, taking a bite, "is everything."

"You better say that," I said with a slight smile.

"I ain't saying it to be polite," he said. "This cake tastes like home."

As the laughter and wine settled into a soft hum, our conversation shifted.

"So . . . about Johnny Boy," I said gently, setting my glass down. "You really think this lead with Sticky Fingers will go anywhere?"

Curtis leaned back in his chair, tensing slightly. "It's early. Could be something, could be nothing. I appreciate you helping me out with this, but I won't put you in harm's way."

"Curtis, I knew what I was signing up for. You didn't drag me into this, even though I knew we were getting into dangerous territory."

"I know," he said, voice low and serious. "You offered. But I need you to understand that this ain't one of your exposés. This man doesn't just put people in time-out. He erases them. If he finds out we're sniffing around, especially with you beside me, he won't hesitate to take action."

"If I didn't want to help you, I wouldn't," I said, steady and clear. "I'm not scared of the truth, and I'm not scared of him.

He looked at me for a long moment, something un-readable in his eyes. "You always were stubborn."

"And you always played like you didn't need anyone," I said, leaning in a little. "But you do. And I'm here. We're in this together."

He reached across the table, his hand resting over mine again, but this time, there was something heavier in the touch. We moved to the couch, and I tucked my legs under me while he leaned back with his wine glass. The city buzzed in the background, but in that moment, it felt a world away.

"Mya, are you happy?" he asked suddenly.

The question caught me off guard. "What you mean?"

"I mean . . . with everything. Your job. Life. Being here."

I paused, thinking. "I'm proud of what I've built. I've seen things, written things, made change in real ways. But I guess I never expected success to feel so lonely sometimes."

He nodded slowly, like he understood too well. "Same."

There was a long silence before I added, "Being here with you, it doesn't feel lonely."

He didn't answer, but the way he looked at me said more than words could. I leaned in, brushing his arm lightly with my fingertips.

"You've changed, Curtis. But you're still you."

"And you," he said softly, "are still everything."

We didn't kiss, but the way he took my hand, the way we leaned into the silence together felt intimate enough to leave its own mark. As the night wound down, I gathered my things, slipping back into my heels reluctantly, and we lingered at the door.

"This was good," I said.

"It was more than good," he replied.

"I'll call you tomorrow?"

"I'll beat you to it."

I smiled and stepped into the hallway, but before the elevator door shut, I turned and looked back at him. "Curtis."

"What?" he asked.

I grinned. "Tell Nee Nee I'm still mad about the tutu."

He laughed as the doors closed, and I floated down with a belly full of good food and a heart that hadn't felt this light in a long time. Somewhere between the wine, the laughter, and the shared memories, I realized something real: I wasn't just reconnecting with Curtis. I was remembering what our friendship was before it got so complicated, and that version of me missed him something serious.

Chapter 18

Johnny Boy

The smoke in The Grand Cigar Lounge was smooth, rich, and slightly suffocating. My cigar burned slowly between my fingers, the scent of rare Dominican tobacco lacing the air with power and patience. The thing I love about cigars is that like revenge, they're best savored, not rushed.

I leaned into the polished mahogany table at the center of the private room, pressing my fingertips into the grain. Every man in that room knew what time it was. Santana, Simeon, and a few of my top lieutenants were the kind of men who didn't flinch when the stakes got high. They also knew I didn't waste words.

"Tonight," I said, my voice low but laced with steel, "we fix a problem."

My Haitian accent always crept in when I got serious; thicker and darker, letting folks know the old me was still right there under the silk ties and custom suits. I looked around the room, catching each man's gaze, letting the weight of my words settle deep in their chests. I wasn't asking. I was declaring.

The exclusive room we were in was on the top floor of The Grand Cigar Lounge. We called it the war room. Every inch of the lounge screamed status: leather seats softer than most politicians' spines, liquor you couldn't pronounce unless your passport had stamps from places with no extradition laws, and artwork that whispered bloodlines and bank accounts. But this wasn't about flexing. This was a war council.

"Senator Richard Winbush got comfortable," I continued, letting his name hang in the air like the smoke from my cigar. "Forgot who cleaned up his messes. Who made people disappear so he could shine in his little suits and preach his little speeches."

I sipped my aged rum, straight, no ice, and let it warm my chest. "Now he wanna stand on podiums, talk about cleaning up crime like he ain't been breaking bread with us for the last six years." I shook my head slowly. "Disrespect don't go unpunished. Not in my world."

Santana, sitting in a leather chair that looked like it wanted to tap out under his weight, grunted in agreement. The scar on his jaw twitched, a sign that he was already thinking ahead.

"He needs to be made an example," he said, his voice sounding rough like concrete dragging across asphalt.

"Not just made an example," I corrected him. "He needs to be a statement: in public, messy and irreversible."

Simeon looked up from his tablet, fingers still moving across the screen like they had a mind of their own. "I've got access to the security cams at the event. Nothing fancy. It's a predictable layout. Static guards. Two extras for show."

"Details?" I asked, turning back to Santana.

He stood, stretching his thick frame, and moved to the wall where the blueprints were pinned. "Anacostia Recreation Center, Winbush's pet project. The senator arrives at seven, speaks at eight, mingles until nine, then departs with his family." His deep voice rumbled through the room like distant thunder. "Security will be focused on the crowd, on potential disruptions inside. They won't be expecting it."

He stepped up to the blueprint, his hand damn near covering the whole block as he pointed to a line of buildings next to the spot. "We'll position Drexel here, on the roof of Ketcham Elementary School, which is adjacent to the rec center. Clear line of sight to the parking area where the senator's vehicle will be waiting. When he exits with his family . . ." Santana made a simple gesture with his finger and thumb, mimicking a gun. "One shot, clean and professional."

The beauty of the plan was in how simple it was. No wild break-ins, no Hollywood-style getaways, no extra moving parts. Just one clean shot that would shake the whole damn city to its core.

"The community center's boxed in by three precincts," I said, eyes locked on the blueprint. "But they don't hit that side of town fast. Average response is seven minutes. We'll be ghosts in two."

Santana gave a slow nod, cool as ever. His shoulders dropped just a little, his way of showing approval. "I'll post up in a ride half a block out. Drexel hits the stairwell after the shot, switches his look, and blends in with the crowd like he ain't done nothin' but hear a bang."

I let my eyes sweep the room one last time, landing on each man just long enough to make sure there was no confusion or hesitation. I wasn't about to open the floor for questions. This wasn't a roundtable discussion. In my crew, doubt didn't get a mic.

I leaned in, voice cool and deadly. "Tonight, we remind this city who the fuck we are. And Winbush? He gon' learn what betrayal really costs."

The crew got up without a word, moving like a machine that had been running smoothly for years. Everybody knew their lane, and there was no need for extra talk. Only Santana and Simeon stuck around after the rest left, leaving the three of us: the core that turned the Gede Gang from corner hustle to political force.

Simeon was already in motion, fingers flying over the keyboard like he was conducting an orchestra. Screens lit up with surveillance footage, security schedules, staff rosters, everything needed to pull off a hit with military precision.

"I'm in their system," he said, his tone sharp and clipped like always. "Got eyes on every feed. I'll be making live adjustments if needed."

He pushed up his glasses, which looked more like designer shades, with one finger, light bouncing off the lenses just enough to hide his cold eyes. "I also built out a backup plan. Traffic lights, emergency calls, full city chaos if we need to create confusion and get out fast."

I gave him a slight nod. He never missed a detail.

Then I turned to Santana. "You trust the shooter?"

"Drexel was military before he came under our wing," Santana said, arms crossed tight over his chest like he was holding in thunder. "Special Forces. Five long-range kills in the field, three more since we put him on payroll. That boy don't miss."

I swirled the last of my rum against the glass. "And the family?"

"Collateral's fair game," Santana said flatly, like he was reading off a shopping list. "But Drexel knows this ain't a massacre. It's a message. The senator's the target. Wife and kids live to suffer the aftermath."

I leaned back, thinking, as the liquor burned a slow path down my throat. Even in my line of work, there was a distinction between setting an example and going full savage. There were lines that, once crossed, changed how the game was played. Dead politicians created martyrs; traumatized families created lasting fear.

"Make sure he don't get creative," I said. "One shot, one kill. Just the senator."

Santana gave a short nod. "Say less. It's handled."

Chapter 19

Simeon

By the time the sun set, I was already locked in my command post in the back of a van that looked like a makeshift NASA control room. Nobody paid me any mind because I looked like a television news production van covering the event live. Monitors were lit up like Vegas with the screens tracking every inch of the community center. I sat posted up in front of the security hub online.

I had a habit of mumbling to myself, talking more to the machines than to anyone listening. "Cameras under control . . . loop backups loaded . . . guard paths tracked and mapped."

The main screen had the live feed of the Anacostia Pool & Recreation Center, every angle covered like a sniper with a 360-degree scope. There wasn't a blind spot I couldn't see. The gang worked in sync like ants, techs tested mics, security patrolled their routes, and the clean-up crew did their best to make it all look like the block didn't just reek of betrayal. I watched it all with cold, calculating eyes, piecing together weak spots, tracking guard habits, mapping the whole scene like a doctor prepping for a surgery.

"Timing window locked in," I muttered, jotting notes on a device so locked down it didn't even know the internet existed. "Best shot's at 9:17, right when the target's moving from the building to the car."

Meanwhile, across town, a man dressed in plain clothes strolled into a raggedy apartment building like he paid rent there. Nobody looked twice at his military build, stoic demeanor, with just a duffel bag hanging off his shoulder, quiet as death. Inside, he laid everything out on a white cloth like it was a ritual. Every piece of his rifle shone like church silver. He wouldn't assemble it until go-time, an old habit from his Special Ops days. Everything was precise and clean.

At the community center, last-minute prep was in full swing as the hour of the ceremony approached. Security teams conducted sweeps, caterers arranged refreshments, and staff placed chairs in neat rows facing the podium where Senator Winbush would soon stand and sell the dream, unaware his nightmare was sitting on a rooftop with a loaded scope, waiting for the cue.

The center was starting to hum with activity as guests began to arrive. Local business owners, community leaders, and political supporters all filtered through security checkpoints, their excitement about the renovated facility and the senator's appearance creating a constant buzz of conversation. Right at seven sharp, a line of all-black SUVs rolled up smoothly to the front of the Anacostia Pool & Recreation Center like royalty had just arrived. The senator's security team jumped into motion, tight and trained, clearing a lane like the sidewalk was a red carpet.

Senator Richard Winbush stepped out of the vehicle like he was unstoppable, with no fear in the world. He was suited and polished, walking like the whole block was built just to witness his presence. His wife and two kids trailed close behind, looking like the poster family for political perfection. Inside the rec center, Senator Winbush worked the room with the skill of a career politician. His handshake was firm but not aggressive, his smile reached his eyes without appearing forced, and he remembered names with the facility of someone who understood that such details translated directly to votes and influence. Every move said, "I'm important," and every nod screamed, "Vote for me."

But across the street, somebody was already clocking him. Dressed in dusty maintenance coveralls, the shooter was already in place. There was no rush, no nerves, just steady movements like he was checking in for the evening shift at work. The duffel bag on his shoulder didn't look like much, but inside was a fully disassembled problem-solver, military-grade and cold as hell. By the time Winbush finished his last handshake, that bag would become something lethal and final.

"This rec center," Winbush said as he stepped up to the mic at exactly eight o'clock, his voice loud, smooth, and trained like he'd been rehearsing it in the mirror all week, "represents not just an investment in infrastructure, but an investment in the future of this community." The crowd clapped, some because they meant it, others just because it was expected. He kept talking, laying it on thick. "When we create spaces for our young people to learn, for our families to gather, for our seniors to share their wisdom, we create the foundation for a stronger tomorrow."

His speech continued for twenty minutes, hitting the expected notes of community pride, governmental responsibility, and optimistic futures. Through it all, Winbush kept his politician's smile locked in place, warm enough to feel familiar but fake enough to know it was practiced. His family watched from the front row, his wife maintaining the perfect expression of supportive admiration, his media-trained children keeping their perfect posture and practiced nods.

As Winbush concluded to enthusiastic applause, I monitored the senator's movements through hijacked security cameras, relaying information through encrypted channels to Santana, who sat in a parked sedan half a block from the center's main entrance.

"The mark's finishing up," I said flatly, no emotion in my voice. "Crowd's hyped. Departure window in seventeen minutes. Everything's in play."

Up on the rooftop, Drexel was locked in, weapon fully assembled, scope dialed in, body tucked tight behind a dusty ventilation unit like he was born to be there. The high-powered rifle sat steady against his shoulder. Through his scope, he had a clear view of the area where the senator's SUV waited. The shot was light work for him. There was barely a breeze in the air, and the distance was child's play for someone with his résumé. He could thread a needle from two rooftops over if he wanted. His breath was slow and measured, just like he'd been trained, with the kind of focus that didn't break, even with a high-profile political target on the line.

Inside, Senator Winbush moved through the crowd and worked the room like a pro: shaking hands, grinning for photos, accepting congratulations, and tossing out one-liners that sounded humble but hit like campaign slogans. To the crowd, he was all charm and polished energy. But it was just a show, all show and no depth. His security hovered close but not tightly enough. Professional, but lazy with the rooftop sweeps. They watched the people in front of them, but never thought to look up.

At exactly 9:14, his aide slid up with a tap to the wrist, indicating time to go. Winbush nodded, wrapped it up like a man who'd done it a thousand times, and motioned for his wife and kids. The squad tightened around them, shifting toward the exit in formation.

In Santana's earpiece, my voice came through low and clipped: "Target en route to extraction. Everything's smooth. No flags."

Santana gave a short grunt in response. "Shooter, check in."

Drexel didn't flinch or blink. He shifted a few inches to track the front doors through his scope. "Ready," he said, voice cool as the rooftop breeze. "Waiting on visual."

The recreation center doors opened, spilling light onto the darkened steps outside. Security personnel emerged first, creating a protective formation through which Senator Winbush and his family would pass to reach their vehicle. A few of the senator's security moved out first, scanning the crowd and never checking the rooftops like they should.

Through his scope, Drexel watched the doors, his finger resting lightly on the trigger, not yet applying pressure. His breathing remained steady, his focus fixed on the door. When the senator emerged, there would be approximately seven seconds before he reached the vehicle. That's all it would take. Seven seconds from the door to the car, and Drexel wasn't wasting a single one.

Winbush appeared right on cue, his hand at the small of his wife's back, guiding her with the same ease he used to shake hands and make promises he never planned to keep. Their children had already gotten in the car. The security detail moved with them, their eyes scanning the surroundings, and they descended the steps with practiced ease, moving toward the waiting vehicle.

Drexel's trigger finger tightened just a little as he tracked the senator's movement. Through the scope, he could see the details of Winbush's face: the confident smile, relaxed brow, and absence of awareness that death was aligning itself with the back of his skull.

Three seconds until optimal firing position. Two seconds.

In that precise moment, a security guard at the outer perimeter of the detail, a man whose name would later be celebrated in news reports and official commendations, noticed something that his training had taught him to recognize: a flicker of light bouncing off Drexel's scope. That split-second glint triggered something deep in his training.

"Gun!" he shouted, already in motion, breaking into a sprint like his life, and the senator's, depended on it. He launched himself at Winbush just as Drexel pulled the trigger. The rifle cracked, loud and sharp, bouncing off brick and concrete like a thunderclap. The guard's shoulder slammed into Winbush's gut, folding the senator in half. They hit the pavement together. The bullet that was supposed to blow the back of Winbush's head wide open ended up tearing through the SUV's door instead, missing him by inches.

Chaos erupted. Screams filled the air, and people began diving for cover like a bomb had just gone off. Security scrambled, drawing down on nothing, trying to shield Winbush with their own bodies as they dragged him toward the vehicles.

"Shit," Santana cursed under his breath, watching the chaos unfold through his binoculars from the parked car up the block. "He's down, but not dead. Repeat, the senator's alive."

On the rooftop, Drexel calmly stripped down the rifle with military precision, breaking it into pieces and sliding each one into his duffel. He didn't waste time attempting a second shot. The moment of surprise was gone, and with it, the clean opportunity. Now his priority shifted to getting the hell out of there without being seen.

Inside my surveillance nest, my fingers flew across the keyboard, activating contingency protocols. Traffic lights at key intersections switched to patterns that would delay police response. The security camera footage from the past thirty minutes began overwriting itself with slightly modified loops that camouflaged the shooter's position.

"Alpha route's blown," I muttered into the earpieces. "Go to delta. Switch to delta. Now." My voice was calm with no sign of panic whatsoever, just the tone of a man who has lived inside the system and knows how to bend it in real time. I watched on-screen as security swarmed the scene, unaware that their real threat was already on his way out of the building across the street, blending in with the crowd like he never existed.

At The Grand Cigar Lounge, Johnny Boy took Santana's call with a silence that said more than any curse ever could. Posted behind his desk, he let him talk while his grip on the phone got tighter and his eyes turned to ice.

"Copy that," he said, calm as ever. "Get everybody out. Fall back."

He hung up slowly, set the phone down like it was made of glass, then reached for his rum. The glass damn near shook in his hand, not from fear, but from the kind of heat that builds just before a storm hits. That was the thing about Johnny Boy. He didn't yell; he got quiet. And when he got quiet, somebody was about to bleed.

Chapter 20

Senator Richard Winbush

Everything moved in slow motion, but with sound on blast.

"Move, move, move!" someone barked from my left. Without looking, I knew it was probably Anderson. He was always the loudest in the room, and right now, hearing him nearby was exactly what I needed.

The air outside the Anacostia Pool & Recreation Center felt thick, like it was fighting us back. My wife clutched our daughter like she was two again instead of ten. My son stood frozen, wide-eyed, his lanky frame still as stone, as if his body hadn't caught up with what just went down.

The bullet wasn't meant to miss. That much I knew in my gut. Security moved with a type of urgency I'd only seen in war zones. With guns drawn and eyes straight ahead, two of them practically carried me down the steps while I tried to keep some kind of composure. But my knees buckled when I looked back and saw the bullet hole in the SUV door.

Shit, that could've been my head, I thought. Instead, here I was, breath short, heart pounding like a bass drum, getting shoved into an SUV like some damn fugitive instead of the senior senator from D.C. For the past decade, I'd been one of the most powerful figures in politics—untouchable, or at least that's how I carried myself. Even with the looming threat of Johnny Boy, I had refused to flinch. When my security team urged me to lay low at a safehouse until things cooled down, I dismissed them. Pride wouldn't let me run. I was too big, too rooted, too influential in the nation's capital to ever back down.

My wife, Beth, was as white as a sheet, but she didn't scream or panic. She was in straight mother mode, keeping the kids close as she was pushed into the back seat beside me like this was just another scheduled stop on the campaign trail.

Once the doors slammed shut and the vehicle pulled off, it hit me. They really tried to kill me. Not scare me, not threaten me, but kill me. I wrapped one arm around my daughter's shoulders and pulled my wife in close with the other. My eight-year-old son sat across from us, gripping the door handle like it might fly open at any minute. I forced my voice steady, like the cameras were still rolling.

"Everybody good? Anybody hit?"

Beth nodded quickly. "We're fine. We're okay."

Our daughter just blinked at me. Her phone was still clutched in her hand like she'd tried to text somebody and forgot mid-press.

My son finally spoke. "Dad . . . what was that?"

I looked him dead in the face, feeling the weight of it all on my shoulders. "That," I said, "was the cost of pissing off the wrong people."

Beth squeezed my hand tighter than she had in years. Any other time, it would be the polished grip she used at donor dinners or ribbon cuttings. This one was different.

"They're gonna try again," she said, voice low and sharp. "We can't go back to that damn house, Richard. Not after this."

"I know," I said. My throat felt dry as paper. "We're not."
Even though I didn't want to go to the safe house like they
had advised, I knew it was the right move—for my family.
Swallowing my pride wasn't easy, but protecting my wife
and kids mattered more than my ego. It wasn't about fear.
It was about making sure they stayed safe, even if that
meant disappearing for a while.

She turned to me, her eyes wide and locked in. "Don't
just say that to shut me up. I need to know you mean
it. I need to know you've got a real plan, not just one of
your political speeches with bullet points and wishful
thinking."

"I do have a plan," I said, trying to keep my tone steady.
"I've called Bradford already. He's the only one I trust to
handle this the right way."

Beth shook her head, glancing out the tinted window.
"The 'right way' almost got your head blown off."

The point she made was a good one.

"I don't mean by the book," I said. "I mean handled
quiet and quick and not necessarily by the book. I've
already started the process."

Her eyes flicked back to me. "What does that mean?"

"It means I put a call in. There's someone . . . he doesn't
work for the government. Doesn't answer to red tape.
He's good. As a matter of fact, he's the best."

Beth looked like she wanted to ask more but stopped
herself. Our daughter had her head on her lap now, trying
not to cry. My son had gone quiet again, his face blank.

"I just want us safe," Beth whispered. "Not just tonight.
Not just until the headlines pass. Really safe. I've followed you through every storm, Richard, but I can't keep
doing this if it means wondering whether we'll survive
the next fundraiser or city hall opening."

I nodded slowly, guilt rising like vomit in my throat.

"We're not going back to the house," I said. "Beth, I've got a secured location already lined up. Security will be there. Private location in Virginia. State-of-the-art system, underground garage, the works."

Beth looked at me for a long time, like she was trying to read the part of me that didn't show up in front of cameras, the part of me she'd married before I ever ran for office.

"This time, I'm trusting you, Richard," she said. "But I swear to God, if anything else happens to our kids, I don't care how many terms you've served or how many bills you've passed. I'm done."

"I know," I said softly. "I know."

The SUV hit a turn fast, tires screeching. Ahead, flashing lights bounced off buildings. Our escort was making sure the road stayed clear, but my mind was already a mile ahead, planning, calculating, and preparing. Because now it was personal, and if Johnny Boy thought the first shot was all he'd need, he just made the mistake of reminding me what kind of fighter I really was.

The moment we pulled through the tall steel gates and down the gravel driveway, I saw the two black Suburban SUVs parked side by side, tinted like limo hearses. Secret Service was already on the front lawn, suited up like this was the White House, with their tight-lipped look showing they weren't there for jokes or pleasantries.

The SUV hadn't even stopped rolling when Agent Carver stepped up to my door. A slim sister in a navy suit, tight bun, and even tighter energy. "Senator Winbush," she said before I could even blink. "This way. You and your family will be escorted to the briefing room."

Beth still had her arm around the kids like a human shield. I stepped in front of her real quick.

"We just ducked a sniper round," I said through clenched teeth. "Maybe let us catch our breath before the damn interrogation."

Carver didn't blink. "Standard protocol, sir. This way."

I could feel Beth's eyes burning into me. She didn't trust this, and hell, I didn't either, but I nodded and followed, not having a choice.

Inside the safe house, thick steel doors were built into solid walls, and bulletproof windows looked out at nothing but trees. Every wall had cameras and mics, as if there were eyes everywhere and even the air was watching.

One agent waved toward a bedroom. "Ma'am, you and the children can rest in here."

Beth hesitated, looking to me. I leaned in and kissed her temple. "I'll just be a minute."

They led me to a study that looked like it had been prepped for a deposition. Inside were two agents and two suits, waiting in silence.

"Tell us what happened," the lead suit said.

I gave them just enough information to satisfy their inquiry, giving minute details about the crowd, the flash, and the tackle. I purposely left out the part where I already knew who was behind it. Instead, I played the victim and let them draw their own conclusions.

When they shifted attention to reviewing footage, I excused myself, lying and saying, "I need to check on my family." Instead, I ducked into the bathroom, locked the door, and pulled out my private cell, the one no government ever tracked, and called Ray.

"You alive?" he asked on the second ring. "You been all over the news."

"Barely," I said, voice low. "He missed by inches. If not for that guard . . ."

"Damn," Ray muttered. "All right. Curtis is moving. You're good."

"No, Ray, I'm not. I don't need good. I need final. I need Johnny Boy erased."

"I hear you," he said. "Just keep your head down. Curtis is focused."

"He better be," I growled. "Because I'm losing everything out here."

I shoved the phone in my pocket, splashed water on my face, and walked out like nothing happened. When I got to the bedroom, Beth was packing up the kids. She didn't yell or give a big speech, just started walking out the door with the kids.

"Where are you going?" I asked.

She didn't look up. "To my parents' house."

"With who?"

"With my babies."

I took a step closer. "Beth, come on . . ."

She stopped walking, finally looking at me. Her eyes were glassy but hard. "You almost died tonight. And I'm still not sure what part of that scares you more: the bullet, or the headlines."

"That's not fair."

"What's not fair is dragging your family into a war we have nothing to do with. I've stood by you, smiled beside you. I've swallowed every whisper. But this? I won't bury my husband over this fucking power trip."

"I'm handling it."

She headed toward the door. "I'm done gambling with our lives."

I looked at my son, who wouldn't meet my eyes. My daughter clung to her phone like it could protect her. I told the Secret Service to make sure my wife and kids got to her parents' house safely and to make sure a security team kept an eye on the house 24 hours a day. Johnny Boy had taken enough. I couldn't let him take them, too. Not my family. I prayed that this Curtis guy was doing what the fuck I needed him to do. My world depended on it.

Chapter 21

Johnny Boy

The heavy mahogany door to The Grand Cigar Lounge creaked open like it knew shit was about to go left. As soon as I stepped inside, conversation dropped like a body, fast and final, replaced by silence so heavy you could hear the sound of ice cubes melting. The place that had become our sanctuary almost never went quiet.

I didn't rush. My stride was smooth, deliberate, each step measured and confident. The soles of my Italian leather shoes tapped against the polished floors like a countdown, and my custom charcoal-gray suit hugged my shoulders like it had been stitched onto me in the dark. My face stayed blank as I scanned the room, checking every look and reaction like a lion sizing up his prey.

As soon as I stepped in, the guys straightened up without making it obvious. Whiskey glasses lowered, cigars paused mid-air. A few nodded with quiet respect, others looked away, pretending to study the rug as if it had suddenly become interesting. Every man in the room made sure their reaction was proper because they all knew slipping up in front of me could cost more than just their pride.

Behind me, Santana walked in like a storm in a wife-beater tank top, all broad shoulders, stone silence, and the kind of presence that made grown men sit up straighter.

Every eye in that lounge clocked him immediately. If I were the one handing down judgment, Santana was the one making sure it got carried out. And tonight, we were both on duty.

In the center of the room sat the reason for all the tension. Tied to a wooden chair like some low-budget sacrifice, he lay slumped over with blood crusted on his shirt and sweat soaking through his collar. His face told the story of his failure in vivid detail: one eye swollen shut, split lip crusted with fresh blood, a cheekbone that no longer aligned properly with the rest of his face. His eye, the one not swollen shut, snapped toward me. And that's when he knew whatever tiny-ass hope he'd been holding onto had evaporated with my entrance.

I didn't say a word. I just walked over, slow and cold, peeling off my jacket and handing it to Santana like we were backstage at a fitting and not about to deliver a message the whole gang would remember. I circled him, calm and quiet, allowing him to feel the weight of the moment and letting the fear marinate in his bones.

"Look at me," I said, low but sharp.

His chin rose, trembling like a leaf in a hurricane. "Johnny . . . please, man. I swear—"

I held up a hand, and that shut him down quickly.

"Do I look like a man who came here for excuses?" I asked, brushing imaginary lint off my lapel. "Senator Winbush is still alive, which means you didn't do what the fuck you were paid to do."

He started stuttering, begging, his words tripping over cracked lips. "They moved him. Security changed last minute. I had him in the crosshairs, I swear. It wasn't my fault—"

"Fault," I interrupted, the word falling from my lips like a judge's gavel, "is fucking irrelevant." I leaned in close, voice dropping into a whisper just for him. "You had one job."

Then I turned to the rest of the room. "Let me be real clear," I said, addressing every set of eyes that dared look at me. "This ain't the kind of organization where you get to fuck up and still breathe the same air as me. I don't pay for almost. I don't reward close calls. We ain't in the 'oops' business."

Santana stepped forward, cracking his knuckles. The floor creaked under his weight. Somebody coughed behind us, but it sounded more like fear choking on itself.

"Please, Johnny," the man begged. "I got a family, kids. Just give me another—"

"You shoulda thought about that before you let my enemies walk out with a pulse," I snapped, then nodded once.

That was all Santana needed. The wooden floor groaned under his weight as he moved forward, the sound sharp in the dead silence. He came to a stop behind the tied-up man, face unreadable, as if he were about to adjust a chair, not handle something that couldn't be undone.

I didn't turn around; there was no need to. Instead, I walked toward the bar, reached for a glass, and poured myself two fingers of good bourbon, twenty-year-aged heat that went down smooth but hit hard, just like I liked it. Behind me, I heard the safety click.

The man's voice cracked as he begged louder, his words tripping over each other as he began offering apologies, excuses, and deals he had no chance of delivering. Panic took over, turning his cries into something wild and guttural, his body shaking so hard the chair rattled across the floor.

BANG!

Silence fell again like a curtain dropping after a final act. I lifted my glass, studying the way the light played through the whiskey. I took a small sip, savoring the burn as the liquid traced a warm path down my throat.

"Execution," I said to no one in particular, "is not just about carrying out an action. It's about carrying it out correctly." I took another sip. "Precision matters."

I set the glass down, grabbed my jacket, and as I headed for the exit with the same measured pace that I had when I entered, I paused long enough to give one final instruction. "Clean that up."

Once the door shut behind me, the room stayed locked in silence for a long, heavy beat. Then, like tension snapping, the air shifted. Conversations picked up again, but softer, lower, and more cautious. The vibe had changed. I'd left behind more than a body. I'd left a reminder: in my world, failure comes with a price, and I always collect.

A few moments later, Santana stepped out front beside me, sparking up a Black & Mild like we hadn't just ended a man's last shot at redemption.

"You think that was necessary?" he asked, not looking at me.

I took a deep pull from my cigar, letting the smoke swirl out of the corner of my mouth. "That shit wasn't just necessary," I said. "It was educational. Order requires examples, especially with this Winbush situation. We can't afford mistakes."

Santana nodded once, accepting the logic that in our world, mercy was often more expensive than brutality. Together, we walked down the dimly lit street, steady and focused, like two men who knew exactly the kind of weight they carried. Behind us, The Grand Cigar Lounge slipped right back into its routine, the night's mess already being wiped away. By morning, there'd be no trace of the man who failed—just like there'd be no trace of anyone else bold enough to threaten what I'd built.

Chapter 22

Curtis

The smooth, soulful voice of Kenny Lattimore poured through the Bluetooth speaker like warm honey. I was laid out on the leather sectional, one arm tossed behind my head, the other resting across my chest, fingers keeping time with the beat like I was born in rhythm. On the coffee table sat a sweating glass of Uncle Nearest, ice melted, drink untouched. I hadn't even taken the first sip. Despite the room being peaceful, I wasn't asleep. I didn't rest the way normal people did, mainly due to my mind never clocking out. It just moved quieter in the dark.

My phone buzzed against the glass table, breaking the calm like a rock thrown through a stained-glass window. The vibration rattled the whiskey glass, sending a shiver of rings through the amber liquid. My eyes snapped open, and instinct kicked in before my body did. I leaned forward and grabbed the phone, checking the caller ID, seeing the name displayed: Ray.

I swiped to answer. "Talk to me."

His voice came through low and tense. "We've got a situation. Winbush was almost taken out at the Anacostia Rec Center."

His statement immediately got my full attention. I sat up straighter, my brain already shifting into mission mode. "Almost?"

"Yeah. A sniper missed him by inches. Security guard spotted the scope glare and threw himself into the senator at the last second. Bullet went through the SUV door."

"Shit," I muttered. "Why didn't he have eyes on the location?"

"He did. But this wasn't random. This was high-level professional. It was a hit, Curtis. A public one meant to send a message."

I ran a hand over my face and stood, pacing toward the window. The city lights blinked back at me like they were in on something I hadn't figured out yet. "So this changes the game?"

"It changes everything," Ray said. "There's no more time to play it safe. Winbush is in full panic mode. Secret Service is swarming, and the news cycle is playing it 24/7."

I nodded slowly, even though he couldn't see me. "I got it."

"You sure?"

"Yeah," I said, my tone flat.

There was a pause on the other end, then a sigh.

"Send me whatever updates you've got. I need to know everything." I told Ray.

"Sending it now," Ray said. "And Curtis..."

"Yeah?"

"Be careful. This ain't just a bounty anymore. It's a damn war."

I ended the call and sat there for a second, staring out at the skyline like the answers might be hiding in the city lights. There were just more questions stacked on top of problems I didn't ask for. My body felt wired, but my mind needed clarity. I headed for the bathroom. Before I dealt with Johnny Boy, I needed to rinse off mentally and literally.

The hot water hit my back like pressure therapy, loosening the tightness in my shoulders. I let it run down my face, eyes closed, replaying Ray's words over and over. Johnny Boy was moving recklessly.

I dried off and threw on some black joggers and a tee, my black Gucci link chain resting across my chest. I picked up my phone, thumb hovering over my contacts. There was only one person I trusted to help me track a ghost like Johnny Boy or clean up loose ends digitally: my genius young cousin, Nevada. He was my go-to for anything that lived in a hard drive or behind a firewall.

I hit his name and put the phone to my ear, already knowing he was about to give me grief for calling this late. He answered on the first ring.

"What you got for me, Li'l Vegas?" I asked, my voice slipping into that low, sharp edge I reserved for work.

"Cuz! Man, you're gonna love me for this one." Li'l Vegas's voice crackled through the speaker, excitement barely contained. "That number you sent me? Ran it through my system, pulled some strings, called in a few favors. Got an address for you."

I sat down on the edge of the couch, body leaned forward now, no more laid-back posture. The calm was gone, replaced by focus. "I'm listening."

"The Grand Cigar Lounge, downtown. Fancy joint, all mahogany and leather, you know the type, where suits go to prove they can afford hundred-dollar cigars."

My pulse kicked up. "You sure?"

"One hundred percent. I ran it against three different databases. That number links to a business line registered there. But that's not the wild part." I could practically hear him grinning through the phone. "They got two power grids, cuz. One for the shop. The other? Quiet. Low-key. Someone's paying to keep something out of sight, and they're paying good money to do it."

I let that sink in, lips pressed together in thought. "Somebody hidin' something."

"Yeah. And payin' a whole lot to keep it tucked."

I stood, stretching just enough to pop the tension in my neck. "Good lookin', Li'l Vegas. You just saved me a week of surveillance."

"What can I say? I'm a technical genius. Are you heading there now?"

"Yeah. Keep your phone on. Might need to check something else out for me."

"Bet. Watch your six, cuz."

We hung up, and just like that, the hunter in me fully woke up. I moved with purpose into the bedroom. The top drawer slid open smoothly. *Holster. Check. Desert Eagle. Check. Extra mag. Burner phone.* All in place. I suited up in a dark leather tailored jacket, one that concealed everything I needed it to. In the mirror, I caught a flash of myself: sharp, clean, eyes hard as granite.

"It's hunting time," I muttered. Then I was out the door.

Hours later, I eased my black Lambo into a parking spot half a block down from The Grand Cigar Lounge. The evening had settled into that time of day when the city blurred between the hustle of folks clocking out and the night owls gearing up for their own brand of business. It was the perfect cover. I cut the engine and took a moment to size up the street.

The neighborhood was a mix of old and new, a place that couldn't decide if it wanted to be the next big thing or keep hold of its roots. The Grand Cigar Lounge stood out like an OG who'd earned his stripes with its heavy wood doors, polished brass handles, and gold lettering. The place had character, like it had stories to tell if you asked the right questions.

I stepped out and adjusted my jacket. The evening breeze was just enough to make the jacket feel right without making me look like I was hiding something. I locked the car and moved toward the shop at an easy pace, like I belonged there and had a reason to walk through those doors.

A movement across the street caught my attention. The familiar, wiry figure weaving between pedestrians was Sticky Fingers, the pickpocket-turned-informant who'd fed me a lie about a different Gede Gang location days ago. I slowed my pace, turning my body toward a nearby shop window. Through the reflection, I watched Sticky exchange a quick word with two men in pricey suits. Their body language was loose, like old friends who'd done more than one shady deal together. Sticky's eyes looked around a little too fast, showing his paranoia. Then, with one last look over his shoulder, he slipped inside The Grand Cigar Lounge.

I counted to ten before crossing the street, slipping into the flow of pedestrians. I wore sunglasses even though the sun was low, making sure nobody saw where I was looking. The crowd parted naturally around me.

The Grand Cigar Lounge looked like old money. The windows gleamed, but the wooden frames had that worn-in charm. A gold plaque by the door read: SERVING DISTINGUISHED GENTLEMEN SINCE 1923. I pushed the door open and let the smell hit me: rich tobacco, polished wood, the subtle cologne of men who thought their money made them untouchable. Clouds of smoke hung like a curtain, catching the light from fancy chandeliers.

Sticky Fingers was inside, heading for the counter like he owned the place. He drummed his fingers on his thigh like it was a signal or secret password. I moved to a display of Dominican cigars, pretending to study the box while I watched him out of the corner of my eye.

The guy at the counter, a middle-aged man in a vest, hair slicked back, looked up as Sticky approached. "What up, Sticky?" the guy said, voice low.

Sticky smirked, leaning in. "What's good, Sam?"

The man's eyes darted around the room, then back to Sticky. "You sure this is the right time? Boss said it's getting hot."

Sticky glanced over his shoulder, then shrugged. "I don't have a choice. He's expecting me."

A silent beat passed between them. The man at the counter exhaled slowly, then gave a tight nod. He reached under the counter, and I heard a soft click. A section of the wooden panel swung open.

Sticky smirked and gave a mock salute. "Appreciate you."

Sticky disappeared through the hidden door, and the panel swung shut like it had never been open.

"Bingo," I whispered. "Let's see what's behind door number two."

My blood was pumping now, that hit of adrenaline telling me I'd found the right spot. This place wasn't just about cigars. It was a front for the Gede Gang, just like Li'l Vegas had said. I kept it casual, pulling out my phone like I was checking a text. Instead, I aimed the camera at the counter, snapping a few shots of the panel where Sticky had disappeared. I even grabbed a quick video, slowly panning across the room, making sure to catch the counter and the guy who had let him through.

The crowd worked in my favor. I edged closer to the counter, pretending to check out a display of fancy lighters. Another customer stepped up, and I watched closely, same routine. A quick glance, a hand under the counter, and the wall panel opened like it had a mind of its own. That was enough. I slipped the phone back in my pocket and headed out at the same easy pace I'd walked in. Nobody called after me. I was just another browser who didn't buy.

Outside, the air felt clean compared to the thick smoke inside. I took a deep breath and made my way to my car, moving like a man with nowhere special to be. Once I was inside with the doors locked, I pulled out my phone and reviewed what I'd caught. The photos were solid. I had shots of the counter, the employee, and the spot where that hidden door opened. The video was even better, showing the panel sliding open and the button being pressed twice. Enough proof to know this place was more than a fancy cigar shop. With Li'l Vegas's intel about the separate power grid, it added up to a secret setup for something shady.

I started the car but just sat there, drumming my fingers on the wheel. My mind raced with questions: *What is behind that door? How many Gede Gang members are on the other side? What kind of security do they have?*

I couldn't just bust in there. The Gede Gang wasn't some sloppy street crew. They were careful, ruthless, and well-protected. This would definitely take a well-organized plan.

I pulled up Li'l Vegas's contact and hit the call button.

"Yo, tell me you found something good," he answered.

"Better than good," I replied. My voice was low even though I was alone in the car. "I found their hideout. A secret entrance inside The Grand Cigar Lounge, just like you said. There's a hidden panel behind the counter, button underneath. Got photos and videos."

"Damn, Curtis! That was fast. What's the plan now?"

"I need intel," I said. "A layout of the place, security systems, number of personnel, guard rotations if they got 'em. Can you pull building plans, maybe hack into their power usage records? Anything that shows me what I'm walkin' into."

His voice dropped into that laser-focused tone I'd come to trust. "I'm on it. It might take a day or two to get the full picture, but I'll start with the basics. You thinkin' of goin' in?"

"Not without knowin' the terrain." I paused, eyes on a passing police cruiser, the glow of its headlights briefly reflecting off the windshield. "Get me what you can. I'll call Mya, see if she's heard anything through her contacts. This might be our shot to hit them where it hurts. If this entrance leads to their main operation . . ."

"Understood. I'll dig in, work my magic. I should have something solid for you by tomorrow night."

"Appreciate it." I ended the call and eased off the curb, my mind already moving at a hundred miles an hour. The Gede Gang had been playing hide-and-seek with law enforcement for years, their operations protected by layers of secrecy and payoffs. But everybody slipped up sooner or later, and I'd just found their soft spot: a secret entrance, hidden in plain sight behind The Grand Cigar Lounge's polished exterior.

As I cruised through the quiet streets of D.C., that old tension crept into my chest, the kind that only came when I was close to making a move. The Grand Cigar Lounge might've looked like a classy spot for cigars and drinks, but I wasn't fooled. Beneath all that fancy wood and leather was something rotten, and I planned to drag it out into the light, no matter what it took.

Chapter 23

Mya

I nursed my coffee like a lifeline, eyes fixed on the door of the café, waiting for Curtis to show. The bitter brew had gone cold, but I didn't care. My mind was too busy running through every possibility, every risk. The Gede Gang had tentacles everywhere in this city, and even in a place like this, with my back pressed firmly against the wall, I couldn't shake the feeling of being watched.

A couple two tables over laughed too loudly, a sharp reminder of how regular people lived, untouched by the darkness that had become my normal. I gave them a quick once-over—just another couple, no threat—then turned back to focusing on the door.

The café pulsed with the usual morning crowd: suits, students, a stray tourist or two. I sat like a rock in the middle of it all, my leather jacket a shield against the world and the .45 tucked snug against my ribs. It wasn't my choice to carry it. Curtis had insisted, practically shoved it into my hand with a lecture about safety and a look that told me arguing was pointless. The weight of it was foreign, uncomfortable, like wearing someone else's shoes. Every time I shifted in my seat, I felt the hard edge of the grip pressing against my side, a constant reminder that I was one step away from a line I'd never imagined crossing.

I'd told him I wasn't a cop, and I damn sure wasn't one of his bounty hunter buddies, but Curtis had just given me that look, the one that said he'd seen too many people pay for their mistakes in blood. He hadn't said it, but I knew what he was thinking: the Gede Gang didn't play fair. So, I carried for him, the story, and the truth that seemed to get more dangerous every time I chased it.

I adjusted my posture, staring at the entrance again. Any minute now, Curtis would walk in, bigger than life, carrying the same darkness he always did, and I'd have to pretend like I wasn't scared to death of what we were about to do. I checked my watch, my dad's old Seiko, scuffed and a little loose on my wrist. He'd worn it every day on his beat as a local cop in Waycross, and now it felt like a piece of him was still here with me, keeping time with my racing heart.

The bell over the door finally jingled, and my breath hitched. Curtis stepped into the café, moving with that effortless confidence that turned heads. Instead of the typical suit-and-tie, he wore a fitted T-shirt that hugged his broad shoulders, dark jeans that emphasized his athletic build, and scuffed boots that spoke to his no-nonsense approach to life. The kind of outfit that said he could handle business and trouble without breaking a sweat.

He saw me instantly, and in that moment, the noise of the café faded away. I let my breath out slowly as he crossed the floor, each step deliberate. I didn't smile; I didn't need to. We had history deeper than any grin could show. He sat across from me, his presence filling the small space between us.

"You took your time," I said, my voice steady, eyes locked on his.

Curtis leaned back a little, that small smirk playing at the edge of his lips. "Had to make sure I wasn't followed. Can't be too careful these days."

I arched a brow. "You find something?"

"Yeah," he said, leaning in. "The Gede Gang's head-quarters. It's inside The Grand Cigar Lounge."

I let out a low whistle, leaning forward. "That place? It's a D.C. institution. Half the damn city goes there to blow smoke and talk power. You're saying it's a front?"

"Not just a front," he said, eyes locked on mine like he could will the truth into me. "It's their command center. Hidden entrance in the back leads to some kind of underground setup."

I drummed my fingers on the table, a nervous habit I'd never managed to kill. "Curtis, that would be huge. But how the hell would they hide something like that in plain sight? That place has been written up in every lifestyle mag in the city."

"It's the perfect cover. Who's gonna question what goes on in the back rooms of a place where half the city's power brokers smoke cigars? Luxury vehicles come and go at all hours, nobody bats an eye."

I felt my reporter's mind shift into gear. "You got proof? Because if this is real—"

He cut me off. "I followed Sticky Fingers there last night."

"Really?" I raised an eyebrow, disbelief threading through my words. "He's working for the Gede Gang now?"

Curtis sipped his coffee, jaw tight. "Yeah. I guess he's one of their runners. Been trailing him for a few days."

I couldn't hide my irritation. "You didn't mention that."

"I'm mentioning it now." His tone didn't change. "I watched him walk right in like he owned the place. He went straight to a guy at the counter, said something low, and next thing I know, the wall behind the counter opens up like a damn movie."

"Jesus," I breathed. My mind raced. "That could be anything. Storage room, wine cellar."

He cut me off, his voice sharp. "Let me finish. I waited. Twenty minutes later, a black Escalade pulls up. Two guys get out. One was Antoine Baptiste. I recognized him from the FBI bulletin you showed me."

My stomach clenched. "Antoine Baptiste," I whispered, the name tasting like poison. "Gede Gang's suspected lieutenant."

Curtis's eyes hardened. "They went in. Same guy at the counter did the whole button routine, then checked a screen, maybe cameras, then opened the wall. Antoine and his boy disappeared behind it. Door closed like nothing happened."

"Shit," I muttered, processing. "So what's our plan?"

Curtis's jaw tightened. "There's no 'we' in this one."

I stared at him. "Don't you dare. You said you would keep me informed."

"You'll get your story," he said, his tone firm. "But I'm not taking you in there."

I stared him down. "Since when do you make the calls on what I cover?"

"Since they started putting bullets in witnesses," he shot back. "Three in the last month. One under police protection. These aren't street kids, Mya. They're professionals."

"I've dealt with dangerous people before," I reminded him. "It's part of my job."

"Not like these ones," he said. "I'm going in alone."

The sting hit harder than I expected. "Then why am I here? Why tell me any of this if you're just going to shut me out? What am I, Curtis? Your research assistant now?"

"Exactly." His eyes softened. "You've got contacts, records, things I don't. And I care about you too much to get you killed."

God, the way he said it made my chest ache. "Fine. What do you need?"

"Antoine Baptiste," he said. "Anything you've got on him, especially who he's close to."

"When do you need this info?" I asked, my voice small.

"Three days," he said. "Maybe four."

"Sure," I whispered with a slight attitude.

He reached across the table, his hand brushing against mine in a way that caught me off guard. "Sorry, but I need you more on the outside, and it's a lot safer," he said, seeing the frustration on my face. "Don't let anyone see what you're researching. Use your home computer, not the *Post*'s network."

"Curtis, I know how to handle sensitive research," I said, my voice firm. "I've been doing this for years, remember?"

"I remember," he murmured.

"I should get started," I said, my tone all business. "The sooner I dig into this, the better your chances of not getting killed."

"Use the secure email only," he instructed, voice low and serious. "And if anything feels off, anyone asking questions, any weird interest in your work, you drop everything and call me."

I gave him a look that was part exasperation, part affection. "Yes, sir, boss man," I said with as much of a playful tone as I could muster as I reached for my bag. "Try not to get yourself shot before I deliver this all-important information you need."

He managed a half-smile. "No promises."

I slung my bag over my shoulder, but before I turned to go, I paused. "Curtis." I made sure he was looking at me, really looking at me. "This isn't just a story for me. Be careful."

His expression shifted, the weight of everything between us settling in his eyes. "You too," he said, his voice
low. "These people . . . they have eyes everywhere."

I offered him a confident smile that didn't quite erase
the worry tugging at my gut. "I've been navigating D.C.
politics for years, Curtis. I know how to be invisible when
I need to be."

As I turned to leave, he called after me. "Mya. No
heroics. Research only."

I rolled my eyes, a motion so familiar it almost made
me laugh. "Pot, kettle, Curtis Duncan," I shot back. "Save
the lecture for someone who doesn't know you."

Then I was moving through the café, my steps quick
and sure, head high. The bell over the door chimed as I
left, and I felt his eyes on my back, heavy with unspoken
words. Out in the bright morning air, I let out a slow
breath I hadn't realized I'd been holding. Three days.
Three days to get every record I could access on Antoine
Baptiste and help Curtis navigate the lion's den he was
determined to walk into.

Chapter 24

Curtis

The fluorescent lights of DCity Smokehouse, a D.C. staple known for its smoked wings, down-home BBQ, and mumbo sauce, beat down on the late-night crowd. A Black-owned mom-and-pop joint, it always felt like community wrapped in spice. I stepped inside, scanning the room until my eyes landed on Sticky Fingers hovering by the counter, jumpy as a rabbit in a foxhole.

I kept my breathing steady, my eyes locked but casual. When our eyes met across the cramped space, recognition sparked in Sticky's face like a lit match: bright with terror and gone just as quick. In that instant, I knew the game was on.

Instead of making a move, I stayed still, a statue in the current of late-night diners. Sticky's fingers drummed the countertop, his body tense, ready to bolt. Three days of tracking his every move, digging through whispers and rumors about Johnny Boy's hidden club, had led me here. And now, the key to it all stood fifteen feet away in a ratty Georgetown sweatshirt two sizes too big.

The carry-out buzzed with the late-night energy unique to D.C. There were party-goers grabbing post-club dinner, college kids fueling all-nighters, neighborhood folks holding court like it was their living room. The tang of smoked wings and mumbo sauce hung thick in the air.

Behind the counter, a cook called out order numbers with the rhythm of a street preacher.

Sticky Fingers ditched his place in line like he had a hot wire on his back, sliding sideways toward the door with a fake casualness that fooled no one. Then, in a burst of panic, he grabbed a tray of food from the pickup counter and hurled it behind him. A family-sized order of wings and fries splattered across the floor, sending people jumping back with startled shouts.

"He's got a gun!" he yelled, even though I held nothing but a napkin.

The place erupted. Chairs scraped, people dove under tables, and a soda exploded across the floor like a crime scene. Someone smacked the emergency button, setting off a piercing alarm. The kitchen staff ducked behind counters, eyes wide.

I moved through the chaos like water finding its path. Sticky wasn't running yet, but he was about to. I kept my eyes locked on the back of his sweatshirt as he slipped through the door. The screams, the noise, the panic all faded. My focus was only on obstacles—chairs, dropped trays, people—and I was already calculating the fastest way through.

Outside, the city's humidity hit me like a hot rag. Rain-slicked pavement glinted under neon signs. Sticky was half a block ahead, weaving through the crowd. I broke into a run. My breath evened out, every sense sharpening like a blade. The rhythm of my boots, the streetlights reflecting off parked cars, the frantic people stepping aside, all snapped into focus. This was my element.

"Move!" I barked at a group of suits blocking the sidewalk. They scattered without a word, instinctively giving way.

Sticky glanced back, panic written all over him. He cut across traffic, a taxi honking and swerving as he dashed between headlights. I waited half a beat, then sprinted after him. A delivery truck screeched by, close enough to brush my sleeve, but I had already anticipated the driver's move, my body adjusting like a well-oiled machine. The driver shouted something, but it didn't register. I was locked in.

The street narrowed into an older part of the neighborhood. Row houses lined both sides, their windows glowing with warm, domestic light that felt out of place against the urgency in my chest. Sticky Fingers knew these streets; that much was evident by the way he veered down an unmarked alley without hesitation.

"You're just making it worse, Sticky!" I shouted, my voice echoing between the brick walls.

He threw a terrified glance back, missed a pile of construction debris, and stumbled. He recovered, but it cost him. The alley opened into a small courtyard. Sticky veered right, aiming for another narrow passage. I anticipated, cut the angle, and closed the gap fast. His breath came in ragged gasps, sweat soaking through the back of his sweatshirt. I reached out, my fingertips brushing his collar. Almost there, I pushed harder, feeling the burn in my thighs.

Sticky Fingers dove into a cramped alley, scraping against the brick. I followed, using the tight quarters to my advantage. He couldn't weave or dodge now. I lunged, snatching his collar like a man with a point to prove. Yanking him back, I used his own momentum against him. His breath hitched as the fabric tightened around his neck.

We stumbled, then I slammed him face-first into the wall with all the force I could muster. The impact cracked through the alley. I kept him pinned, his right arm twisted up high enough to make him whimper. I leaned in close, my breath steady, letting him feel the heat of my words.

"That was stupid," I said, low and even. "Real goddamn stupid."

"C-Curtis, man, I didn't—"

I twisted his arm a little higher, cutting off whatever excuse he thought he had. Sticky Fingers whimpered, his cheek pressed to the grime of the alley wall. Blood trickled from his nose.

"The Grand Cigar Lounge," I said, my tone calm but firm. "The secret entrance. Where does it lead?"

Sticky Fingers tried to shift, looking for relief from the pain. I answered by driving my knee into his back, hard into a pressure point. His leg buckled.

"I can't—he'll kill me. You know he will."

I said, voice casual like we were talking over drinks, "If you don't start talking, you're not gonna have to worry about him killing you because I will."

A rat scurried by our feet, slipping into a drain. A window slammed shut somewhere nearby. The alley stank of piss and rotting takeout, that signature city funk that didn't bother me anymore. A single bulb above a service door threw just enough light to cut harsh shadows across our faces.

"I don't know exactly," Sticky Fingers said, voice cracking. "I swear to God, Curtis."

I let go of his arm, but before he could relax, I spun him around and cracked him across the jaw. Not enough to knock him out, but just enough to let him know I wasn't playing. He slumped back, still pinned to the wall by my grip.

"Try again," I said, shaking him like a rag doll.

Sticky's eyes rolled, then refocused. "Inside The Grand Cigar Lounge. There's a secret entrance, looks like a wall but gives you access to the front part of the back room. The main office, where Johnny Boy handles his private business, got a keypad lock."

"Code?"

"I don't know the code. I never been inside. I swear!"

I studied his face, reading the fear, the lies fighting to live. He was telling the truth, or at least part of it.

"Who goes in and out?" I asked.

"Johnny Boy, of course. His guys. Some girls, too—real high-end, you know?"

I nodded slowly. It matched what I'd been piecing together these past couple of days. Johnny Boy had built himself an invisible fort, tucked away in the cracks of D.C., the perfect operation for a man who liked to keep one foot in the street and the other in the halls of power.

"That's good," I said, loosening my grip slightly. "That's helpful."

Hope flickered in his eyes. "We cool then? I told you what you wanted."

I stepped back, letting him straighten his sweatshirt with trembling hands. "We're cool. But if I find out you tipped me off . . ."

I turned to leave, taking three deliberate steps toward the entrance of the alley. From the corner of my eye, I caught a reflection in a puddle near my feet. In the greasy reflection of the puddle, I caught Sticky Fingers's hand dipping under his sweatshirt.

Time slowed. I processed the movement, recognized the telltale reach. My hand moved to the small of my back where my Desert Eagle rested in its holster. The motion was smooth, practiced through a thousand repetitions. The weight of the gun felt natural in my hand, an extension of my arm.

I pivoted, weapon already level. Sticky Fingers had just cleared his own piece from his waistband, a cheap .38 snub-nose, the kind sold in back alleys with the serial numbers filed off. His eyes widened as he realized he was too slow.

The shot thundered through the alley, echoing off the brick. The recoil punched up my arm as the bullet hit Sticky Fingers square in the chest, lifting him before he dropped like a rag doll. His cheap .38 hit the ground with a dull clatter.

I approached slowly, gun steady, but it was done. He lay there, staring up with empty eyes, a dark stain spreading across his sweatshirt. His lips moved once, no sound coming out, then nothing.

I exhaled slowly, my adrenaline still humming but fading. My hands stayed steady as I holstered my piece. I didn't want this, but he made it happen. The difference between me and most was the fact that I was always ready for how things might end.

I crouched to check and confirmed that there was no pulse. I didn't bother closing his eyes. Someone else would handle that. I slipped his .38 into my jacket pocket, thinking it might be handy later.

Standing, I rolled my shoulders, letting the tension drain. The night felt quieter now, like the city held its breath. No sirens yet, but they'd come. This neighborhood was just gentrified enough that gunshots drew attention. I stepped out, pulling my jacket tight to cover the holster.

The street moved like normal: couples, college kids, a homeless man sorting his stuff. No one looked at me. D.C. taught people quickly how to mind their business. Four blocks later, I slid into my car and sat for a second, hands on the wheel, feeling the last of the adrenaline ebb.

After sitting for a few minutes, I started the engine. The clock read 12:43 AM. As I drove, my mind shifted from the mess behind me to the war ahead. Johnny Boy wouldn't go easy. He'd have security, escape plans, and safehouses. But now I knew where to find him. The light ahead turned red. I stopped, drummed my fingers once on the wheel, then fell still. In the rearview, my eyes were calm. America's Baddest Bounty Hunter was on the hunt, and the night's first blood had already been spilled.

Chapter 25

Curtis

My eyes burned from hours of staring at the intelligence reports scattered across the couch. The harsh fluorescent light cast shadows across the papers, photos of tattooed men with cold eyes staring back at me like trapped spirits. Somewhere in this mess of surveillance photos and cryptic messages from Li'l Vegas was the thread I needed to help unravel their entire operation.

I rubbed my temples, trying to piece together the fragments of information. Li'l Vegas had outdone himself this time. The intelligence was solid: bank transactions linking shell companies, surveillance photos from The Grand Cigar Lounge, and transcripts of intercepted phone calls. I reached for my pen, circling a name that appeared in three separate documents. Not a coincidence.

My finger traced a line between photocopied ledger entries, connecting invisible dots that the police had missed. The Gede Gang had their fingers in everything from East Coast narcotics to political bribes in D.C., but they were careful, professional. I didn't earn the title of America's Baddest Bounty Hunter by chasing amateurs. I'd been hunting fugitives like these my entire career, men who thought themselves untouchable.

The cell on my desk buzzed, dancing across a stack of papers like an angry insect. I frowned at the interruption, almost letting it go to voicemail. Then I glanced at the screen, and my expression softened immediately. Lauryn. My baby sister had timing that veered between terrible and perfect, often in the same call.

"Hey, troublemaker," I said, leaning back in my chair for the first time in hours. My spine cracked in three places.

"That's no way to greet your favorite sister." Lauryn's voice carried that particular blend of confidence and warmth that always made me smile. "Especially when I'm your only sister."

"All the more reason you should work harder at being my favorite." I reached for my cold coffee out of habit, grimaced at the taste, but swallowed it anyway. "What's got you calling your big brother in the middle of a workday? You finally decide to ditch that fancy office job and join the real world?"

"Yeah. I'm so tired of that 'fancy office job,' but it pays for my bills. Unlike some, I would rather get into a profession that involves getting shot at." Her laugh was bright, infectious. "Enough about me. I'd rather talk about what you are up to these days. Anything worth mentioning, or are you just scaring jaywalkers again?"

I glanced down at the intelligence reports, at the grim faces of men who'd ordered executions for lesser offenses than curiosity. "Nothing special. Just some paperwork, boring stuff. Tracking a small-time bail jumper who thinks crossing state lines means I can't touch him."

"Liar," Lauryn said, but there was no malice in it. "You've got that tone. The one where you're trying to make something sound smaller than it is. You're on something big, aren't you? Come on, Curtis, spill it."

My sister had always been too perceptive for my comfort. Even as kids, she could tell when I was hiding Halloween candy or covering for a broken window. I sighed, shifting the cell phone to my other ear. "It's just a job, Lauryn. Nothing for you to worry about."

"Nothing for me to worry about, or nothing you want me involved in?" The edge in her voice was slight but unmistakable. "Because those are two very different things, big brother."

I closed my eyes for a moment. "Look, it's complicated. These are dangerous people, and I'm still putting the pieces together. That's all."

"That sounds exactly like something I could help with." The excitement in Lauryn's voice picked up, and I could picture her sitting up straighter, eyes lit with that familiar spark. "I could be there in less than three hours. I've got vacation days saved up, and you know I'm good at research. Remember that fugitive in Idaho? You said yourself I spotted the pattern in his movements."

"Lauryn." I cut her off more sharply than I intended, so I softened my tone. "This isn't Idaho. These people, they're different. They're organized, connected. The kind who disappear witnesses and bribe judges."

"You mean the kind the finishing school trained me to handle." The playfulness had disappeared from her voice. "Curtis, you promised after the last job that you'd let me in on the next big one. You said I was ready."

I pinched the bridge of my nose. She was right, I had promised. But that was before I knew I'd be going after the Gede Gang, an organization that had left bodies across three states and had half the D.C. police department in their pocket.

"This isn't about you being ready," I said carefully. "You're good, Lauryn. Damn good. But this operation has too many moving parts, too many unknowns. Even Li'l Vegas is being cautious with this one."

"If Nevada is in, then you definitely need another pair of hands." She wasn't backing down. "Curtis, I've been training for this my whole life. What's the point of all those skills if I never get to use them?"

The guilt slid into my chest like a cold knife. She was right again. Lauryn was highly trained, maybe even more than I had been. She was number one in her class at Chi's Finishing School, but every time I pictured her in the field, standing across from men like the ones in the photos on my desk, my confidence closed up. If anything happened to her, somebody was going to die.

Bringing Mya in was risky enough, but at least she was a needed resource, and I wasn't about to tell Lauryn about it. The only reason I even considered letting Mya help was because I needed her relationships in the area, her sharp mind, and maybe, if I was being real with myself, because I just wanted to see her. The thought of explaining that to Lauryn stressed me out even more. That wasn't happening. Some guilt just had to stay tucked away where it belonged.

"Next time," I said, softening my voice. "I promise. But this one . . . these guys make the Idaho mission look like an elementary chess club. The Gede Gang doesn't take prisoners, and they have eyes everywhere. I'm only telling you this much because you're my sister, and I trust you to keep it quiet."

The silence on the other end of the line stretched long enough that I wondered if she'd hung up.

"You promised last time," she finally said, her voice quiet but icy. "And the time before that. I'm starting to think America's Baddest Bounty Hunter is also America's Biggest Liar when it comes to your sister."

"That's not fair," I replied, though in my heart, I knew she had a point. "I'm trying to protect you."

"I don't need protection, Curtis. I need respect." The hurt in her voice was worse than anger would have been. "I need my brother to see me as the killer I am, not as the six-year-old he taught to ride a bike."

I leaned forward, resting my forehead in my free hand. "I do respect you, Lauryn. That's not what this is about."

"Then what is it about? Because from where I'm sitting, it looks like you'll always find a reason why this job is different, why this one is too dangerous."

She was right, and we both knew it. I would always find a reason, because the alternative, which was putting Lauryn in harm's way, was unthinkable. But she deserved more than excuses.

"Look," I said finally, "after this job wraps, I promise, and I mean it this time, we'll work something together. Something real. No sidelines, no research-only role. Partners."

The silence returned, but shorter this time.

"Partners," she repeated, testing the word. "Equal partners? As in, I get a say in the planning, I'm in the field, the whole deal?"

"The whole deal," I confirmed, already wondering if I'd regret the promise I was making. "But you have to give me this one, Lauryn. Let me finish what I've started with the Gede Gang. They're the real deal, and I've already got my approach mapped out."

I heard her sigh, a mixture of resignation and cautious hope. "Fine. But I'm holding you to this, Curtis. No more excuses, no more delays. When this job is done, we work together. For real this time."

"For real," I agreed, relief easing through me. "And hey, maybe between now and then, you can tighten up that left hook. Last time we sparred, you wound it up so bad I could've taken a coffee break before it landed."

Her laugh returned, though slightly muted. "In your dreams, old man. Next time we train, you're the one who's going to need ice packs."

The tension eased, sliding back into the comfortable rhythm we'd perfected over decades. "I love you, Lauryn.

You know that, right? Even when I'm being overprotective."

"Especially when you're being overprotective," she corrected. "I love you too, Curtis. Just . . . be careful with these Gede guys, okay? I want my partner in one piece when you're done."

"Always am," I replied, though we both knew that wasn't entirely true. My collection of scars told a different story. "I'll call you when things calm down."

"You better," she said. "Love you, big brother."

"Love you too, troublemaker."

The call ended, and I set the phone down gently on the end table beside me, staring at it for a long moment. The silence in the living room seemed heavier now, weighted with promises made and the knowledge that someday soon, I'd have to make good on them. Even though I wasn't excited about the idea of her joining the bounty hunter business, I knew she was right. Lauryn was every bit the professional I was, maybe in some areas even better. Attending the prestigious Chi's Finishing School made her very qualified. I knew I couldn't keep her on the sidelines forever.

I turned back to the couch, to the spread of intelligence that had consumed my day. The faces stared back at me: hard men with dead eyes, the inner circle of the Gede Gang. My new promise to Lauryn added another layer of urgency to an already high-stakes hunt. I needed to wrap this case cleanly, definitively, before I could think about bringing my sister into the business.

I picked up a surveillance photo of The Grand Cigar Lounge, the Gede Gang's unknown headquarters. Behind its legitimate facade of expensive cigars and craft whiskeys lay the nerve center of their operation. Somewhere in that building were the answers I needed, the evidence that would put these men away for good.

After pulling out a fresh notepad, I began jotting down entry points, security measures, rotations. The familiar rhythm of planning calmed me, focusing my scattered thoughts. This was what I did best: breaking down seemingly impenetrable defenses, finding the weak points that others missed.

As the night deepened outside my window, my determination solidified. I would finish this job, not just for the substantial bounty on these men's heads, but for what came after. For the promise of partnership with my baby sister, for the chance to finally see her as the equal she had always been.

The Gede Gang had no idea what was coming for them. I was on their trail, and I never, ever gave up on a hunt. Not when there was this much at stake.

Chapter 26

Mya

I stretched across my leather couch, the cool surface pressing against my skin as I juggled three laptops open on the coffee table. The screens cast a pale blue glow across my face, fighting the late-night shadows creeping into the corners of my brownstone. The rich aroma of French roast coffee cut through the hush, a lifeline in the marathon hunt I'd signed up for. My fingers flew across the keyboards, each keystroke a defiance against the unknown. This was different, more personal, more dangerous, but the rhythm of the work kept me grounded, one step at a time.

Maps and surveillance photos covered every available surface, transforming my living room from a stylish crash pad into a full-blown war room. I reached for my coffee mug. It was lukewarm, but I drank it anyway. My eyes stayed locked on the center screen, where satellite images of The Grand Cigar Lounge rotated, revealing every angle of Johnny Boy's supposed fortress.

"The Gede Gang has expanded into three more neighborhoods since last month," I muttered, barely glancing at my notes. The glow of the screens reflected in my glasses as I flipped a page in my notebook, eyes scanning scribbles that had started to feel like my own code.

Curtis's voice cut through the hum of electronics from where he stood near the window, arms folded across his chest, silhouette hard in the faint city glow. "Johnny Boy's getting bold. What about his political connections?"

I flipped another page, my handwriting barely legible, but the information sharp as ever. "Three city councilmen, a police captain, and a judge, all spotted at the lounge after hours. My source says they walk in the front but leave out the back. Nobody's cracked how they disappear yet."

Curtis nodded slowly, absorbing it all. "They're using those connections for cover," he said, voice low. "Classic move. The real question is—"

A sudden buzz sliced through the room. Curtis's phone vibrated against the table, screen lighting up with an incoming FaceTime call. The name "Li'l Vegas" flashed across the display, and every muscle in my body tensed. Curtis and I locked eyes. We'd been waiting on this call all night.

"Right on time," Curtis said, voice steady as he propped the phone against one of the laptops so we could both see the screen.

Nevada's face filled the screen, his grin bright enough to chase the tension from the room for a second. He was nineteen but carried himself with a confidence that felt older, like he'd inherited it along with that Duncan bloodline. He was handsome in a boyish way, with tight curls that framed his forehead, a light mustache, and sharp brown eyes that danced with mischief even in the dim glow of his car's dashboard.

Before I could say anything, Curtis leaned in a bit and gestured toward the screen. "Mya, this is my cousin Nevada, aka Li'l Vegas. Li'l Vegas, meet Mya."

"Nice to finally meet you," I said, giving him a quick nod. "Curtis talks about you all the time."

That grin of his got even bigger. "Yeah, he told me you're the best at getting info. So, let's get this party started." Nevada's voice was smooth, but I could hear the undercurrent of adrenaline, like he'd been waiting for this moment as long as we had.

"Li'l Vegas, what you got for us?" Curtis asked, his voice a notch lower, all business now.

"Oh, y'all gonna love this," Nevada said, shifting the camera to reveal the leather interior of his tricked-out SUV before refocusing on his face. "I ran some deep background on the Gede crew like you asked. Their security detail rotates every week, but it's got a pattern: four guards outside, two at the main entrance, and at least six inside at all times. Shift changes at 2 a.m. and 2 p.m."

Curtis's shoulder brushed against mine as I leaned in, sending every nerve in my body on alert. "That lines up with what my source hinted at," I said, my voice tight but steady.

"That's just the appetizer, though," Nevada continued, his grin fading as his tone dropped, all serious now. "Johnny Boy's got five main lieutenants. They're all Haitian nationals with military backgrounds. They carry concealed Glocks, wear body armor under their suits. Real pros."

Curtis's eyes darkened with that familiar intensity, the one that said he was already planning his next move. "Security systems?"

"State of the art," Nevada said. "Motion sensors. Facial recognition at the entrance. Cameras with a direct feed to a control room in the basement. But . . ." He paused, letting the weight of that single word hang between us. "There's always a but."

"What did you find, Nevada?" I asked, my breath catching just a little.

Nevada's grin came back, but it was sharper now, all edges. "The blueprints I got—don't ask how I got 'em—" he added with a wink that made me chuckle despite myself, "show something real interesting."

The screen shifted, and a grainy architectural drawing of The Grand Cigar Lounge filled the space between us.

Curtis leaned in, eyes locked on the screen. "That's what we've been waiting for."

"This is their headquarters?" I asked, leaning closer to study the screen. Nevada's grin, so much like Curtis's that it made my stomach flip, spread across his face, bright and full of mischief.

"Legit part, yeah," he said, his finger tapping the blueprint. "High-end cigars, fancy whiskey, membership fees that'd make the mayor sweat." He slid his finger across to a smaller section at the back. "Right here is where it gets interesting."

I narrowed my eyes, picking apart the scribbles and notations like a puzzle. "Storage room?"

"Supposed to be," Nevada said, his tone a little too pleased with himself. The screen shifted, annotations everywhere. A red circle pulsed in the corner of the storage room. "This right here? Not on the official plans filed with the city."

Curtis leaned forward, his forearms resting on his knees. "Hidden entrance," he said, his voice low and dangerous.

Nevada's grin widened, all confidence. "Exactly. Johnny Boy had it built during renovations five years ago. Tied it straight into the D.C. sewer system with a secret tunnel to the outside world. When shit hits the fan: poof, gone."

I shook my head, the realization sinking in. "That's why nobody ever sees them leave."

Curtis's jaw tightened. "Makes sense." He shifted his weight, eyes locked on the screen. "How secure is it?"

Nevada's face got serious. "A heavy steel door with an electronic lock." He leaned in like he was telling a secret. "It's designed to open quick if they need to bolt. That means it's solid, but there's a vulnerability if you know what you're doing."

Curtis's expression darkened, his eyes flicking between me and the screen. "And the sewer system? How complex is it?"

Nevada's grin was back, flashing white teeth. "That's where I come in. I got the whole map, Mya. It's old but accurate. There's a maintenance junction or tunnel three blocks from the lounge. A perfect access point. From there, it's a straight shot to that hidden door."

"Show me," Curtis said.

Nevada shifted his tablet, showing us the overlay, which was a messy tangle of sewer lines superimposed on the building blueprint. "The blue line is your main route. The red line is your exit if things get hot. I marked depths and potential obstacles."

I stood, grabbing my notebook. My mind was spinning. "This changes everything. We need a new plan." I flipped to a clean page. "I can stake out the maintenance junction, provide backup."

Curtis shook his head. "No. You're not going in there."

I glared at him. "Curtis . . ."

"You'll be on the outside," he said firmly. "You got sources and reach I don't. I need you alive, not in a body bag."

"I agree with Curtis on this one," Nevada cut in, his voice steady but carrying that familiar hint of mischief. "But I've got something that might make both of y'all sleep a little easier." He leaned off-screen and reappeared holding what looked like a modified tactical vest. "Body camera with live feed capability," he said, eyes glinting. "I can monitor everything Curtis sees in real time from my end and relay it to you, Mya. Plus,"— he lifted a small, flesh-colored device between thumb and forefinger— "next-gen earpieces. Practically invisible and completely secure. Sent 'em straight to Curtis's Airbnb. They'll be there first thing in the morning."

A rare smile tugged at my lips, despite the tension in the air.

"Li'l Vegas, you just earned yourself a decent Christmas gift," Curtis said.

"Damn right." Nevada laughed. "This equipment wasn't easy to come by."

I moved back to the couch, dropping into the cushions and leaning forward, elbows on my knees. "When do we move on this?"

Curtis's gaze locked on the blueprint spread across the table. I could see him weighing every risk, every possibility, just like he'd taught me to do back when we were kids playing hide-and-seek that felt like training. His jaw tightened, and when he spoke, it was with the kind of finality that made my stomach flip.

"As soon as that package arrives," he said, voice like steel. "We go in prepared, not a second before."

Nevada nodded, his grin fading as he slipped into business mode. "I'll finalize the overlay and send it your way within the hour. The equipment'll be at your door before sunset—couriered by someone I'd trust with my life."

"I'll compile everything we know about the interior layout," I added, the words tumbling out as my mind raced.

Curtis stood, rolling his shoulders like he was warming up for a fight. I could see the shift in his body, the calm, measured readiness I'd come to know too well. He might be a bounty hunter now, but that same Duncan blood still ran through him, always a step ahead, always calculating.

"Li'l Vegas, I need those sewer routes to be precise," Curtis said, his voice carrying that no-nonsense edge that even made me sit up straighter. "No room for error down there."

Nevada's expression softened just a hair. "Have I ever let you down, cuz?" he asked. "But be careful. These Gede boys ain't playing. Word is they've disappeared three people in the last month alone, people who asked too many questions."

"Then it's time we gave them something to answer for," I said, flipping through my notes. "Curtis, I'll dig deeper into their emergency protocols. Find any clue about how they might react if they realize they're cornered."

Curtis nodded. "Good." His eyes met mine, that unspoken understanding passing between us like a shared breath.

"We move tomorrow night midnight," he said. "Li'l Vegas, I'll check in at ten for final prep."

"Copy that," Nevada said, giving a mock salute before the screen went black.

The atmosphere went quiet, but the air was electric now, crackling with purpose. I turned back to my screens, my mind already running through the worst-case scenarios and how we'd beat them, one by one. My attention turned to Curtis for a moment, his focus so intense it felt like the air around him had thickened.

"Curtis." I waited until he looked up, that familiar intensity in his eyes. "This isn't just about the bounty, is it?"

He held my gaze, and for a second, I thought he'd dodge the question like he usually did. But then he sighed, voice low and steady. "Johnny Boy's operation has destroyed too many lives. The bounty's nice, sure. But taking him down, that's what matters."

I turned back to my screens, pulling up the satellite imagery of the area around the maintenance junction.

My fingers moved with mechanical precision, but my mind was already racing ahead, mapping possible snags, planning contingencies. The mission was crystallizing inside me, every detail slotting into place like a puzzle only I could solve.

Twenty-four hours from now, I'd be at my laptop, watching every move Curtis made as he navigated the city's guts, tunnels most people didn't even know existed. Twenty-four hours from now, I'd either be getting the call that Johnny Boy was in cuffs or that Curtis had run into a storm none of us could handle. One way or another, by tomorrow night, the Gede Gang would know someone was hunting them, and I'd be there, backing him up, no matter what, even if it was on a computer miles away.

Curtis stood by the window, his broad shoulders silhouetted against the city lights. The tension in his stance eased just slightly when he turned to face me, his expression softening in a way it rarely did.

"Hey," he murmured, voice lower than usual. "I just wanted to say . . . thanks. For being here. For all of this."

The words hit me like a warm wave. I tried to keep my own face neutral, but my lips curved despite myself. "There's nowhere else I'd rather be, Curtis."

He crossed the room, his steps slow, deliberate.

"You've always had my back," he said, stopping just inches from me. His eyes, the color of good bourbon, searched mine like he was looking for something only I could give.

I held his gaze, refusing to drop it like I usually did. "You've always been my best friend, Curtis. No matter what."

His jaw flexed, that telltale sign he was holding something back. Maybe it was the same thing sitting at the base of my throat, too tangled and dangerous to voice. He reached out, his hand hovering near my cheek before pulling back at the last second, like he'd thought better of it.

"Best friend," he repeated softly, but there was a weight to the words that said they meant more.

A silence stretched between us, thick with unspoken things. I let it hang there, not filling it with easy jokes or safe talk. Sometimes the truth lies in what isn't said.

After a moment, he straightened, the bounty hunter mask sliding back into place. "Get some rest, Mya. Tomorrow's gonna be a long day."

"Yeah," I breathed, the unspoken echo of everything we'd left unsaid settling in my chest.

As he turned to leave, I watched him go, every line of his body familiar in a way that was both comforting and complicated. He'd always been my best friend, and maybe that's why it hurt so much—because we had always been too afraid of losing what we had to risk making it something more.

Chapter 27

Curtis

Each step I took pacing the living room was slow and deliberate, like a predator circling its prey, waiting for just the right moment to strike. The glow from a single lamp threw long shadows across the floor, shifting with each move I made. My fingers brushed against the Desert Eagle at my hip, not because I was nervous, but because I needed to feel that weight, that promise of finality that came from fifteen years of hunting fugitives who didn't want to be found. Tonight, Johnny Boy's time was up.

The penthouse felt constricted, too small for the weight of the mission ahead. I paused at the window, parting the blinds with two fingers to scan the Washington, D.C. night. Rain threatened in the heavy clouds that hung like bruises over the capital. Perfect weather for hunting. Precipitation kept casual witnesses indoors, limited visibility, muffled sounds. Nature was on my side for once.

My gear lay on the kitchen table, arranged with military precision. Each piece had been checked three times already, but I ran through them again. The ritual soothed me, sharpened my focus. There were extra magazines for the Desert Eagle, positioned for smooth retrieval. Reinforced zip ties. Tactical flashlight with fresh batteries. My knife was cleaned and sharpened to a wicked edge. The body camera, compliments of Nevada, was small enough to conceal but powerful enough to capture evidence that would stand up in court.

I checked my watch. Two hours until go time.

I grabbed my encrypted phone, the one that couldn't be traced, and dialed a number from memory. Three rings, then a familiar voice answered.

"Bradford."

"It's me," I said, my voice dropping into that low, professional register I reserved for business. "Just confirming again, tonight it goes down. Make sure you're on standby and ready for that handoff. Johnny Boy's at The Grand Cigar Lounge for his weekly meeting with his lieutenants. I've checked it through three separate sources."

Deputy Raynard Bradford's pause was short but deliberate. "You're sure about this, Curtis? We get one shot at this. If we miss—"

"I don't miss." I cut him off, not from impatience but from certainty. "I'll enter through the southeast utility access. There's a maintenance tunnel that leads to the lounge's storage room. I'll handle the inside work. Your team should position at the three exit points I marked on the map."

"And you want us to stay back until you give the signal?" Bradford's voice carried that professional concern I'd come to respect.

"That's right," I said, moving to the window again. The street below was quiet, but I knew eyes could be anywhere. "The Gede Gang has people everywhere. If they spot the Marshals converging, Johnny Boy'll vanish like smoke. I need eyes on him first. I need to confirm he's there, then take him down. When I give the signal, you move in for the secure and transfer."

"What's the signal?"

"You'll hear me say 'package secured' on the comms. That means I've got Johnny Boy in custody and am moving him to the east alley exit. Have your team ready, but invisible, until then."

Bradford sighed, the sound of a man who'd walked this tightrope before. "You know this isn't standard procedure, Curtis."

"Nothing about Johnny Boy is standard," I replied, looking at my watch again. "That's why you called me."

"Yeah," he agreed. "I know the risks. Just . . . be careful in there. I've seen what happens to people who cross the Gede Gang."

"I hear you," I said, voice like iron. "I'll signal when I got him."

The call ended, and I returned to the table to get ready. I picked up the body camera, a marvel of modern surveillance tech no bigger than a shirt button. I clipped it to my leather Benjamin Beryl jacket lapel, adjusting the angle for the best coverage. Next came the earpiece, a custom piece that let me talk to my team while staying invisible to the untrained eye.

I powered both devices on and spoke softly. "Testing. Li'l Vegas, Mya, do you copy?"

Nevada's voice came through immediately, that familiar mix of technical confidence and familiar warmth. "Reading you loud and clear, big cuz. Camera feed's perfect. I can count the hairs in your nose, which, by the way, might need a trim."

I allowed myself a small smile. "Save the grooming tips, Li'l Vegas. What's my route looking like?"

"Sending the final sewer map to your phone now," he replied. "I've marked three patrol sweeps from city maintenance. Avoid the yellow sections between 11:15 and 11:30. They're checking for blockages after last night's rain."

"Copy that." I checked my phone as the map popped up. "Mya, you there?"

"Right here, Curtis." Her voice was steady, professional, but I could hear the concern beneath it, something only someone who'd known her as long as I had would catch. "I've been monitoring the police bands and Gede communications. Johnny Boy rolled in twenty minutes ago with four lieutenants. Security's standard. Two at the front, four at the back, probably two more inside."

"Any sign they're expecting trouble?"

"Negative. Looks like a regular night."

I checked my watch. It was time to move. "He's quiet because he thinks he's untouchable. Tonight, we're gonna prove him wrong." I slid the tactical knife into its sheath. "I'm heading in. Keep the comms open."

"I will. Be careful."

"Li'l Vegas, stay on the police bands. If anything changes, I need to know right away."

"On it. It's hunting time, cuz."

I took one last look around the penthouse, making sure not to leave anything personal. I switched off the lamp, plunging the room into darkness. Then I slipped out the door, locking it behind me.

Chapter 28

Senator Richard Winbush

The safe house smelled like stale coffee and old carpet, a place that had seen too many secrets and heard too many lies. I'd been here for days now, moving from room to room like a ghost, my every step echoing in the emptiness. Every time I caught a glimpse of myself in the mirror, I barely recognized the man staring back.

I thought about Attorney General Bowens often. He'd been more than a colleague. He'd been a friend and a business partner. We'd shared cigars and secrets, thinking we were untouchable. Now his death was a stark reminder of how wrong we'd been. Every time I thought about the plan he and I had hatched, the favors exchanged, the blind eyes turned, I felt like throwing up. It had all seemed so foolproof. Now, all I saw was the price tag: lives lost, trust shattered, and my own family in hiding.

Ray was the only person who still called. He would mention that bounty hunter, Curtis, all the time. Ray said he was the best shot we had. I'd never met the man, but I'd heard his name whispered like a prayer and a curse in D.C. circles. America's Baddest Bounty Hunter. If that was true, maybe—just maybe—he could put Johnny Boy down for good.

I'd avoided their questions as best I could—the agents, the reporters, all of them asking for statements, for answers I didn't have. Every knock at the door felt like it might be the one that brought Johnny Boy's people instead. Every shadow outside the window felt like a scope trained on my head. Alone in this place, I'd replayed every conversation I'd had with Attorney General Bowens, every shady deal and off-the-record promise. What had it been worth? A bigger bank account? More influence? None of it could buy back the lives lost or the security of my family.

I sank into the worn-out couch in the living room, staring at the darkened TV screen. My reflection stared back, accusing. I rubbed my hands over my face, felt the roughness of a beard I hadn't bothered to shave. The phone rang—secure line. I snatched it up like a drowning man grabbing a lifeline.

"Senator, it's Deputy Bradford." His tone was clipped, efficient. "The operation is proceeding tonight."

There was a pause, then the sound of a door closing as I moved into the living room, putting distance between me and the kitchen where the Secret Service detail liked to hover. When I spoke again, my voice was lower, stripped of its usual smooth authority. "You're certain?"

"As certain as I can be. Johnny Boy will be at The Grand Cigar Lounge within the hour. Curtis is moving in tonight, and my team will be there as backup."

"And the evidence?"

"Curtis will be wearing a body camera—it'll capture everything. If Johnny Boy says anything, we'll have it on record. Either way, knowing Curtis, he'll be in custody by midnight."

I let out a heavy sigh, relief washing over me. "Good. Very good." I closed my eyes, letting the tension ease just a fraction. "You understand the delicacy of this situation,

Deputy Bradford. If the Gede Gang's connections to certain political interests were to become public without proper context . . ."

Bradford's voice hardened slightly. "I understand politics, Senator. I'm not interested in it. I'm interested in bringing in a man who killed a United States judge and attorney general. Your interests are safe with me as long as you keep your end of our arrangement."

My body tensed. "The million-dollar payment for Curtis is already prepared. Once Johnny Boy is in custody, it will be released."

"Then we understand each other." Bradford ended the call without waiting for me to reply.

I let the phone rest against my palm for a moment. A knock rattled the front door, sending a bolt of panic through my spine. I replaced the receiver and stood, forcing my legs to steady. Agent Carter from the Secret Service, a middle-aged man with an ironed suit and eyes that never blinked, stood on the other side.

"Senator," he said, stepping inside without an invitation. "We need to go over your statement again. There are inconsistencies in your account of the shooting at the community center. The Bureau wants to know exactly what you saw."

I turned away, crossing my arms. "I've told you everything I can. The gunman fired, the crowd scattered, I was pushed to the ground. That's all I know."

Carter's jaw tightened. "Senator, with respect, you're a key witness and a target. We can't protect you effectively if you're not honest with us."

I snorted. "Protect me? Like you protected the attorney general? He's in a box now, Carter."

The agent's expression hardened. "We're doing our jobs, Senator, but we can't help you if you keep stonewalling us. The more you tell us, the better chance we have of bringing this man down."

I turned back, my stare cold. "I told you everything I know."

Carter opened his mouth to argue, but thought better of it. "We'll be outside if you change your mind," he said stiffly, retreating with a final glance over his shoulder.

"Curtis," I muttered to myself, "you'd better be every bit the legend Ray says you are." Because right now, that bounty hunter was my only hope of living long enough to see my family come home.

Chapter 29

Curtis

Thirty minutes later, I dropped down into the tunnels beneath the city. The entrance was hidden in a forgettable alley three blocks from The Grand Cigar Lounge. I shoved the heavy iron cover aside with a grunt and found a ladder vanishing into the dark.

I climbed the ladder steps one at a time, my tactical flashlight cutting through the thick darkness. The air was surprisingly fresh for a tunnel—no damp stench, no rot, no constant drip of water. This was man-made, a clean, functional passage connected to the city's sewer system but without the filth you'd expect. I could see why people could slip out of the cigar lounge unseen. The tunnel was discreet and well-kept. I moved slowly, carefully toward the cigar lounge storage room entrance.

"Li'l Vegas, confirm my position," I whispered, barely louder than the underground sounds around me.

"You're on track," he replied, voice crisp in my earpiece. "Two hundred meters ahead, hang a right at the junction. That'll take you straight under the storage room."

Following his directions, I carefully weaved through the maze of the clean, brick-lined sewers and modern conduits. Up top, politicians and hustlers walked the city's streets, clueless that I moved beneath their feet. Every so often, the city's hum reached me: a car engine, a distant siren, the buzz of electricity. I kept my breathing slow and quiet, one more shadow in the darkness. At the junction, I turned right. The tunnel tightened, forcing me to crouch a bit. My flashlight caught the ladder I'd been searching for, a maintenance shaft ending at a hatch.

"I'm at the access point," I murmured.

"That's it," Li'l Vegas confirmed. "You should be right under the storage room.

Each rung I climbed tested my patience as well as my strength. At the top, I found the hatch: a simple metal door with a basic lock. I pulled out my picks and went to work. To my surprise, it was a cheap lock, meant for casual thieves, not a professional. I felt each pin fall into place, the mechanism giving way in under thirty seconds. The click of success was the only sound I allowed myself.

I eased the hatch open, wincing at the faint creak of hinges that hadn't seen oil in years. Total darkness welcomed me above as I pulled myself into the crawl space, closing the hatch behind me with barely a sound.

"I'm in the crawl space," I whispered. "Moving over top of the storage room."

This crawl space wasn't so clean. Dust and cobwebs clung to me as I crawled forward. I caught glimpses of the storage room below through the narrow vents: liquor bottles, boxes of cigars, cleaning supplies. The place looked empty. *Perfect.*

I found a maintenance panel and pressed on it gently. It moved, loose enough to lift. I slid it aside and peered down, happy to see that it was still clear. My landing after lowering myself into the room was soft and silent like a ninja. The air smelled of tobacco and leather, the signature scent of The Grand Cigar Lounge. I heard the faint sounds of jazz and muted conversation through the walls.

"I'm in," I breathed. "Heading to the main floor."

I pressed my ear against the door but didn't hear anything. I cracked it open, revealing an empty hallway, dimly lit, that I slipped through, pulling the door shut behind me. The hallway connected to the main lounge. I pressed against the wall, staying in the shadows. The music got louder.

When I reached the beaded curtain that separated the hallway from the main floor, I peered through, getting my first look at Johnny Boy's domain. The space glowed with amber light, thick with cigar smoke that hung like a haze near the ceiling. Leather armchairs and small tables dotted the room in intimate clusters. At the far end, a polished mahogany bar gleamed. The clientele was small but select, men in sharp suits, a few women in elegant dresses.

I scanned the room carefully. There in the roped-off VIP section, Johnny Boy sat in a big wingback chair, flanked by four of his top lieutenants. They leaned in close, talking low, glasses of whiskey in hand.

"Target in sight," I whispered. "Moving to phase two."

I studied the guards, one near the VIP entrance, another at the main door, a third behind the bar. His tailored jacket couldn't hide the outline of a shoulder holster. There were too many eyes, and a direct approach would be suicide. I needed to thin the herd.

To my right, I spotted a service door that I slipped through. It led into a small, orderly kitchen. Inside was one chef with his back to me, plating food. I moved in close, pressing a nerve at the base of his neck. He crumpled silently, and I eased him to the ground. A swinging door on the other side of the kitchen led to the main floor, near the bar. I moved to it and peeked through, relieved to see that it was perfectly located just beside the bar. I slipped through when the music hit a high point, letting the sound cover my movement. The bartender's back was turned. I took three steps toward him, then rendered the same nerve pinch. He went limp, and I lowered him behind the bar.

One down. Two to go.

I scanned the room from my new vantage point. The guard at the main entrance focused on the door, his attention turned outward. The VIP guard, though, was sharper, his eyes constantly moving, taking in every detail.

I picked up a cocktail tray from the bar, moving with practiced ease toward the main entrance, just another staffer on the job. When I reached the door guard, I staggered slightly, tipping the tray. The guard reached out to steady me, making a rookie mistake. A quick jab to the solar plexus knocked the air out of him, and a couple of quick punches I had learned from my big cousin Vegas left him slumped against the wall, looking like he'd dozed off.

Three down, one to go.

The VIP guard hadn't noticed, distracted by one of Johnny Boy's lieutenants. I set down the tray and moved around the room, using the other patrons as cover, closing the distance to the VIP section. When the guard glanced toward the main entrance, I slid into his blind spot. A sharp strike to the kidney and two quick chops to the back of the neck folded him in half. A third blow to the base of his skull finished it. He collapsed silently to the plush carpet.

Four down. Only Johnny Boy and his lieutenants remained.

I stepped into the VIP section, drawing the Desert Eagle as I moved. The lieutenants looked up, their surprise turning to alarm. Before they could react, I had the gun on them.

"Nobody move," I said, my voice steady. "Hands where I can see them."

Johnny Boy looked up, a flicker of irritation crossing his face before he settled into a practiced calm. "Who are you?" he said, his Haitian accent thick. "Do you know who I am? I will fuckin' cut your heart out and feed it to the birds."

"You not gonna do shit but put your hands behind your back," I said, eyes steady on the group. "You're coming with me. There's a federal warrant with your name on it."

One of the lieutenants, a big man with a scar across his brow, tensed. His hand drifted toward his jacket. I adjusted my aim slightly.

"Don't," I warned. "I'm not here to kill unless you make me."

Johnny Boy let out a dry laugh, no real humor in it. "You come in here alone and think you'll walk out with me? That's not too smart."

"I'm not alone," I said. "The building's surrounded by U.S. Marshals. You're done. You leave in cuffs or in a body bag. Your choice."

He gave me a hard look, like he was weighing his options. Then, he nodded. "A businessman knows when to cut his losses. My men will stay seated. I assume you have transportation ready?"

"Stand up. Hands behind your back," I ordered, the Desert Eagle steady on him.

Johnny Boy stood, slow and deliberate, hands positioned as I said. I stepped forward, zip ties in hand, and secured his wrists. A quick pat-down found a pistol in an ankle holster, which I took for myself. I also relieved his lieutenants of their weapons. There was no point in leaving any threats.

"Move," I said, steering Johnny Boy away from the table, the barrel of my gun at his side. To the lieutenants, I said, "Stay seated for ten minutes. After that, I don't care."

I backed away, keeping Johnny Boy between me and them, then moved through the lounge. People watched, then looked away fast when they met my eyes.

"Package secured," I said into my comms. "Moving to the east alley exit."

"Copy." Bradford's voice came through. "Team is moving in. Two minutes."

I guided Johnny Boy outside into the night air, where rain misted down, glistening on the pavement. The alley was empty except for the distant glow of a streetlamp, perfect for a clean handoff.

"You've made a mistake," Johnny Boy said as we walked. "You know who I'm connected to in this city?"

"Save it for your lawyer," I replied, keeping my pace steady toward the pickup location. "Your connections can't help you now."

Johnny Boy let out a dry laugh that bounced off the alley walls.

My expression remained neutral. "Move."

We were halfway down the alley when a sharp and final shot ripped through the night. Johnny Boy jerked, his body folding like a rag doll. I dropped into a crouch, my Desert Eagle up and eyes cutting through the dark for the shooter. But there was nothing. The alley was empty.

"Nevada, Mya! Shots fired!" I hissed into the comm. "Johnny Boy is down. Repeat, Johnny Boy is down."

I checked his pulse. One clean entry wound in the back of the head, execution style. No pulse. He was gone.

"Curtis, get out of there, now," Nevada's voice snapped in my ear. "Police bands are lighting up, and reporting that's coming through the police scanners is bounty hunter killed Johnny Boy during an attempted capture. They're saying it was you. It's a setup. Got outta there now!"

A cold realization settled in my gut. The timing was too perfect: the shot, the response, the instant blame. Someone wanted me out of the way.

"Raynard, abort extraction," I said into the comm. "Situation's compromised. Johnny Boy's dead, killed by an unknown shooter."

Only static answered me.

"Raynard? Bradford, do you copy?"

"Curtis, these comms are being jammed," Mya cut in, her voice crackling with interference. "Someone's messing with our signal. You need to move, now! This was a setup from the start."

I stood, my mind firing through options. The body at my feet, the gun in my hand, and the wail of sirens getting closer, all of it forming the perfect frame for murder.

"I'm moving," I said, already backing away from Johnny Boy's corpse. "Li'l Vegas, wipe the system. Full disconnect. I'll reach out through the emergency channel when I'm clear."

"Already on it. Be safe, Curtis."

I holstered my weapon and slipped into the shadows as the sirens grew louder. My mind buzzed with questions. *Who set me up? How deep does this conspiracy go?*

I slipped into the city's shadows with practiced stealth, blending with the night like smoke. Rain started falling harder, washing away footprints and scent, nature's way of erasing my tracks. One thing was certain as I vanished into D.C.'s maze of alleys: I was the hunted now, not the hunter. But they'd made one big mistake. They'd left me alive, with nothing to lose and everything to prove.

Chapter 30

Mya

My feet traced an invisible figure eight across my living room, wearing down the thin carpet with every anxious pass. My phone that I clutched like a lifeline in my right hand remained stubbornly silent despite the dozen calls I'd made in the past hour. Outside my brownstone windows, the night had settled in with that slick, D.C. kind of darkness where even the streetlights felt shy, like they were waiting for the drama to unfold.

"Pick up, Curtis. Damn it, pick up," I muttered, jabbing the redial button harder each time, as if my urgency could somehow cut through the silence and reach him.

I got his voicemail again. Curtis Duncan's deep voice, sounding professional and emotionless, told me to leave a message. I ended the call without saying a word. What was there left to say that I hadn't already tried in the last five messages? Curtis had gone to confront Johnny Boy hours ago, and now he wasn't answering. As a *Washington Post* investigative journalist, I'd learned that silence could mean a lot of things, none of them good when dealing with someone like Jonathan Boykins.

Normally, my brownstone near Catholic University felt like a refuge, a place where I could work on exposés and pick apart the D.C. power structure. Tonight, it felt like a cage, the walls pressing closer with every unanswered call. I paused at the window, peeking through the curtains. The street was empty. The wet pavement reflected streetlights in shimmering pools, the rain having washed the air clean but left the ground slick. There was no sign of Curtis's car or him.

The phone buzzed in my hand, and my heart leapt, only to sink as I saw it was just another news alert. I swiped it away without reading. Capitol Hill's latest scandal could wait. The only breaking news I cared about was Curtis being safe and alive.

My instincts fought each other. The reporter in me wanted to trace his steps, call contacts, find the story behind the silence. But the girl who'd grown up with Curtis in Waycross just wanted to scream. Just as I was halfway through dialing another number, three sharp knocks rattled my front door. I froze at the sound, still cradling my phone between my shoulder and ear. Those weren't casual knocks. They were urgent and insistent, carrying an edge of something more than impatience. I disconnected the call and quickly found the small .38 Special in the side table drawer, the same gun that Curtis had given me earlier to protect myself.

As I moved slowly to the door, I angled my body away from the center, just in case. The peephole revealed a distorted fish-eye view of my porch, and the broad-shouldered figure standing there sent a wave of relief crashing through me so forcefully that my knees nearly buckled.

Curtis.

His face was tight, eyes scanning behind him like he expected a ghost to jump out of the shadows. But he was alive, uninjured from what I could see, and standing on my porch. I tucked the gun into the waistband of my jeans, my loose blouse hiding the outline, and unlocked the door with trembling fingers. I cracked it just enough to grab Curtis's wrist and yank him inside, slamming it shut and twisting the deadbolts back into place.

"Jesus, Curtis," I breathed, equal parts relief and scolding. "I've been calling you for hours."

He stood there in my foyer, muscles wound tight like a coiled spring. In one smooth motion, he shifted away from the door and the windows, pressing his back against the wall where he could see everything. His eyes, usually warm brown, crinkling at the corners when he laughed, were cold and watchful now, sweeping my living room like it was a battlefield.

"Had to ditch my phone," he said. "Couldn't risk being tracked."

Then he reached for me, pulling me into a hug so fierce it took my breath. His arms were steel bands around my shoulders, and I felt the shudder of his exhale against my cheek, like letting go of the weight he'd carried all night. When he pulled back, his expression was still hard, but there was something softer at the edges—relief, maybe, or the kind of determination that comes from having nowhere left to run.

I stared at him, my mind already racing with what I knew. He'd gone after Johnny Boy at The Grand Cigar Lounge, the plan was solid, and everything was supposed to end tonight. Instead, everything had gone sideways.

"Curtis, the plan was airtight. You had him. What happened out there?"

Curtis rubbed his hand against his forehead, that old familiar gesture from Waycross that was his way of buying a moment to think, to steady himself.

"Let's move away from the windows," he mumbled.

He led me deeper into the house, steering us toward the living room where the blinds were already down tight. Even there, he posted up in a spot where he could peep every exit. My heart beat harder just watching him, shoulders squared, jaw set, every muscle on high alert like he was ready to move at a moment's notice.

"I had Johnny Boy," he said, his voice tight, eyes locked on mine. "Had him zip-tied, walking him out to the alley to hand him over to Ray. All the evidence we worked for, his whole damn operation. And then—" He stopped, jaw clenched, fighting for composure. "One shot, Mya. From behind. Straight through the back of his head."

I swallowed hard. I'd covered enough crime in D.C. to know what that looked like without needing the details.

"Professional hit," Curtis continued, his voice like gravel. "One minute he was my prisoner, the next . . ." He spread his hands, that same small explosive gesture I'd seen him use a dozen times.

Relief and worry fought for space in my chest. My throat felt tight, but I managed to reach out and lay a hand on his forearm. "I'm just glad you made it out," I said, sounding nervous and unsteady. "If anything happened to you, I'd . . ." My voice broke, and I had to look away, unable to bring myself to finish the thought.

He turned his hand, covering mine with a gentle squeeze. His eyes met mine, his gaze intense and haunted.

"Somebody set me up, Mya."

"Come on, sit down," I said, gesturing to the couch next to me.

Curtis hesitated, then gave a sharp nod and sank onto the edge of the couch, still looking angry and confused. His eyes kept darting to the windows, the door, the corners where the shadows pooled.

"Okay, who stands to gain from Johnny Boy being dead?" I asked, my mind already running connections and motives like I was building an investigation board. "Was this a move from inside his own crew or something bigger?"

Curtis shook his head, looking deep in thought. "Could be internal. The Gede Gang's got plenty of hungry lieutenants. But the timing's too perfect." He paused, eyes narrowing. "This wasn't just about taking Johnny Boy off the board. Whoever pulled the trigger wanted me there to catch the blame."

I felt a cold twist in my gut.

"Which means somebody knew you'd be there," I said slowly, every word weighted.

"Exactly. And only a few people knew about that meeting. You, me, Li'l Vegas, and—" Curtis's face darkened, and the realization hit his voice and eyes at the same time. "Ray. He's the only one in law enforcement I trusted enough to loop in."

"Ray?" I frowned. "You said he's been your guy at the Marshals for, what, ten years? Why would he flip on you now?"

"I don't know," Curtis admitted, the raw uncertainty in his tone rare for him.

"You think Ray's dirty?" I asked.

Curtis let out a breath, heavy and tired. "I don't know what to think."

The shrill ring of my phone shattered the tension, slicing through the silence like a blade. I snatched it up from the coffee table, seeing Nevada's name flash across the screen.

"It's Li'l Vegas," I said, glancing at Curtis. He gave me a sharp nod, his expression locked in that intense focus. I hit the answer button. "Nevada, talk to me."

His voice was rapid-fire on the other end, each word spilling out faster than the last. "Mya, you gotta tell Curtis he's being set up. I've been listening to the police scan. His name's all over it."

Curtis's eyes met mine, cold and dangerous. "Put him on speaker."

I tapped the screen, the phone's tiny speaker filling the room with Nevada's anxious voice. "I've been hacking the city cams and police chatter. Somebody's making this look like you executed Johnny Boy, Curtis. Even Deputy Bradford said he doesn't know what's going on. I heard him on the scanner."

Curtis tensed. "Ray. Knew it."

"Curtis, you gotta get outta there," Nevada said urgently. "MSNBC's already running your picture, talking about a warrant. It's gonna get real messy, real fast. They're running it on the main segment," Nevada answered.

Curtis turned to me. "Turn to MSNBC, Mya."

My fingers scrambled for the remote, heart pounding as I stabbed the power button. The screen flickered to life, and the anchor's serious face filled the screen, his tie perfectly knotted against a blue backdrop. A red **Breaking News** banner scrolled across the bottom.

"Sources confirm that notorious crime boss Jonathan Boykins, known to authorities as the leader of the Gede Gang, was found dead this evening in an alley behind The Grand Cigar Lounge," the anchor was saying, his voice calm but urgent. "Police are looking for Curtis Duncan for questioning in connection with the shooting. Law enforcement sources say evidence at the scene strongly suggests Duncan's involvement, though no formal charges have been filed at this time."

The screen split, showing a professional headshot of Curtis next to a blurry crime scene photo with yellow tape and distant flashing lights. My stomach twisted.

"Initial reports indicate that Deputy U.S. Marshal Raynard Bradford provided information that Curtis had Jonathan Boykins in custody. Bradford reportedly had knowledge of an arranged capture between Duncan and Boykins earlier today."

"I think Ray sold me out," Curtis announced, his face a mixture of fury and disbelief.

On the screen, the anchor was now grilling some retired FBI agent about bounty hunters who operate "outside the law," the conversation tilting hard to paint Curtis as some trigger-happy vigilante who'd finally snapped. I shook my head, a bitter laugh stuck in my throat.

"What the hell is happening?" I muttered, half to myself, half to Curtis.

Curtis ran a hand over his face, pressing his fingers to his eyes like he was trying to squeeze the headache out. When he looked at me, the raw honesty in his eyes stopped my breath. "I didn't kill him, Mya. I was there to bring him in, by the book. But someone wanted a different ending."

"I know," I whispered, reaching across the space between us and resting my hand on his arm. "I know you didn't."

Nevada's voice came through the phone. "You need to get off the radar, Curtis. Like, now. This ain't no misunderstanding. Someone set this up, and they're making it stick."

"Yeah," Curtis said. "I'll figure it out, and then I'm gonna find out who's behind it."

"I'll dig into Ray's movements on my end. But don't trust nobody," Nevada warned, then ended the call.

The room fell into that kind of thick silence that presses on your chest. The TV was still churning out footage: Johnny Boy's fancy cigar lounge, reporters spitting half-truths and speculation. I muted it and turned fully toward Curtis.

"You can stay here tonight," I said, hearing the vulnerability in my own voice and not caring. "Nobody's gonna think to look for you here, at least not right away."

Curtis shook his head, that stubborn tilt to his jaw. "No. I'm not bringing this to your doorstep. If they find me here, your career, your safety, all gone." His expression softened just a hair. "But thank you."

I folded my arms across my chest. "So what's the plan?"

Curtis stood to his feet, moving to the window like a restless cat, checking the street below. When he turned back, that cold fire was in his eyes, the one I'd seen when he squared up to bullies back in Waycross.

"I need to talk to Ray," he said, his tone low and dangerous. "Look him in the eye when I ask him why he sold me out."

My stomach flipped. "That's risky, Curtis. If he's involved, he'll expect you to come to him. Could be another setup."

"Maybe." He shrugged, but it was the kind that said I'm going anyway. "But Ray's got answers. About the case, Johnny Boy's operation, who might want me out of the picture. Whether he's working with them or being used, he's the key."

Once Curtis Duncan set his mind on something, God himself would have to show up with a burning bush to stop him.

The TV glowed behind us, silent but damning, Curtis's face locked next to Johnny Boy's in a way that made my blood boil. Curtis looked at the screen, his expression like stone.

"Whoever did this," he said, "they think they've boxed me in." He turned to me, eyes like steel. "They just gave me a reason to hunt them down."

"I'm gonna find Ray," he said, reaching for his jacket. "And get the truth."

"And then what?" I asked.

"Answers first," he muttered, sliding his piece into his waistband. "Justice later."

I watched him go, knowing there was no stopping him now.

Chapter 31

Santana

The blue light from the TV made everything in the living room look haunted—walls, furniture, even my face in the reflection. On screen, Tiffany Cross kept her voice even, but the words she spoke might as well have been gunshots.

"Criminal kingpin Jonathan Boykins, also known as Johnny Boy, was found dead behind The Grand Cigar Lounge earlier this evening. Authorities are now searching for bounty hunter Curtis Duncan in connection with the murder."

My jaw locked. Tension pressed against my teeth, and it felt as if something inside me cracked, like a windshield being hit by a brick. Johnny Boy was dead, and Curtis Duncan was on the news like he was some damn rogue cowboy. I stared at the surveillance footage being displayed. It was grainy, black and white, as if it had come from an old camcorder, but I'd recognize the silhouette on the screen anywhere: Johnny Boy, standing with that cocked head he always had when he was peeping game. Across from him, this asshole Curtis Duncan was all coiled up like he already knew something wasn't right.

"Where the hell was everybody, Johnny?" I muttered, my voice low with more pain than anger because I knew Johnny Boy would never answer me again.

The two men looked like they were arguing. Curtis was pushing Johnny Boy along. Then the feed jumped, and the time stamp in the corner showed 10 seconds missing. When it came back, Johnny was laid out on the pavement, blood leaking under him onto the concrete, and Duncan was already backing away.

My fists clenched so tight I didn't even feel my nails digging into my palms. Pain didn't matter. Nothing did.

Johnny Boy is dead. The words echoed in my head as if I needed a reminder. Johnny Boy, the same man who had yanked me off the corner when I was wild and half-starved. The one who saw past the heat in my eyes and the chip on my shoulder, who molded that rage into something sharp, something useful. Who made sure the streets said my name with respect. That man was now laid out in some alley, dropped by a bounty hunter like he was trash. Like he didn't mean a damn thing.

I stood up, knocking over the coffee table, but I didn't even feel it. My hands were shaking, and my lungs didn't know how to breathe. I couldn't wrap my head around Johnny Boy, the man who gave me a shot when I didn't have a damn thing but rage and Haitian blood in my veins, was gone. The crib felt tight all of a sudden, like the walls were closing in on me, choking on memories I didn't ask for. Johnny Boy posted on that same couch, legs crossed, puffin' on a cigar while laying out blueprints for expansion like we were a Fortune 500 company, or posted at the window, nodding toward the corner store across the street.

"That's our next front, once we grease the right palms," he'd said.

Now, none of our plans would be happening, I thought, as I began pacing back and forth, my mind cycling through disbelief, rage, and sadness. Finally, I forced myself to focus. A brief moment of clarity was enough to straighten my spine and steady my breathing. I picked up my phone from the floor, thumb hovering over the screen before I finally tapped a contact.

Simeon answered on the third ring. "Yeah?"

"You watching this shit?"

There was a slight pause, then he answered. "Yeah. I'm watching."

"Get everybody. The Lounge. One hour," I instructed.

"Police got it on lockdown. They're still processing the scene," said Simeon.

"That's right. The back-up spot. One hour." My tone left no room for negotiation.

"What about—" Simeon started.

"One hour, Sim. I'm not asking." I hung up.

I flung the phone onto the couch and just stood there, still as death. Gave myself five seconds, no more, no less. Enough time to let the weight of it all settle in my chest like wet cement. I began to feel that burn behind my eyes as I remembered Johnny Boy's heavy hand landing on my shoulder when I handled business just how he liked it. Then, I remembered the closest thing I had to family had just gotten laid out in the damn street like trash, and I sprang into action.

I moved toward the far wall that held a generic painting of blue and gray brush strokes that wasn't art. It was a cover. I lifted it easily, revealing the wall safe tucked behind it. My fingers spun the dial like they'd done it a thousand times: right to 24, left to 8, right to 45. Johnny's birthday had always been the code and always would be.

Inside were crisp stacks of hundreds, emergency money that never got touched. There were three passports with my face and three different names, a velvet pouch with loose diamonds, and the tools: a Ruger .22 for the up-close whispers, a beat-up Smith & Wesson from my uncle back in Miami, and the Glock 19: matte black, no nonsense, dependable like sunrise.

I reached for the Glock first. The weight hit different and felt heavier. Johnny used to say your piece should be cleaner than your conscience, and I kept mine spotless. A memory hit me sideways: Johnny at the range, adjusting my grip, his tone cool but sharp.

"Ain't the movies. Two hands, stable base. You ain't here to look cool. You here to go home."

I blinked and tucked the Glock into the small of my back, then grabbed a stack, ten bands in hundreds, and slid it into my jacket. It was enough to open doors or close mouths. Either way, it'd come in handy.

Back in the bedroom, I pulled the drawer open and grabbed the second phone. It was the ghost line: no SIM, no ties, just what I used when shit needed to stay off the grid. As I powered it on, I caught my reflection in the mirror. I looked the same, but something was different. Something was gone, and I looked like a man who had nothing left to lose. The man in the mirror looked like me, but colder. I wasn't Santana the lieutenant anymore. I was the heir to a war.

I returned to the living room long enough to turn the television off. I didn't need to hear anymore. I had all the information that mattered.—Johnny Boy was dead, Curtis Duncan killed him, and now, I was going to kill Curtis Duncan.

I slid into the Audi, jet black, windows smoked just shy of illegal. The engine purred like a predator. As I rolled through the streets, my mind raced. Curtis Duncan was in the wind, probably leaning on those bounty hunter connects of his, pulling favors, ghosting in places only folks like him know exist. I knew the cops would be looking too, but they'd move how they always do: endless paper trails, chains of command, waiting for the right judge, the right time, the right press release. We were the Gede Gang. We didn't have to wait or ask, just take.

Three blocks out, I parked and walked, taking the back route through the alley behind the restaurant. This was where business was handled when Johnny wanted things really quiet. Inside, the private room of a bar called Sammy's was lit by Simeon's laptop. He nodded at me without standing.

"The others are on their way. I've got the security feeds from last night queued up. Higher quality than what they're showing on the news."

I nodded once as I dropped into a chair across from him. "What else?"

"Police report says one shot, that's all it took." Simeon made a small gesture with his hand. "M.E. puts the time of death between midnight and two a.m."

"Witnesses?"

"None that have come forward."

I let the info hit me, heavy and hard, each word dropping like bricks in my gut. Johnny Boy was careful, always careful. He made sure he had layers of protection and eyes everywhere. The Grand Cigar Lounge was supposed to be untouchable, like Fort Knox. But somehow, Curtis Duncan got in and snatched Johnny like it was nothing. The fact that he'd walked through all that security like he had a damn key was unacceptable.

"That ain't security slipping. That's someone inside." I clenched my jaw. "Nobody's that good," I said, my voice low and certain. "Everyone leaves traces. Everyone has connections. Everyone has weaknesses."

Simeon looked up, meeting my stare directly. "What's the play?"

I leaned forward, resting my forearms on the table. In my mind, Johnny Boy's voice echoed clear as day: *"When someone hits you, you hit back twice as hard. But you do it smart. You do it right."*

"We find Duncan," I said, each word deliberate and heavy with promise. "We find the people he really cares about. We take them, and then we sniff him out with the people he loves. And then we make him understand exactly what it means to have taken Johnny Boy from us."

Simeon gave a tight nod. "Say less."

I stood and looked around. This space used to feel like the command center of an empire. Now it felt like a tomb. Johnny Boy's ghost was in the walls, and Curtis Duncan had brought all this down with one bullet.

"I don't care if it takes months or even years," I said. "We'll flush him out. Piece by piece. And when we do—" I didn't finish the sentence. I didn't have to.

Chapter 32

Lauryn

The big screen in Mama's formal living room had seen its share of news, but nothing like this. Not with *his* name crawling across the ticker in bold red letters.

I sat frozen on the edge of the leather sofa, knees bouncing, palms sweaty against the cool glass of my phone. The television cast flickers of light across Mama's face, but she didn't blink. Her eyes stayed locked on the screen like it might change something. As if she stared hard enough, the truth would shift, and my brother wouldn't be who they were looking for.

"Curtis Duncan, wanted for questioning in the murder of alleged crime boss Jonathan Boykins, the man said to be behind the Gede Gang . . ."

I could barely breathe.

"Turn it off," I whispered. Mama didn't move. "Mama. Turn it off."

Still nothing.

I grabbed the remote from the table and jabbed the power button, cutting off the anchor mid-sentence. Silence filled the room.

"He's not answering," I said, standing suddenly. The words scraped against my throat. "It goes straight to voicemail. Ma, he's not answering. He always answers for me."

Mama's hands trembled as she reached for the hem of her cardigan and wrung it like a dishcloth. Her voice cracked, soft but sure. "You need to find him."

I stared at her. "What?"

"You need to go to Washington, D.C., Lauryn, and find your brother."

My mouth opened, but nothing came out at first. "Mama, what . . . how am I supposed to—"

"You heard me." She leaned forward. "Curtis taught you everything he knows. If anyone can find him, it's you."

There was something about what she said that lit a fire in my chest.

"I don't know where to even start," I muttered, but the words felt like a lie the second they left my lips because deep down, I did know. Curtis always taught me: no one disappears without leaving a trace. No one. Not even him.

Mama stood slowly, smoothing her skirt. She crossed the room, placed her hands on my shoulders, and looked me straight in the eye. "Go and get your brother and bring him home. Alive."

I nodded, and then I was moving, stuffing my duffel with basics, grabbing my license, backup ID, burner phones, two changes of black clothes, and the silver knife Curtis gave me the day I graduated from Chi's. A flashback hit me, and I remembered the day as if it had just happened.

The courtyard behind the old brick convent had been lit with candles and moonlight, elegant and eerie all at once. I stood at the center in black, with a blade in one hand and crimson roses in the other. Around me were the other graduates: trained in everything from close-quarters combat to surveillance, seduction, and clean exit strategies. We were women who could move in silence, disarm with a smile, and vanish like smoke.

When the headmaster, Brother Minister, placed the crimson sash over my shoulders, he whispered, "You're not like the others. You fight for something deeper. Don't ever let that turn into weakness."

Later that night, I called Curtis.

He answered on the second ring. "What's up, big head?"

I hesitated. "I graduated."

"Already? Damn. I'm proud of you, Ryn."

"I want to partner with you."

The phone went silent.

"I'm serious," I continued. "You hunt dangerous people. I've been trained to take out dangerous people. We could be a team."

He released a sigh, the kind that carried years of weight behind it. "Lauryn, you don't know what it's like out here. I mean, you think you do, but this ain't school. There ain't no mock mission and debrief. Out here, it's blood, betrayal, and bodies. I can't have you in that."

"I'm not a little girl anymore."

"No. But you're still my little sister."

"I could have your back," I said, sharper than I meant to. "Who else does?"

He paused. "I do this alone. Always have."

"You don't have to, Curtis."

"I do," he said quietly. "Because if something happened to you on my watch, Ryn, I wouldn't survive it."

Click. The phone went dead, and that was the last time I asked.

Now, he needed me now more than ever, whether he wanted to or not. My mother had given me my marching orders, not him. I strapped on my boots, slung my bag over my shoulder, and walked back into the living room where Mama stood like she hadn't moved.

"Okay, Mama, I'm leaving. I'll find him," I said. "And I'll bring him home."

She hugged me tight, tighter than she had in years. "Don't trust nobody up there. And if something don't feel right, Lauryn, you listen to your gut. Always."

"I will."

I left through the side door, cutting across the gravel path toward the detached garage where my matte black motorcycle sat under its cover. Curtis had helped me fix it up when I first got back from Chi's. Told me every spy needed a fast ride. He said it suited me: slick, powerful, and dangerous if you didn't know what you were doing. The second the engine roared to life, I felt it.

This was no mission; it was personal.

Curtis had always been my anchor in the storm, and now, he was drifting into the kind of trouble that people didn't come back from. I didn't care if the feds had a BOLO out. I didn't care if there were shooters on every block. I was coming. I tightened my gloves, leaned forward, and opened the throttle. Waycross blurred behind me, D.C. was ahead, and nothing was going to stop me.

Chapter 33

Curtis

I moved through the darkness like a prayer—silent, deliberate, and full of fire. Every step I took on the hardwood floor was calculated, my weight shifting just right to avoid the telltale creak that might give me away. I knew this house. I had been there hundreds of times, but tonight, it felt foreign. Like betrayal had rearranged the furniture.

Three days. That's how long it had been since I went to bring Johnny Boy in and walked into a setup instead. Three days of digging through silence, smoke, and lies. Three days since I'd gone to collect Johnny Boy's bounty and walked into an ambush instead. Three days of the same question hammering in my mind. Who knew I'd be there? And all roads kept leading back to one answer: only Ray Bradford. Deputy U.S. Marshal Ray Bradford was my friend and my brother in everything but blood. He was the only other person who knew about the plan to bring Johnny Boy in.

I paused at the end of the hallway, ears tuned to the low hum of the news coming from his living room. I could hear the steady drip of a faucet somewhere in the kitchen and smell the last of last night's jerk chicken. Normally, it would have made me feel at home. Tonight, it felt like a cover for something rotting.

The Desert Eagle in my grip was heavy, comforting. I adjusted my hold, palm slick with sweat. That weight had always felt like power. Now, it felt like revenge.

The scene from Johnny Boy's murder replayed in my head: his body slumped on cold concrete, my name already in the mouths of detectives before the blood even dried. The setup was clean, surgical almost. Someone with authority made sure the story hit the streets fast, like they were waiting for it to happen.

I tensed, fighting through the anger threatening to cloud my judgment. My mama always said to think before you move, treat decisions like ingredients in a recipe—measure twice, stir slow, watch the heat. But this betrayal was bitter, no matter how I tried to dress it up. Ray wasn't just U.S. Marshals Service, bound by law and a badge. He was the one who'd sat at my table, cracked jokes over plates of fish and grits, shared secrets over late-night bourbon like blood didn't matter when loyalty was thicker.

I stepped into the living room without hesitation. Ray sat on the leather couch, looking worn down and haunted. The loosened collar, the undone cuffs, none of it matched the man I used to know. When he saw me, the glass in his hand slipped, splashing dark rum across the table before it hit the floor.

"Jesus—" he started, his eyes locked on the gun.

"Don't move." My voice sliced through the air, cold and controlled. I didn't raise it. I didn't need to. The Desert Eagle I had trained on him did enough talking.

Ray immediately went pale. His hands went up, slowly, measured, a gesture of surrender. "Curtis, man, listen to me . . ."

"Three days ago, I walked into a fucking ambush and watched a man die." My voice remained steady, a feat considering the storm raging inside me. "Only person I told where I'd be was you."

"Curtis, I swear to God, I would never—"

"You're the only one I told, Ray!" The control slipped, just for a moment, volume rising with my anger. "The only one. You set me up."

Ray's eyes darted to the gun, then back to my face. A sheen of sweat had broken out across his forehead, glimmering in the low light. "I didn't set you up. I would never do that. You're like a brother to me."

"Then explain how anyone knew. Explain how Johnny Boy's head gets blown off at a location only you knew about." I took another step forward, close enough now to see the rapid pulse at Ray's throat. "I trusted you."

Silence. He looked like he wanted to run but knew better. That training the U.S. Marshals beat into him held him down. He swallowed hard, eyes jumping between me and the gun.

"I told Senator Winbush."

My stomach turned. "You what? Why the fuck would you do that?" I shouted.

"Winbush was the one who set up the bounty, Curtis. He asked for you specifically. He called me on the phone one night and said Johnny Boy threatened to kill him and his family. He seemed scared." Ray's words tumbled out, rushed but clear. "When you said you'd located him, I told the senator because it was his operation."

My grip on the gun tightened, the metal warming against my palm. I stared at him, the words hitting but not sinking in. "So you went behind my back and told a politician where I was going to be?"

"Curtis, I swear I didn't know someone would kill him. I had nothing to do with it."

I studied his face, every twitch, every drop of sweat. The man I used to trust didn't look like a liar. He looked like a fool who got played.

"So, you're telling me Senator Winbush knew where I was dropping Johnny Boy off to you?" My tone remained flat.

Ray took a deep breath, his shoulders dropping slightly as he leaned forward. "I'm telling you Winbush was scared, Curtis. Genuinely scared. Whatever Johnny Boy told him, it was enough to make a United States senator risk his career to set up an off-the-books bounty."

"But why, Ray?" I asked. "Why would Johnny Boy want to kill Senator Winbush and his family is the question."

Ray shook his head. "I don't know. I've asked myself the same question. But my main focus was getting Johnny Boy off the streets."

I leaned back slightly, shifting the pieces in my mind. If Ray was telling the truth, there was a bigger story that needed to be told.

"Did Winbush tell anybody else?" I asked, watching him closely.

Ray hesitated. His expression changed, like something just clicked. "He might have. He's got staffers, drivers, security. He moves with a whole damn entourage now. You know how politicians roll."

I studied him for another long beat. "I need to know every name. Every person who had eyes on that location or heard anything about that bounty. You get me that list, Ray. Fast."

I finally lowered the gun, but I didn't holster it. The weight of the past three days pressed down on me. I wanted to believe Ray. After all, ten years of friendship had to count for something. The countless times he'd passed me information, helped clear jurisdictional hurdles, or simply shared a drink after a difficult case, these weren't trivial connections.

"If I find out you're lying to me," I said, my voice heavy with finality, "if I discover you had anything to do with what happened, I will hunt you down. Badge or no badge. Friendship or no friendship." The words tasted acrid, but necessary.

"I'm not lying." Ray's voice was steady now, his hands finally lowering to rest by his side. "You're my brother, Curtis. I'd take a bullet before I'd set you up."

I looked Ray in the eyes one last time, searching for the friend I'd trusted with my life on countless occasions.

"I need to find out who knew about Johnny Boy," I said finally. "And why they wanted him dead and why they set me up."

I left without looking back, the door closing with a soft click behind me. Something wasn't right, and I didn't earn my reputation by letting shit like this slide.

Chapter 34

Mya

The forest closed in around me like a secret whispered and never repeated. The branches hung low and heavy, brushing my shoulders like they were checking credentials. Pine needles blanketed the ground beneath my boots, each step swallowed in silence—like even nature knew to mind its business. The air in Front Royal carried the scent of woodsmoke. Curtis was already here.

After checking my watch, I scanned the perimeter. Thankfully, there were no vehicles in sight. Curtis had stashed his car behind the cabin, in a beat-up garage, and out of view from the gravel road. Mine was tucked more than a half-mile back at a hiker's lot. A pain, but necessary. When something you're chasing can get you killed, you don't take the scenic route. You move like your life depends on it.

I paused at the edge of the clearing, letting my instincts and training take over. The journalist in me scanned the scene like it was my beat: just me, the wilderness, and a whole lot of questions. The cabin looked like it had seen better decades with faded cedar planks, a roof missing a few shingles, and windows so clouded they looked like they had a coat of tint on them. It didn't scream "safe house," but that's exactly why it worked. To somebody else, it probably looked like an abandoned hunting shack.

To me, it was perfect, tucked away, forgettable, and about as far from D.C. politics and microphones as you could get.

I stepped up onto the porch, each creaky wooden plank bowing a little under my weight. My bag shifted against my hip, the recorder inside pressing against me like it was itching to come out, but I didn't reach for it. Not yet. Some conversations didn't need timestamps or red lights blinking. Some truths were better whispered and scribbled, the kind that could vanish if spoken too loudly. I raised my hand and knocked. Three quick taps, just like we planned. The door opened immediately. Curtis had to have been watching me through the dirty windows.

"You weren't followed?" Curtis asked without greeting, his eyes already looking past me to the tree line.

"No." I stepped past him into the cabin's warmth. "Took the long route, doubled back twice."

He shut the door and bolted it. The sound of metal hitting wood echoed through the space. He wasn't just being cautious; he was expecting trouble.

Inside, the cabin was warmer than I expected. The stone fireplace was alive with a steady flame, casting shadows that danced across the walls. A wooden table sat under a low-hanging lamp, cluttered with maps, documents, and what looked like surveillance photos. Mismatched chairs surrounded it, along with a couch sagging in the middle and a faint scent of coffee hanging in the air.

"Cozy," I said, unwinding my scarf. "Didn't expect rustic charm."

"Used to belong to my Uncle Lou. He'd come out here every hunting season. After he passed, Uncle LC kept it in the family trust. The keys are hidden in a secret spot we all know about," Curtis said. "We've got the place as long as we need it."

"Have you talked to your Uncle LC about being all over the national news?" I asked Curtis.

"No," he said. "I don't want to drag him into my mess. I know if I really needed him, he'd step in without a problem. But this . . . this is something I have to handle on my own. I need to stand on my own two feet."

The lamp illuminated scattered papers already spread across the wooden surface holding photographs and a map of D.C. with certain areas circled in red. I could see that Curtis had been busy. I took off my coat and laid it over the back of a chair. From my bag, I pulled out a leather notepad and pen, flipping to a clean page. Curtis remained standing across the table, his hands planted firmly on the edge like a man holding himself up.

"How long have you been here?" I asked.

"Three hours," he said. "Wanted to make sure the place was secure."

He looked . . . different. Not just tired, changed. Worn down, but not broken, more like sharpened. His fingers traced the edge of a photograph of Senator Winbush shaking hands with someone whose face was just outside the frame.

I gestured to the scattered photos. "You been pretty busy, huh? How did you get those?" I asked.

"I had Li'l Vegas send them to me." He slid the photo across the table, his eyes never leaving the picture.

"So, what do you have?" I asked.

He sat down, the chair creaking beneath him. "Ray told Winbush the day, time, and location of the bounty."

"Deputy Bradford? Why the hell would he give Winbush that information?"

Curtis's mouth tightened. "That's the same question I asked."

"What did he say?"

"He said that he told Winbush because he was the one that ordered the bounty."

"Why would Winbush need to order a bounty on Johnny Boy?" I asked.

"Ray told me that Johnny Boy threatened to kill him and his family."

Curtis must have sensed my confusion. He nodded slowly. "Ray told me that himself."

I started scribbling, connecting dots as fast as they formed. "That doesn't make sense. Why would a crime boss tell a senator from the United States government that he was going to kill him and his family? Something doesn't add up."

"Exactly. Also, Ray said the million-dollar reward came from Winbush."

My pen stopped mid-word, leaving an ink blot that bled into the paper. "Wait. Winbush put up the bounty on Johnny Boy?"

"One million dollars."

"He wanted Johnny Boy found bad enough to pay seven figures."

The scratch of pen against paper filled the silence as I processed. Senator Richard Winbush, respected legislator, family man, chair of three powerful committees, secretly financing a bounty on one of D.C.'s most notorious crime bosses. My hand moved across the page in a blur.

"Jesus. That changes everything. This . . . this is big, Curtis."

Curtis stood and started pacing, his voice gaining urgency. "It gets deeper. Winbush flew to Haiti three times last year. Each trip matched up with major shipments of rare metals coming in from Johnny Boy's crew."

"You think Winbush was working with him?"

"I think Johnny Boy had something on him. And I think Winbush wanted that something gone." He stopped pacing and stared into the fireplace, the flames casting sharp shadows across his face.

"What else did Ray say?" I asked, trying to keep my voice steady.

"That's the thing. He said Winbush didn't want me to know he was the one that assigned the bounty. He wants to keep it off the record so it doesn't hurt his upcoming campaign. Said it was off the books. Private."

"Is that legal?"

"No," he answered, then asked, "Why would a senator assign a million-dollar bounty off the record to a crime boss he supposedly has no connection to?"

I watched Curtis closely. His jaw was set, his eyes narrowed, but underneath it all, there was that same fire I remembered from when we were kids in Waycross. He was chasing the truth the same way I chased a headline, with purpose, not permission.

"So what's your theory?" I asked.

Curtis turned to face me. "I think Johnny Boy knew something that could ruin Winbush. Maybe even land him in prison. And I think Winbush decided a million dollars was cheaper than letting that happen. Elimination was simpler than negotiation."

"That's a serious accusation against a sitting senator," I said and underlined Winbush's name twice.

"I know. That's why I need proof." Curtis crossed his arms. "I've got a hunch, but hunches don't hold up in court or in print. I'm gonna get Li'l Vegas to start digging."

Curtis pulled out his phone, checking something on the screen before looking back at me. "I need more on Winbush. Financial records, travel history, phone logs, everything."

"I can help with that," I offered. "I've got sources at three different agencies who owe me favors."

Curtis nodded as he tapped his phone screen and put it on speaker. After three rings, a voice answered. "Yeah?"

"Li'l Vegas, it's me." Curtis's voice shifted slightly with a warmth reserved for family. "I need everything you can find on Senator Richard Winbush's connection to Haiti or to Johnny Boy."

I watched Curtis as he spoke, noting the subtle changes in his posture. The bounty hunter became more relaxed, more human when talking to his cousin.

"How deep do you want me to go?" Nevada asked, his voice echoing in the quiet cabin.

Curtis looked at me, then back to the phone. "All the way. If he's got offshore accounts, I want to know. If he's got a secret Twitter handle where he argues about sports. If he bought a fucking latte under a fake name in Miami, I want to know."

Li'l Vegas whistled low. "This guy dangerous?"

"Potentially more dangerous than Johnny Boy, just with better suits and security clearance," Curtis said. "He wears suits and gives speeches, but he could be just as deadly."

"Got it. I'll start now. Give me twenty-four hours for the first sweep."

"Thanks, cuz."

Curtis ended the call, slipping the phone back into his pocket. "Li'l Vegas is the best at what he does. If there's dirt to find, he'll find it."

I closed my notepad, tapping it against the table thoughtfully. "And if we do find a connection between Winbush and Johnny Boy? Then what?"

"Then we have leverage. Information to keep us both alive while we figure out the next move." Curtis returned to his seat, the weight of the situation evident in the set of his shoulders "Because if Winbush is willing to spend a million dollars to find Johnny Boy, he won't hesitate to spend more than that to silence anyone who knows why."

Our eyes met across the table, understanding passing between us.

"If we're right, this story could destroy him," I said.

"Or get us both killed."

"Then we'd better be smart. We need to move carefully," I said. "Winbush has friends in every agency in D.C."

Curtis nodded, his eyes steady. "And we need to move fast. Winbush will find a way to get to you. Whatever you know, he wants it buried."

I stared at him, my decision already made. "I'm in. Whatever this is, wherever it leads."

"Time to find out what a D.C. politician and a Haitian crime boss had going on behind closed doors." He sighed.

And so here we were, Curtis and I, tucked away in a cabin deep in the Virginia woods, a far cry from the heat of Waycross and a world away from the chaos waiting back in D.C. In the stillness of that cabin, surrounded by nothing but trees, shadows, and secrets, two kids from Georgia prepared to go up against the kind of power that didn't just ruin lives but erased them.

Chapter 35

Santana

I sat in the driver's seat, still as stone, the shadows inside my G-Wagen wrapping around me like grief. The only light came from a streetlamp flickering down the block, catching the edge of my jaw just enough to spotlight the twitch that betrayed the storm inside me. The cigar between my fingers burned low, its smoke curling in the cabin like sorrow I couldn't shake. Johnny Boy was gone. He wasn't just my boss or mentor; he was the architect of everything. And now, he was nothing but a body bag and a memory.

The passenger door creaked open, slicing through the quiet. Simeon climbed in without a word, his presence lean and cold, like winter slipping into a room uninvited. He shut the door with careful precision, not slamming it. That was never Simeon's style. Everything he did was controlled and methodical.

"They processed the scene," he said, his voice calm. "No witnesses. Professional hit."

I nodded once, not needing any further confirmation of the details. I could already see the blood outside the cigar lounge, already hear the shots again in my head. Whoever did it knew exactly what they were doing and exactly who they were hitting.

"Curtis Duncan," I muttered, the name like acid on my tongue. "America's Baddest Bounty Hunter."

It sounded like a damn joke.

Simeon didn't respond right away. He stared straight ahead, fingers tapping once against his knee before going still again. His calm was deceptive. I recognized the subtle tells of his rage, the slight flaring of his nostrils, the too precise movements. When Simeon was quiet, people disappeared.

"We move now," he said, voice low. "We hit him where it hurts before he vanishes. Collecting bounties was business. Now this, this is personal."

"Personal," I repeated as I blew out a stream of smoke. "Johnny Boy built all this, brick by brick. Nobody gets to erase that without consequences."

"What would he want us to do?" Simeon asked, though we both knew the answer.

He reached into his coat and slapped a photo onto the dash. It landed flat, but the sound echoed like a gunshot in the tight cabin.

"This is our way to him," he said.

I leaned forward. The picture was grainy, taken from a distance, but it was clear enough to show Curtis Duncan walking alongside a woman. She was tall and confident, pretty in a way that didn't scream for attention. Even though she wasn't hanging on him, they walked like people who shared history. Curtis's head was turned toward her, his expression soft.

"Who is she?"

"Mya Wynn," Simeon answered. "Investigative journalist for the *Washington Post*. Built a career exposing corruption and embarrassing powerful people."

"And her connection to Duncan?" I stared at the photo.

"She is his friend from Waycross, Georgia. They go back. Way back." Simeon continued, "From my research, they were best friends, then her family moved to Prince Georges County because her dad was relocated to Andrews Air Force Base."

Simeon nodded. "They've been spotted together a lot lately. Dinner spots. Her place in Northeast. Late nights. She's in his orbit, and she's got a reputation for digging into the type of information Curtis could use to capture fugitives."

"She knows something." I said it more to myself than to him. "So, she writes about corruption and politicians with dirty hands."

"She probably helped Curtis track down Johnny Boy," Simeon added, a slight smile touching his lips without reaching his eyes.

I nodded slowly, pieces falling into place. "You think she's feeding Curtis information about our gang?"

"Absolutely," Simeon said. "And her movements are quite predictable. We've been tailing her. She jogs every morning, hits the same café for coffee, and lives in a brownstone near Catholic University and the Brooklyn train station. We take her, we draw Curtis out."

I studied the photo again. She didn't look like a threat, but that's what made her valuable.

"Duncan's slippery," I said, crushing the cigar into the ashtray. "He disappears like smoke."

"But he won't leave her hanging." Simeon's voice was quiet but sure. "That's our window."

"We take her," I said. "Use her as bait. Let him come to us."

"We trail her until she hits a stretch with no eyes, no cameras, no foot traffic. Quiet and clean."

"And then?"

"We wait." Simeon kept it short, but there was a lot packed into what he said. "Duncan will come looking. When he does, we'll be ready. We finish what he started."

I leaned back, running the plan in my head. Johnny Boy always said, "Think three moves ahead, even when grief clouds your sight." I'd been grieving since I got the call, but now . . . now I had a target.

"How soon?"

"Tomorrow we will start tracking her every move." Simeon reached for the door handle, pausing before opening it. "I'll pull six men for the grab, keep another twelve on standby. We'll stash her at the Ivy City warehouse. It's ready."

"Good. Make it clean." I nodded my approval. "Keep me informed."

He nodded, then opened the door and stepped into the night, leaving me in the dark, right where I needed to be. Alone again, I reached for the photo, bringing it close enough to catch every detail. Mya Wynn looked calm, composed, walking through her day. She had no idea what was coming. In the shot, she looked regular, unassuming. But to me, she was a pressure point, a crack in Curtis Duncan's armor. I didn't hate her. She was just leverage, nothing more than the key to opening the door Curtis had slammed shut. I tucked the photo into my jacket.

"Sorry about your luck," I murmured. "But you're how we get to him."

I started the engine. As I pulled away from the curb, my mind was already mapping out the confrontation to come. Curtis Duncan had made a fatal mistake when he'd decided to take on the Gede Gang. He'd taken something irreplaceable from us. Now, I would return the favor.

Chapter 36

Mya

I moved with intention; my heels clicking sharp against the pavement with the kind of stride that said I had somewhere to be and wasn't there to waste time. My press credentials hung around my neck, partially obscured by my blazer, visible enough to grant access, but subtle enough not to draw attention. In my mind, I rehearsed the cover story I'd prepared, a follow-up interview regarding the senator's infrastructure bill, scheduled weeks ago with his junior aide. There was no such interview, of course. I learned the junior aide had left for vacation yesterday; just another breadcrumb I gathered while casing Winbush's office routine like a pro. The senator was across town at a fundraising luncheon with everyone in his office and a ton of security. This meant he would be occupied for at least another hour, giving me just enough time to find what I needed.

The senator's office was tucked inside a sleek, modern building with mirrored glass and a name no one ever remembered. I'd spent the entire week studying the layout: tracking camera blind spots, clocking security rotations, even noting the exact time the receptionist stepped out for her daily coffee break. Every detail was filed away, not just for curiosity's sake, but because I knew I'd need every advantage once I made my move. I walked into the lobby like I belonged.

"Mya Wynn. *Washington Post*," I said, flashing my press pass and a polite smile. "I have a four o'clock meeting with Jake Thomas from Senator Winbush's office."

The guard scanned his screen, frowned. "Not seeing anything."

"Check again," I insisted, holding up my phone and showing the email I'd crafted myself, carefully worded and legit enough to pass first glance. "I confirmed this morning. Look, here's his response."

He glanced at it, shrugged. "Fourth floor. Visitor badge visible."

"Always," I said, clipping the plastic badge on beside my press credentials. "I appreciate it."

The elevator carried me up, but I stopped on the third floor, just like I planned. The stairwell camera between floors glitched every seventeen minutes. I waited until the red light blinked out, then climbed fast. My pulse picked up, but my hands stayed steady. This wasn't my first time creeping through the shadows in hallways of power.

The fourth floor was quiet. I ducked past a water cooler across from the reception desk. From the corner of my eye, I watched as the receptionist checked her watch, then reached for her purse. The woman stood, smoothed her skirt, and walked toward the elevators, offering me a polite smile as she passed.

Two minutes. That's all I needed.

The front office door gave way easily. I slipped inside the suite, heart steady. The second door, the one that led to Winbush's private office, was unlocked. Inside, the scent of leather and expensive cologne hit me, then a hint of cigar smoke. The blinds were half-closed. I quickly scanned the space. There were photographs of Winbush grinning beside three presidents, a chess set, pieces frozen mid-game, his Georgetown law degree, all props in the show.

But it was the mahogany desk that commanded my attention—specifically, the second drawer on the right, which was slightly cracked. I opened it with the precision of someone who knew exactly what she was risking. Inside were manila folders, arranged alphabetically. My fingers moved through them carefully, making sure I didn't disturb their order and leaving no trace of my search. Adams . . . Anderson . . . Banks . . . and there, nearly hidden between budget reports: Boykins, J. My stomach turned. Jonathan Boykins. The untouchable, ruthless man behind the Gede Gang. And now, tied directly to Senator Winbush.

I flipped open the folder. There wasn't much, but what was there was enough to start a fire. Inside was a single photograph of Winbush and Boykins shaking hands in what appeared to be the back room of an upscale establishment, most likely The Grand Cigar Lounge that served as Boykins' hang out. Beneath the photo lay a typed memo outlining payment schedules and delivery dates. There wasn't anything mentioned specifically about what was being delivered, but the amounts, in the hundreds of thousands, suggested nothing legitimate.

"Got you," I whispered, enjoying the moment of victory.

I reached into my bag for my phone, ready to snap a few quick shots, when I heard footsteps. My fingers froze above the folder. The receptionist wasn't due back for at least ten more minutes. It couldn't have been her. It was decision time. I either had to leave the evidence or take it. The footsteps grew louder. I slipped the folder into my bag and zipped it closed. If need be, I'd have to bluff my way out and claim that I got lost looking for the bathroom, was waiting for an aide, anything to explain my reason for being there. I started toward the door, slipping on my usual face of calm professionalism: chin up, eyes steady. That's when I heard the voices: deep, male, and definitely not anyone from the senator's staff.

"Check the desk first," someone said. "Boss says he's looking for something specific."

Shit.

There was no time to play innocent. The office had two doors: the main entrance where the men were about to appear, and a side door that likely connected to a private bathroom or conference room. Moving fast, I slipped through the side door and into a narrow hallway that led to the service elevator. The service elevator required a key card, but the stairwell beside it didn't. I bolted into the stairwell, taking the steps three at a time.

Three floors down, I hit the door and kept moving. My car was parked away from the main entrance in a back lot that I'd chosen on purpose. The lot was always empty at this hour, with just a few vehicles belonging to people working late. My five-year-old Audi waited in the corner, partly hidden by a delivery van. Now I just had to make it there. I fumbled in my pocket for my keys, adrenaline making it difficult. I reached my car, inserted the key with shaking hands, and just as I pulled open the driver's side door, I heard the squeal of tires entering the lot too fast. I turned just as a black van with no plates came flying around the corner with no headlights or hesitation. It blocked my car before I could even open the door.

For one frozen moment, I stood paralyzed, keys dangling from my hand, bag clutched to my chest. Then the training I'd learned in the self-defense classes I'd taken after my first death threat kicked in: the escape plans I always formulated.

Three men jumped out in dark clothes, ski masks, and gloves with trained movements. I locked the door and fumbled for the ignition, my fingers slippery with sweat, but it was too late. Before I could shift into reverse, they broke the driver's side window and rough hands yanked my door open. I screamed. My sharp sound was cut short as I was dragged from the vehicle. I fought as hands yanked me out, elbowing someone hard enough to make him curse.

"Let me go!" I shouted, hoping someone, anyone, might hear. "Help! Security!"

No one came. One man pinned my arms, while another produced a cloth from his pocket. The sweet, overwhelming chemical smell hit me before the fabric did. I held on as long as I could, kicking and thrashing. Then everything tilted. My body betrayed me, and my grip on the bag loosened. The men bundled my limp body into the van effortlessly. The door slammed shut. Tires squealed as it sped off, leaving behind my car, door open and contents exposed. The last thing I saw was the folder with *Boykins, J.* written on the front. Then, nothing.

Chapter 37

Curtis

I stared at Mya's contact longer than I should have. I'd already called her twice, each time with the easy confidence of a man who expected an answer. But she hadn't answered. A low buzz at the base of my skull, a kind of signal I'd learned to respect after years of tracking fugitives, told me something wasn't right. The phone rang once, twice, three times. By the sixth, I was already tense.

"This is Mya Wynn. I can't take your call right now, but leave a message, and I'll get back to you as soon as possible."

I exhaled slowly. Her voicemail was as crisp and professional as she was. Mya always picked up for me. Always. That was our rhythm, even back when we were just kids chasing fireflies through the heat of Waycross summers.

"Mya. It's me." I kept my tone calm and steady. "We were supposed to meet for coffee an hour ago. Just checking if you're okay. Call me when you get this. Please."

I ended the call, my eyes locked on the screen. Our last text was at 7:13 this morning. That was nearly twelve hours ago. Twelve hours since she told me she was up to something big. Twelve hours of silence.

The walls suddenly felt tighter, like the place was closing in on me. I should've asked more questions or picked up on the shift in her voice this morning when she mentioned that she had a plan.

Without hesitating again, I made another call.

"What up, cuz," Li'l Vegas answered, playful like always. I could hear keys clacking in the background, telling me that he was on the computer.

"I need your help," I said, skipping the small talk. "Mya's not answering. We had plans. She's never late. And she told me this morning she was working something heavy."

Typing stopped. "She's missing?"

"She's not picking up. And that's not like her. Can you ping her cell?"

"I'm on it," he said, the usual swagger dropping from his voice. "I still got access to her cell carrier database from last month. Totally legit, of course." He was lying, but I didn't care. "Gimme thirty seconds."

I started pacing the length of the kitchen. Ten steps up, ten back. My cousin's fingertips tapped in rapid rhythm in the background, the sound like a clock ticking louder in my ears.

"She's still on the grid," he said finally. "The good news is, her phone's on. But it hasn't moved in three hours."

My stomach tightened. "Where is it?"

"Just sent you the coordinates. Old parking structure near the Capitol. Government lot. Not much happens there these days except government overflow parking. It's kinda deserted this time of day."

My phone buzzed with his incoming text.

"Got it," I said. "Thanks, Li'l Vegas."

"Hang on. I'm not done being useful yet. You want me to keep tracking the phone? Maybe see if I can access her recent calls or messages?" he offered.

I hesitated for half a second. Under normal circumstances, I wouldn't cross that line with Mya, but normal had left the building hours ago.

"Do it. Quietly. And Li'l Vegas . . ."

"Yeah?"

"Be ready if I need more. This shit doesn't feel right."

Nevada sounded just as worried as I was when he responded. "I got you. Always."

I grabbed my keys and headed for the door, my Desert Eagle already at my hip. I thought about the rest of the arsenal I had tucked away in the closet but left it. I wasn't headed into war. At least not yet. First, I had to find her. Whatever came after would have to be handled with what I had on me.

Evening traffic moved slowly, like the city was conspiring to waste time I didn't have. Every red light tested my patience, but I stayed cool. I didn't earn my rep by rushing in blind. I waited, planned, and then when it was time, I moved with precision.

By the time I pulled up near the location, it was after 7 PM, and the streets had grown quiet. I parked half a block away. When I arrived at the parking lot, my senses were on high alert. I quickly searched around, and that's when I spotted Mya's black Audi in the rear of the lot. It was barely visible behind a van, parked crooked, and the driver's window was shattered.

I froze for a beat, then moved in, scanning the space for cameras, witnesses, any threats in the dark. The car was empty, and thankfully, there was no blood in sight. But the glass told me everything. She'd been taken fast, and it wasn't random. I walked around the car, noting the details: keys still in the ignition, engine cold, and on the ground near the driver's door, dark skid marks scarred the concrete. Obviously, someone had been dragged. I moved to the passenger side and spotted a manila folder sitting on the seat like someone had placed it there intentionally. The name on the tab punched me straight in the chest: Jonathan Boykins.

"Goddamn it, Mya," I muttered under my breath. "What the fuck were you thinking?"

I pulled a cloth from my pocket, out of habit, and used it to grab the folder. I flipped through the folder quickly: financial records, photographs of meetings between Boykins and various D.C. officials, transcripts of conversations obtained through means I could only guess at. Something caught my eye. A red light was blinking across the lot on the side of the building, angled toward the parking spaces. I took out my phone and called Nevada.

"That was quick," he answered. "You find her?"

"No. I found her car," I told him. "There's a security camera on the east wall, aimed right at where Mya's car is parked. I need that footage."

"Parking garage cameras." Nevada sighed. "Usually the worst quality and the best security. Give me the exact address. Whatever's on there, I'll pull it."

I provided the details, adding, "Her window smashed in and signs of a struggle. It looks like she was snatched."

"Damn," Nevada responded.

"And, Li'l Vegas, she has a Jonathan Boykins folder in her car."

The pause that followed told me everything. He knew how deep that name ran.

"I'll get that footage if I have to hack every system in D.C.," he finally said. "Give me an hour, maybe less. I know a back door into most of the public security networks. I'll burn through the city's firewall if I have to."

"Make it fast." I ended the call and turned back to the Audi, scanning it once more for anything I might have missed. The interior was immaculate, as Mya always kept it. Her phone was on the floor on the passenger side, laptop too, but no sign of the recorder she always carried. Whatever had happened, she hadn't planned to vanish. But someone else had.

I closed the door gently. My brain was already switching modes: tracking, hunting, anticipating. If Mya was still out there, I'd find her. If someone had taken her because of what she'd uncovered, they had just declared war.

The city blurred as I drove away. The folder wasn't just evidence; it was a map, one that might lead me to her or to the people who planned to make sure she never wrote another word. Somebody had made a critical mistake. They'd taken someone I cared about, someone who mattered in a world where I allowed very few people to matter. They'd made their move, and now it was my turn.

Chapter 38

Mya

Consciousness came back to me slowly, unwelcome and dragging pain behind it. The world tilted and swayed behind my closed eyelids, and when I finally forced them open, darkness greeted me. There was a dull ache in my head that throbbed in sync with the slow rise and fall of my breath, and my mouth was dry and bitter with the taste of chemicals and copper. Something sharp and sour lingered in my nose, a ghost of whatever they'd used to knock me out.

Chloroform? Ether? My brain tried to catalogue the options even as my stomach threatened to turn inside out.

"Focus," I whispered to myself, voice rasping like sandpaper.

I tried to move my hands and felt the burn of the rope against my wrists. They were tied tight, pulled behind the back of a cold metal chair. My chest was pinned by another loop of coarse rope, legs locked down to the chair's frame. Whoever tied me up knew what they were doing, using just enough pressure to hold me, but not enough to cut off circulation.

As my eyes adjusted, the space around me came into view: wide, dim, and industrial. Concrete floors and steel beams stretched in every direction. I could tell that

I was in a warehouse. A single bulb swung from a chain overhead, its weak light swaying. Dust floated in the air, and somewhere in the dark, water dripped slowly and steadily, as if it were counting down time I didn't have.

I tried to piece together what had happened. I'd left Winbush's with a folder with Boykins' name written in bold across the tab. I'd made it to the garage. I remembered my keys in hand, the click of the unlock button. Then, a black unmarked van sped into the parking lot, while a group of men in black snatched me from my car. A cloth went over my mouth, causing my lungs to burn. Then nothing. Now, I was here.

My watch was gone, so there was no way to tell how long I'd been unconscious or even what time of day it was. They'd taken the watch, and my phone and my recorder were missing. There were no windows or a clock. Just shadows along with silence and the sense that something bad was about to happen.

The door scraped open behind me, and heavy footsteps followed. I stiffened, my back pressing against the hard chair. I refused to turn my head and didn't flinch in order not to give whoever it was the satisfaction.

"The sleeping beauty awakens." The voice was deep, smooth, with an accent. Something in it curled under my skin. "I was beginning to worry that my associates had been too enthusiastic with the chemicals."

He came around the side, stepping into the weak circle of light. Tall, with broad shoulders, his skin was the color of old mahogany. There was a long scar riding the edge of his jaw like a warning. He wore a wife beater that fit him perfectly and seemed too clean for this dirty place. Santana Baptiste. I'd seen his name in files, heard whispers in D.C.'s darkest corners. He was second in command of the Gede Gang, the one who handled the messier problems and the kind of man whose presence meant somebody was about to disappear.

"Ms. Wynn," he said, smiling like a snake. "You've been busy. I've just become familiar with your work. My apologies for the accommodations. Not up to the standards you're accustomed to, I'm sure."

My heartbeat thundered in my ears. I swallowed hard, trying to summon moisture to my dry mouth.

"What do you want?" The question came out weaker than I intended, a betrayal of the courage I was trying to project.

Santana chuckled. "Straight to business. I appreciate that in a journalist. What I want is simple. Information."

"I don't reveal my sources," I said automatically, my professional ethics kicking in even in the face of fear.

"Admirable, but irrelevant." Santana slowly walked around my chair in a circle, forcing me to stretch my neck to follow him. "I'm not interested in who's been talking to you. I'm interested in who you've been talking to."

"I don't understand," I said, confused by his statement.

"Curtis Duncan." The name slowly rolled off Santana's tongue like he wanted to savor the taste of it before spitting it out. "Your childhood friend from Waycross, if I'm not mistaken."

"Curtis and I haven't spoken in years," I lied.

Santana stopped his circling, standing directly before me. "Ms. Wynn, please. We both know better." He rested his hand on the back of a second metal chair and dragged it closer, the legs screeching against the concrete floor. He sat down, leaning forward until his face was level with mine, close enough that I could smell his aftershave. "Curtis and I have something really important to discuss."

"Then call him yourself," I said, my voice finding strength in defiance. "I'm not your secretary."

Santana's smile tightened. "But you are leverage. You see, Curtis has proven difficult to reach. He's a cautious man. But for you . . ." He reached out, tucking a stray lock of hair behind my ear. His fingers lingered just long enough to make my skin crawl. "For you, I think he'll answer."

I jerked my head away from his touch. "You're wasting your time. Curtis doesn't care about me that way."

"Oh?" Santana raised an eyebrow. "Maybe not romantically. But something tells me Curtis Duncan, for all his reputation as a cold-blooded tracker, has a weakness for the people he cares about, and I think you fall in that category."

"You're wrong," I whispered.

"Don't insult me by pretending you're not close." His hand moved to my shoulder, fingers pressing just hard enough to promise pain without delivering it. "He won't let you suffer if he can prevent it."

"I haven't talked to him in years," I said flatly.

He chuckled, slow and dangerous, leaning back. "You're a better liar in print. Let's skip the part where I explain how serious this is. You're leverage, Ms. Wynn. You're bait. And Curtis is the type to bite."

I lifted my chin. "He's smarter than that."

"He's emotional. That makes him predictable. You're going to call him. Right now."

"Why would I help you?"

"This is not a request, Ms. Wynn. Not a negotiation." He stood suddenly, towering over me. "You will call Curtis. You will convince him to meet with me, or there will be some serious fucking consequences."

"Threaten me all you want," I said, summoning the courage that had carried me through dangerous investigations and hostile interviews. "I won't be used against my friend."

He didn't answer right away. Instead, he snapped his fingers. Another man entered, knife in one hand and a phone in the other. Santana didn't look at me as he spoke.

"Your mama still lives in Waycross, doesn't she? Cute yellow house on Dorothy Street, white hydrangeas out front."

My blood ran cold.

"And your father's still got that small practice near McDonald Street? Real convenient for someone his age. See, I know they moved back to Waycross after he got out of the Army. It would be a shame if something happened."

"Leave them out of this," I said through clenched teeth.

"I'd love to," Santana said smoothly. "Your parents seem like lovely people. The salt of the earth. Their safety is tied to your cooperation. It would be a shame if something were to happen to them because their daughter refused to make a simple phone call. You know how this works."

The man stepped forward, the knife flashing under the bulb.

"Stop, just stop." My voice cracked. "I'll do it."

My parents were innocent and unaware, their lives built on kindness and community service. They didn't deserve to be pulled into this darkness.

"I'll give you what you want," I said in bitter defeat. "Curtis's number. But I want your word that my family will be left alone."

Santana's smile returned, triumphant and terrible. "You have my word, Ms. Wynn. Your cooperation ensures their safety."

He nodded to his associate, who slid the knife back into a sheath at his belt.

Santana handed me the phone. "The number."

I recited the number slowly, feeling more guilty with each digit. Part of me hoped Curtis wouldn't answer. The other man dialed the number and handed Santana the phone.

"Thank you," Santana said in a sarcastic voice.

He smirked, watching. It rang as he held the phone to my ear.

Once. Twice. Three times.

I closed my eyes, torn between hoping Curtis would answer and praying he wouldn't.

"Curtis." His voice hit me like a rush of air after drowning.

"It's Mya," I said quickly. "I—"

Santana snatched the phone. "Mr. Duncan. I believe you've caused our organization a lot of grief with your actions. You took someone that was very special to us."

There was a pause, then Curtis's voice came through the phone, sharp and cold. "Put her back on."

"She's fine. For now," Santana replied. "And she stays that way if you cooperate."

"If you hurt her . . ." Curtis warned.

"Your threats don't fuckin' mean shit to me, Mr. Duncan," Santana interrupted. "You have something I want. I have something you want. A simple exchange."

"What is it that you want from me?" Curtis said.

"You," Santana replied in a calm, still voice.

There was another silence, longer this time. In my mind, I could almost see Curtis formulating a plan.

"How do I know she'll still be okay?" Curtis finally asked.

Santana held the phone to my ear again. "Tell him you're okay," he instructed.

"I'm here, Curtis," I said quickly. "Don't—"

Again, Santana pulled the phone away. "Satisfied? Now, here's what's going to happen. You will come alone to the abandoned warehouse on Kenilworth Ave. in Northeast Washington, D.C. Midnight tonight. Bring yourself, and Ms. Wynn walks free."

"And if I don't?" Curtis asked, his voice dangerously calm.

Santana's laugh was soft and serious. "You will. You're smarter than that. You know how these things work. Come alone, or she dies. Simple."

"Listen to me. If she's not in exactly the same condition as when you took her," Curtis said, each word precise and heavy with promise, "there won't be a hole deep enough for you to hide in. I will find you, and what happens next will make your worst nightmare look like a children's birthday party."

"Colorful," Santana remarked, unimpressed. "Midnight. Don't be late. Tick tock, Mr. Duncan."

He ended the call and slipped the phone into his pocket. I sagged back in the chair, shaking.

"There. That wasn't so hard, was it?" Santana looked down at me, pleased, then checked his watch. "Just under six hours until your knight arrives."

"Curtis isn't stupid," I said. "He knows this is a trap."

"Of course he does," Santana agreed. "But he'll come anyway. That's what makes him predictable. Now, we wait."

As he disappeared into the shadows, I let the fear take root for a second. Then I buried it, reminding myself: *Curtis is coming.* And if anyone could turn this into a rescue, it was him. I closed my eyes, trying to steady my breathing. *Six hours.* A lot could happen in six hours, and Curtis Duncan was nothing if not resourceful.

Chapter 39

Curtis

The warehouse loomed against the night sky, its metal siding catching the moonlight like dull armor. I lingered in the shadows across the street, slowly exhaling as I recalled the important facts of the phone call I had received. *We have Mya. Come alone. You have until midnight.*

The message had been clear: come alone or she dies. I knew it was a trap from the moment I talked to Santana on my phone, but Mya was in there because of me. It was my fault that this was happening. Putting her in harm's way was the last thing I wanted. She'd gotten too close to the same fire I was trying to put out. Now she was paying the price.

I'd taken a calculated risk and came unarmed. If the Gede Gang searched me and found heat, they'd assume backup wasn't far behind. Mya's safety depended on them believing I walked in alone. I rolled my shoulders, the leather of my jacket creaking. My guns were in the glove compartment of the SUV parked three blocks away, rented using one of the fake IDs, courtesy of Li'l Vegas, and a credit card in the same name.

I checked my watch, confirming that there were twenty minutes remaining until Santana's deadline. It was now or never. I crossed the street with precision, wasting no movement. When I got to the entrance, I pressed my palm to the cold steel of the door handle, took a breath, and pushed.

The door groaned open. I stepped inside, taking three steps before it slammed shut behind me with a loud, metallic clang. I didn't flinch. I felt rather than saw the movement in the darkness. Men stepped out from the shadows, weapons raised and ready. There were three, maybe four, each one armed and watching me with a predator's stillness.

"That's far enough, Duncan." The voice came from straight ahead, deep and measured, the accent unmistakably Haitian.

I stopped, hands held out from my sides. "I'm here. Where is she? Where's Mya?"

A deep laugh bounced off the walls, followed by slow, deliberate footsteps. Santana Baptiste stepped into the light. He was bigger than I remembered from the file: broad shoulders, thick arms, the left side of his face twisted by a scar that curled his lip into a permanent sneer. Dressed in a tank top and dark jeans, his hands were empty, but I knew better than to think he was unarmed.

"So you really do care about her," Santana said, circling me like a shark in the ocean. "Johnny Boy was my brother. And what you did . . . shooting him from the back. That was a bitch move."

I didn't blink. "I didn't kill Johnny Boy."

Santana stopped in front of me, eyes hard. "He's dead. Shot once in the back of the head. And you were the last person to see him alive."

"I was turning him over to the U.S. Marshals. That was the plan. What happened . . . the shooting. Wasn't me."

"Bullshit," he spat.

He stared at me for a long beat, jaw tight. His men didn't move, but I could feel the tension rising like heat off blacktop. He didn't want to believe me. He wanted a name to blame and somebody to punish.

"You expect me to believe someone else killed my brother while you had him?" he asked.

"No," I said flatly. "I expect you to use that brain behind those eyes. Someone set me up. Someone who knew exactly when I'd have him. Someone who wanted to send a message."

Santana's expression shifted slightly, but enough for me to know he heard the logic. That didn't mean he believed it yet.

Movement in the corner caught my eye. Mya was slumped against a support beam, hands tied behind her, head bowed. Even in the dim light, I knew it was her—shoulders still squared, holding on to whatever strength she had left. My chest tightened at the sight of her.

"She ain't got nothin' to do with this," I said. "Your problem is with me."

Santana shook his head slowly, stepping closer to Mya like he was making a damn point. He crouched, lifted her chin with one finger. She jerked away, her face tight with pain but her eyes sharp, still full of fight.

"That's where you're wrong," he said, standing again. "Ms. Wynn here's been pokin' round, askin' too many questions about things she should've left alone. Those questions got real specific after she linked up with you."

Mya's eyes found mine. Her stare was full of fear, but also something harder—defiance. It was the same look she used to wear when we were kids, when she would climb the old water tower or sneak into the football stadium after dark. Some things never change.

Then came the shift, a moment where the atmosphere changed. He took his time walking back toward me, boots loud on the concrete. The rest of his boys moved in closer, a slow tightening of the circle. Seven of them, not counting Santana. Tension rose as they closed in.

He pressed the cold metal of his gun against my forehead. "You thought you could just walk away after killing my brother?"

"Like I told you before, somebody is setting me up.

Before he could answer, the warehouse cracked open with a gunshot that echoed like thunder. Santana shouted in pain, spinning as the bullet ripped through his shoulder. His gun fell. I didn't hesitate to drop, punching my fist into his gut, knocking the air out of him. Another shot rang out, followed by a voice I hadn't heard since Georgia.

"Curtis! Down!"

Lauryn. My sister had found me despite my instructions, and right now, I couldn't be more grateful for her disobedience.

I dove, rolled, and came up with Santana's gun in my hand. A third shot hit one of the gang members center mass. He dropped like a sack of bricks. I scrambled behind a stack of pallets and started returning fire.

Chaos erupted. Screams, gunshots, splintering wood. I moved fast, precisely, just like Pops trained me: low and sharp, conserving ammo, counting bodies. I clocked three more down, three still up, Santana bleeding and scrambling like a wounded animal. Pushing forward, I cut through the smoke and noise until I reached Mya. She was still tied up, breathing hard, watching it all like a war reporter caught in the middle of her own damn story.

"You hurt?" I asked, already working at the restraints.

"I'll live," she said, wincing. "They weren't expecting your sister to crash the party, and I damn sure wasn't either."

"That makes two of us." I helped her to her feet, guiding her behind a stack of metal crates for better cover. "Stay low. When I say move, we're heading for that side door."

I handed her a pistol I had taken off one of the fallen men. "You remember how to use this?"

She gave a slight nod. "Point and shoot, right? Like when you used to drag me into those arcade games at the truck stop."

I smiled. "Close enough. Just aim for the assholes and try not to shoot me or Lauryn."

We huddled low. Three gang members remained, including Santana, who was clutching his bleeding shoulder but still managing to fire wildly in Lauryn's direction after pulling an extra pistol from his pant leg. Our escape route would take us directly through the line of fire.

"Lauryn!" I shouted. "We're movin'! Give me cover!"

"Copy!" she called back, continuing to fire shots without hesitation.

I caught Mya's eye. "Ready?"

She nodded once, her face full of determination. "Lead the way."

I glanced at Mya. "On my mark. Three . . . two . . . one—move!"

We took off. I led, keeping my body between her and the bullets. One of Santana's men tried to cut us off, and I put two in his chest without breaking stride. We reached the exit door. I hit it hard with my shoulder. For one awful second, it didn't budge. Then it groaned open.

Lauryn fired three clean shots, each one hitting a Gede Gang soldier square in the chest—like she was back at Uncle LC's estate in New York, cool and steady on the shooting range. When the smoke cleared, only Santana was left standing..

She dropped from the rafters like a damn ghost, hitting the floor and sprinting toward us with fire in her eyes. She slid through the door past us, turned, and dropped to a knee.

"I got it covered!" she shouted. "Let's go!"

"No," I said. "That motherfucker Santana is still inside, and there's no way I'm letting him walk away from this." I turned to Lauryn. "Get Mya out of here. Now."

She hesitated for a beat—just long enough for our eyes to lock—then gave a quick nod and led Mya toward safety. She grabbed Mya's hand and pulled her into the alley behind the warehouse.

I headed in the opposite direction to find my target. The warehouse was dark, the air thick with the scent of oil, rust, and smoke. Broken crates and metal beams cast jagged shadows beneath the flicker of a failing overhead light. I moved like a ghost, my footsteps silent against the concrete floor, my gun drawn and low. Somewhere in the distance, a pipe clanged. A trap? A distraction? I didn't flinch. Then came the voice.

"You should've saved yourself, Curtis."

Santana stepped out from behind a row of stacked pallets, blood on his shoulder from Lauryn's gunshot. He had an evil smirk on his face. He held his gun low but ready.

Santana laughed. "You think you're walking out of here?"

I rolled quietly and popped up behind a forklift. Santana ducked behind a support pillar, breathing hard. I circled wide, using the noise of a flickering generator to mask my movement. I spotted Santana's reflection in a broken mirror. I crept to a catwalk stairwell, quickly climbed up, and positioned myself from above. I waited until Santana moved to where I had just been.

"Too late!" I shouted.

I dropped from the catwalk, landing behind him with a thud. Before Santana could turn, I knocked the gun from his hands, the weapon clattering loudly across the cold concrete. A brutal fight ensued. Fists flew with vicious intent, elbows jabbed with sharp precision, and knees struck with bone-crunching force. Santana fought dirty, a devilish look in his eyes as he pulled a hidden blade from his belt. He lunged forward, the blade glinting menacingly under the dim light, and slashed me across the shoulder, leaving a jagged trail of searing pain in its wake.

I grunted and then headbutted Santana, causing him to stagger backward. We grappled fiercely over the knife. As Santana lunged, I twisted his body, wrested the blade from his grip, and slammed him against a crate. With a growl, I plunged the knife into his stomach. His eyes widened in shock as he gasped for air. I locked eyes with him, ensuring I was the last person he saw before he descended into darkness.

"It's hunting time, motherfucker," I whispered in his ear just before he shut his eyes.

I stood over him, breathing heavily, blood trickling down my right shoulder, but my gaze remained steady. Then I turned and walked out of the warehouse.

As I exited the warehouse, Lauryn and Mya gave me a big hug.

"How the fuck did you find me?" I asked Lauryn, the adrenaline finally starting to fade, making space for the questions piling up in my head.

Lauryn gave me that look, equal parts annoyed and proud. "You taught me how to track people. I told you I was ready."

"I see," I responded.

As we arrived at my car, I halted for a moment, my hand resting on the cool metal of the door. The outside air was thick with unspoken emotions.

"Thank you," I uttered, my voice soft but weighted with gratitude. "I told you to stay out of it. But . . . I'm glad you didn't listen."

She offered a tight smile as she swung open the car door. "When have I ever listened to you?" she replied, her smile slipping away to reveal a more intense expression. Her eyes, sharp and unwavering, met mine. "You're my brother, and you always told me family comes first."

As we drove off, the silence in the car was thick with unfinished business. Johnny Boy was dead. Santana was dead. Mya and I had nearly paid the price for being close to the fire. The pieces weren't adding up yet, but I'd find the pattern. I always did. Whoever orchestrated this forgot the first rule of the hunt: you never back a predator into a corner unless you're ready for the bite. And I was about to tear off the head of the snake.

Chapter 40

Curtis

It had been a long night. Lauryn had taken the guest room. Mya was in the master. I crashed on the sofa, though sleep didn't come for any of us. I could tell by the silence. It was the kind that presses in too thick to be peaceful. Lauryn's light had clicked off just after two, but I heard her pacing behind the closed door until almost dawn. And Mya . . . Mya hadn't made a sound. That was how I knew she was wide awake.

I knew she was shaken. Not by what she saw—she'd always been tougher than she looked—but by what it meant, how close she came to not making it out. I'd stood outside her door twice, hand raised to knock and go in, hold her in my arms, and promise she was safe now. But both times, I backed away. She needed space, and after everything, I owed her that. So, I stayed in the living room and let the night pass without rest.

Now, it was morning. Mya sat on the arm of the leather sofa, notebook closed for once, and Lauryn leaned against the kitchen doorway, arms crossed, watching me pace back and forth. The quiet between us wasn't awkward. It was loaded, brimming with the same tension that hadn't eased since the warehouse.

"He'll call," I said with a tone of conviction and certainty. "Li'l Vegas doesn't miss details."

"You think the documents are that bad?" Lauryn asked, slicing through the tension like a blade.

"I think it's either nothing," I said, finally pausing to look at her, "or it's everything."

The place looked like a war room, with files sprawled across the dining table, coffee mugs stacked beside half-eaten takeout, and my tactical vest slung over a chair like a warning to anyone who might knock. Sunlight filtered through slanted blinds.

Mya tracked my movement, her eyes staring at my shoulders clenched beneath my t-shirt. She knew the signs. She'd seen me wound tight before, back when we were just two kids in Waycross daring the world to break us. The difference now was that the world had actually tried.

"Your carpet's about to file a restraining order," she said, her voice warm.

Her attempt at being comical gave me slight relief for several reasons. I was about to respond with a quick comeback, but the phone buzzed. The three of us froze as the burner skittered across the glass table, lighting up with Nevada's name.

I snatched it before the second ring, thumb tapping the speaker. "Li'l Vegas."

"Cuz, you sittin' down?" His voice came through, tight with fear.

"I am now." I dropped onto the couch beside Mya, who shifted to make room. Lauryn stepped in from the kitchen.

"These documents you sent . . . Jesus, Curtis. I've been through them three times to be sure." Nevada's words tumbled over each other. "You were right to send them. They're a goddamn treasure map to corruption."

I leaned forward, elbows on my knees. "Tell me."

"Those Johnny Boy transcripts in the file you found in Mya's car are crazy. They're between Attorney General Scott Bowens, Senator Richard Winbush, and our dead friend Johnny Boy. They're careful, using code words and keeping it vague, but it's all there if you know how to read between the lines."

"What are they saying?" I pressed.

Mya quickly grabbed her notebook, pen poised above a clean page. Lauryn remained standing, her eyes narrow as she concentrated.

"They're partners, Curtis. All three of them held ownership stakes in a company called Bon Bagay Mining. It's registered in Haiti, but the paperwork traces back to shell corporations in Delaware and the Cayman Islands." Nevada paused, the sound of fingers tapping on a keyboard audible through the connection. "Winbush and Bowens each own twenty percent. Johnny Boy had the controlling interest at sixty percent."

I felt a cold weight settling in my stomach. "A mining company? Johnny Boy?"

"Yeah, and not just any operation. They secured exclusive drilling rights to a region called Miragoane. The Haitian government granted the concession three years ago, right after Senator Winbush's 'diplomatic mission' to Port-au-Prince."

I exchanged looks with Mya, writing rapidly across the page.

"What's in Miragoane?" Lauryn asked, her tactical mind already figuring out the angles.

"Gold. Copper. Rare earth minerals," Nevada explained. "Geological surveys estimate about twenty billion in extractable resources. The emails show they've been moving the minerals through Johnny Boy's import-export businesses, keeping the operation off the radar while they establish infrastructure."

I pushed up from the couch, pacing again as the weight of it all hit me in waves, each revelation stacking on the last, building a clearer picture of just how deep the betrayal ran, and how I'd been maneuvered into this impossible corner.

"Wait," I said in disbelief. "Johnny Boy owned a mining company? The man ran drugs, weapons, and girls. Since when was he interested in legitimate business?"

"That's the thing," Nevada replied. "This was his big move he'd been planning to step into respectability. But here's where it gets ugly. The last batch of emails, dated two weeks before Johnny Boy's murder, show Bowens and Winbush discussing a 'change in operational structure.' They were planning to cut him out."

The floor seemed to tilt beneath my feet. My hands stayed still, but cold crept into my fingertips while a slow burn ignited in my chest.

"Senator Winbush killed him," I said, flat and sure. It wasn't a question; it was a fact. "That's why Johnny Boy put a bullet in Attorney General Bowens. He realized they were about to cut him out."

"The evidence lines up," Nevada said. "They wanted that sixty percent, and Johnny Boy wasn't letting it go. There's an email from Winbush, with real careful language. But he mentioned 'terminal solutions to partnership disputes.' If that ain't clear, I don't know what is."

Mya looked up from her notebook, her eyes locking on mine. "And you . . . you were the perfect fall guy."

The realization hit me hard.

"Winbush sent me after Johnny Boy," I murmured, my words tasting like poison. "He knew I'd find him. Played Ray into giving up the drop location. Sent somebody to pull the trigger, then left me standing over the body."

"Exactly," Nevada said. "With you holding the bag, the case gets closed, quick and clean. Meanwhile, they trigger some clause in the partnership agreement, Johnny Boy dies, and his shares transfer."

My jaw clenched, a muscle ticking in my cheek. "Twenty billion reasons to set me up."

"At least," Li'l Vegas replied. "Those mineral projections keep rising."

Lauryn moved to the window, sweeping the blinds with a precise flick, scanning the street below. "We've got to move with this. Fast. They're not gonna stop until you're in the ground."

I nodded slightly, my thoughts already moving ahead, calculating angles and contingencies with the same cold precision I used tracking fugitives. "Nevada, what you found . . . it gives me motive. It proves someone else had a reason to kill Johnny Boy."

"It's bigger than that," Mya said, her voice sharper now, the reporter in her fully awake. "This isn't just a setup. It's conspiracy at the highest level. We're talking about an attorney general and a sitting senator orchestrating a murder to protect their business interests. I've covered a lot of stories, but this . . . this is something else."

"I'm uploading everything now," Nevada said. "You'll have the full packet and my analysis in less than an hour." His voice dropped an octave, weighted with fear. "But, Curtis . . . these people? They don't just pull strings. They own the whole damn puppet show. Winbush can bury evidence, reroute investigations, make witnesses disappear. And you already know he's not afraid to have someone killed."

His warning landed hard. I'd been trained to navigate danger, even expect betrayal, but not from men who could rewrite the law mid-sentence and get away with it.

"I hear you," I said quietly. "And I appreciate you, cousin. But this isn't your war."

"Family's always my war," Nevada shot back without hesitation. "Just promise me you'll be smart. What you're holding isn't evidence. It's detonation. Use it right."

The call ended. I stood there, stuck in place, the phone still warm in my hand. Around me, the room felt smaller, the walls drawing in. The truth sat heavily in my chest. Winbush, the man who pretended to want justice, had played me from the beginning. Hired me under the guise of cleaning up the streets when in reality, I'd been moved like a pawn across a board he thought he controlled.

"Curtis?" Mya's voice cut through the storm in my head and brought me back to reality. "What are you thinking?"

I turned toward her, the haze of shock lifting, replaced by something colder, sharper. "I'm thinking they didn't expect me to find those documents. They underestimated the wrong man."

"They always do," Lauryn said from across the room, her smile thin and knowing. "That's what makes you dangerous."

I moved to the dining table, placing both hands flat across the scattered papers. What once looked like disconnected fragments now fit together, each sheet another piece of a puzzle I hadn't known I was solving.

"We've got to be smart," I said, the weight of it all tightening my voice. "Winbush has people buried deep. Justice Department, law enforcement. If we push too fast or too loud, the evidence vanishes. So do the witnesses."

Mya stepped beside me, frowning and focused, already building a strategy in her mind. "We run parallel plays. Legal exposure and media pressure. If enough of this gets out, fast and wide, they won't be able to contain it."

"And we back it all up," Lauryn added. "Multiple copies, multiple places. Deadman switches. If something happens to us, the whole thing drops anyway."

I nodded, that old sense of clarity settling in—the kind that only came when I had a target locked in my sights. For days, I'd been reacting, dodging bullets, outrunning law enforcement, piecing together fragments while staying two steps behind a setup designed to bury me. But now, I saw the whole board.

The burner chimed. Li'l Vegas's first batch of files hit my inbox, encrypted and loaded. One by one, they populated the screen, each document a sharpened weapon of proof, motive, and trail. Together, they spelled out the blueprint of a betrayal meant to destroy me. The knowledge burned hot in my chest.

"They thought they were hunting me," I murmured, eyes still on the screen. "But what they did . . . they built a hunter with nothing left to lose."

Mya heard the shift in my voice, the storm gathering beneath it. She'd seen it before, when we were young. When I found purpose, locked in, there was no pulling me off the path. She stepped closer, placed a steadying hand on my arm. That quiet tether to something real, something human.

"We do this the right way," she said softly. "No short-cuts. No matter how much they deserve your brand of justice."

I covered her hand with mine, grounding myself in her touch. "They made it personal when they framed me. But this ain't just about revenge anymore. This is about power unchecked. Corruption dressed in law and privilege. And making damn sure it never happens again."

More files continued loading, each one another crack in the foundation Winbush and Bowens had built. As the evidence stacked up, so did my resolve. They'd plotted Johnny Boy's murder, turned me into the fall guy, and weaponized the system to finish the job. But they had miscalculated. They left me breathing, and now the trap was theirs.

Chapter 41

Mya

I sat at the edge of the borrowed desk, papers spread before me like the aftermath of a storm, each page a piece of a puzzle that could destroy the powerful men who had taken everything from Curtis. The safehouse we'd moved to for me to work in wasn't glamorous, with bare walls, mismatched furniture, and a single window that stayed locked, but it offered what we needed, anonymity.

Lauryn stood by the door, her hands in her pockets, glancing between me and the hallway every few minutes. Her presence was subtle but undeniable, like a bodyguard moonlighting as a statue. Curtis had insisted she stay with me, and though I'd rolled my eyes at the idea, I didn't argue for long. A couple of days ago, I'd been abducted and thrown into a warehouse like some pawn. I still felt the phantom ache of zip ties around my wrists and the grit of that cold floor beneath me. Even through the trauma, I still had to do my job.

"You know I don't need a babysitter," I murmured, not looking up from the documents.

Lauryn didn't flinch. "I'm not a babysitter. I'm a failsafe."

I looked up at her, raising an eyebrow. "Failsafe?"

"If something happens, I make sure you still get to tell the story."

I stared at her for a beat. I didn't have a snarky comeback or defense. She was right. I was sitting on a grenade, and she was the one shielding me from the blast.

The burner phone on the table buzzed, no ringtone, just the low hum of vibration on cheap laminate. I snatched it up, checked the number, then answered.

"Nevada?" I asked, already reaching for my pen.

His voice came through sharp and clear. "Everything you've got lines up. The mining contracts, the shell companies, the emails. This is bigger than you thought."

I let out a slow breath. "That's saying something."

"You've got names, dates, digital signatures. Winbush. Bowens. Johnny Boy. All connected through Bon Bagay Mining and a trail of dirty money that stretches from Haiti to Delaware to D.C."

Lauryn had moved closer, scanning the table behind me. I flipped through the folder, stopping on a flagged document with a wire transfer from a known political donor to an account linked to Johnny Boy's front company. The senator's signature sat bold and smug on the approval line.

"They thought they buried this deep enough where no one would find it," I said.

"They didn't count on you," Nevada replied.

I scribbled fast. "How long until I get the rest?"

"Two hours. Encrypted drop. I'll send the key separately."

I hung up and dropped the burner onto the desk, its weight suddenly heavier than before. My hand hovered over the file. I should've felt victory, but all I could feel was the target forming between my shoulder blades.

Lauryn stepped beside me. "You good?"

"No," I said. "But I will be."

She nodded, her expression unreadable. "Just remember, you're not alone. Not anymore."

I met her gaze. She was loyal to the bone and the kind of woman who'd go to war for her brother and now, maybe, for me too.

"Thanks for staying," I said quietly.

Lauryn shrugged. "You're family now."

The weight of her words settled over me, stronger than fear, stronger than the story itself.

And suddenly, I didn't feel like a pawn anymore. I felt like a player.

Hours later, I heard the soft creak of the sofa and the quiet, purposeful sound of boots crossing the hardwood. Lauryn entered the room, arms folded across her chest, the glint of her sidearm visible beneath her jacket. She'd been shadowing me all day like a silent bodyguard, watching, waiting, keeping threats at bay while I worked. Her presence was steady, unshakeable. The kind of comfort you didn't ask for but were glad to have.

"You finished?" she asked, glancing down at the portfolio in my hand.

"Two hours of cross-referencing and double-checking," I said. "It's airtight. Everything ties—Johnny Boy, Bowens, Winbush, the mining operation, the cover-up. Curtis gets cleared. And if this gets the traction I think it will, they all burn."

Lauryn studied me for a moment, then gave a slow nod, her face unreadable but her eyes sharp.

"I need to walk this in myself," I added, straightening the collar of my blouse. "I don't trust sending it over the wire. This goes directly into Michael Lawson's hands. He's the only one I trust with it."

She didn't argue. Instead, she stepped aside and gestured toward the door. "Let's go."

It was simple, said with the calm finality of someone who had your back without question. I tucked the portfolio beneath my arm and followed her out, my heels echoing softly in the hallway. This was it. The truth was no longer just in my hands. It was headed for the light.

The walk to Michael Lawson's office felt longer than usual. Same worn linoleum, same desks I passed every day, but tonight, it felt like the weight of the entire newsroom pressed against my spine. My heels struck the floor in sharp, even beats, each one echoing with purpose. I'd walked this path a hundred times before, but never like this and never carrying evidence that could bring down a sitting senator and the legacy of an attorney general.

A memory flashed in my head: me as a little girl, sitting on my grandfather's porch with skinned knees and a sense of pride, promising him I'd always stand up for what was right. That promise echoed now, clear as his voice had been that day. The distance between that fearless tomboy and the woman walking into a war with words felt both miles apart and one breath away.

The door to Michael's office was cracked just enough to let a sliver of light bleed into the hallway. I stopped, took a breath that stretched against the fabric of my blouse, and firmly knocked three times.

"Come in," he called out.

I stepped inside, closing the door behind me. The familiar smell of fresh coffee and printer toner hit me immediately. Lawson looked up from his screen, glasses low on his nose, his gray-flecked beard trimmed neat like always. He didn't smile.

"Mya," he said slowly, reading my face like a front page. "Welp, there's that look."

I raised an eyebrow. "What look?"

"The one that tells me I'm not making it to my dinner reservation tonight." He motioned to the chair in front of his desk. "Let's have it."

I sat, placing the leather-bound portfolio on his desk like I was laying down a loaded weapon.

"I've got a story," I said, voice even. "And it's not just a headline. It's a career ender. It's about Senator Winbush. Something big."

Michael's eyebrows rose slightly—the closest thing to surprise he ever showed. Senator Richard Winbush was not just any target. He was a power broker, a dealmaker with fingers in every political pie in Washington. His distinguished appearance and family-man image had won him five terms, with speculation that he was positioning for a presidential run.

"Define *big*," Michael said, leaning forward.

"Corruption. Bribery. Money laundering through foreign mining operations." I unzipped my portfolio and removed the folder. "All of it documented, verified, and ready to print."

I spread the documents across his desk like a dealer laying out a winning hand. Michael's eyes went from page to page, his experienced eyes taking in the implications faster than most could read the actual text.

"These are emails between Winbush and Jonathan Boykins," I explained, pointing to a printout. "Boykins, who goes by Johnny Boy in certain circles, ran a mining operation in Haiti that's officially extracting gold, copper, and rare earth minerals, but is actually a front for multiple illegal activities."

Michael picked up one of the emails, scanning it with the intensity of a man who'd built his career on spotting the story between the lines. "And the senator is involved how, exactly?"

"Winbush pushed through legislation that directed USAID funds to rebuild Haiti's infrastructure after the earthquake. Those funds were diverted to build roads and power facilities that exclusively served Boykins' mining operation." I slid another document forward. "Here's the bill, with Winbush's amendments highlighted. And here"—I tapped another paper—"are the bank transfers showing how the money moved from USAID through three shell companies before ending up with Boykins' operation."

Michael's fingers traced the money trail, his expression darkening. "And what does the senator get in return?"

I produced a flash drive where I'd stored the information from Nevada. "Offshore accounts. Campaign contributions laundered through legitimate-looking donors. And a twenty-percent silent ownership in the mine itself. According to my sources, we're talking about profits in the billions, all hidden from financial disclosures."

"Your sources?" Michael asked, the question loaded with journalistic caution.

"Multiple and verified. Including a Senate staffer who provided these." I pulled out another folder. "Internal memos showing Winbush personally intervened when the EPA started asking questions about environmental permits for Boykins' stateside processing facilities."

Michael leaned back, absorbing the full scope of what I'd presented. His office suddenly seemed smaller, as if the magnitude of the story had expanded to fill the available space.

"You've triple-checked all of this?" he asked, though the question was more ritual than doubt.

"Quadruple-checked," I confirmed. "Dates match. Account numbers verify. Sources corroborate independently. It's solid, Michael."

He nodded slowly, picking up the photo of Winbush and Boykins at a charity gala, their smiles revealing nothing of the criminal enterprise they shared.

"You understand what this means," he said. "Winbush isn't just any senator. He chairs the Appropriations Committee. Has friends in every agency from the FBI to the Park Service."

"I know exactly what it means," I replied. "It means we're doing our job."

Michael studied my face, looking for any signs of uncertainty. When he didn't find any, he allowed himself a small smile.

"You know they're going to deny this," he said, gathering the documents into a more orderly arrangement. "Winbush's people will call it a political hit job. They'll question your sources, your motives, probably your professional ethics."

"Let them," I said, a steel edge entering my voice. "The documents speak for themselves."

Michael nodded, making his decision. "Front page. Tomorrow's edition." He glanced at his watch. "That gives you four hours to write it up. I want it comprehensive but accessible. Hit the highlights in the first three paragraphs, then build the case methodically."

"Already done," I said, handing him the exposé I'd spent most of the day penning. Relief and excitement surged through my body, a journalist's particular high that came from speaking truth to power. "Thank you, Michael."

He raised a cautionary finger. "Don't thank me yet. A story like this, there will be blowback. Powerful men like Winbush don't go down without dragging others with them. Be careful, Mya. Watch your back."

"Always do," I replied, gathering up my evidence.

"And Mya?" Michael called as I reached the door. "This is good work. The kind that reminds me why we do this job."

I nodded, a silent acknowledgment of what we both knew: that sometimes journalism wasn't just about reporting facts, but about changing the course of events.

I stepped out of the building into the thick D.C. night, the weight of what I'd just handed over settling in my chest like a stone. Lauryn stood beside the black SUV at the curb, one hand resting on the open passenger door, scanning the sidewalk before noticing me.

She didn't ask if I was okay. She didn't need to. As I climbed in beside her, she shifted into gear and merged into traffic with smooth efficiency.

"Well?" she asked without looking over. "How'd it go?"

I exhaled slowly, watching the city lights blur past my window. "It went well," I said. "My byline's about to be permanently attached to one of the biggest political scandals this country's ever seen."

Lauryn nodded once, staying focused on the road ahead. "And how do you feel about that?"

I gave a small, tired smile. "Like I did what I was born to do. And for once . . . I'm satisfied."

The SUV rolled on into the night, two women with purpose, the weight of truth in the rearview, and a storm still waiting up ahead.

Chapter 42

Senator Richard Winbush

The *Washington Post* landed on the desk with the soft, decisive thud of a death sentence. I barely registered it at first. My hand reached for the coffee without thinking, fingers brushing the handle of the mug out of habit. But then I saw it. The headline. Bold. Black. Unforgiving. My hand froze in midair. The mug slipped from my grip and shattered against the floor, coffee bleeding into the carpet like a wound.

The headline read: CORRUPTION UNVEILED: SENATOR WINBUSH AND AG BOWENS EXPOSED IN BILLION-DOLLAR SCANDAL. Beneath it, in sharper type, SOURCES LINK PROMINENT LEGISLATOR TO MURDER OF HAITIAN CRIME BOSS.

My pulse raced as I read the first few lines. There were names, dates, and dollar amounts. A reporter's scalpel had torn through years of well-placed insulation and careful maneuvering. The article meticulously detailed financial irregularities, secret meetings, murder, and a paper trail leading directly to my office. My legacy, fifteen years of calculated ascension, ripped open in the space of a single column.

Just last week, I'd convinced Beth to come back. She and her parents had taken the kids and tucked away at her sister's place in Madrid, Spain, after the assassination attempt. Once Johnny Boy had been confirmed dead,

I told her it was all under control, that I'd taken care of everything. And now here it was, in black and white. Not just a scandal, an implosion. She was going to be pissed, but I had to tell her before she learned from anyone or anywhere else. I had no time to spare.

"Beth!" I called out, my voice raw with urgency. "Beth, get in here!"

I snatched up my phone and scrolled to the name I never used unless the world was on fire: my pilot. I didn't waste any time with pleasantries or an explanation, just the clipped commands of a man whose world was collapsing.

"Ready the jet. Immediate departure. Same airfield. No delays."

Beth appeared in the doorway, elegant as ever in her taupe slacks and cashmere wrap. She was already dressed for the charity auction. She frowned at me when she saw the look on my face that was part confusion, part fear.

"Richard? What is it?"

I shoved the paper toward her. "Pack now. Essentials only."

Her eyes dropped to the front page. I watched the color drain from her face.

"But the kids . . ." she said, her voice faltering. "They're still at school. And I'm supposed to co-host the—"

"Twenty minutes," I insisted as I pulled books from the shelf behind my desk, revealing a hidden safe. "Tell the children it's a surprise vacation. Paris, tell them Paris."

My fingers fumbled with the combination, muscle memory failing me twice before the door swung open. Inside lay the insurance I'd hoped never to need: our passports with unfamiliar names but familiar faces, banded stacks of hundred-dollar bills, and a slim USB drive containing account numbers for funds untraceable to my name. I stuffed these into a leather briefcase alongside a loaded Glock 19, another insurance policy for desperate times.

Beth still hadn't moved. She stood in the middle of the room, clutching the newspaper like it was going to rewrite itself.

"Call Warren," she whispered. "He always said if something happened, he'd protect us."

Warren was the head of the FBI. He manipulated federal investigations, destroyed evidence, silenced whistleblowers, and misdirected the media. For years, he was the firewall between me and Bowens, as well as any real accountability. He wasn't just a tool of corruption—he was an architect of it.

"Warren was quoted in paragraph six. He's already jumped ship," I told her. "Get the children. Now!"

I stuffed the contents of the safe into a leather briefcase and slammed it shut. Grabbing my personal phone, I yanked the SIM card out and crushed it under my heel, then reached into my desk drawer and pulled out a prepaid, unused burner phone and powered it on. I made one quick call.

"We still good?" I asked.

"For now," the voice replied.

I hung up and stood still for a second in the middle of the room: just me and the broken mug. *Fuck!* I'd told Beth it was safe to come home, and now everything was burning.

Fifteen minutes later, my family slid into the black Suburban, the early-morning chill brushing against designer coats and sleepy eyes. The children were confused but compliant, pacified by promises of warm croissants and views of the Eiffel Tower. Madison clutched her stuffed rabbit to her chest, while Preston sat quietly beside her, his expression unreadable.

Beth settled into the passenger seat without a word, her Hermès bag gripped like a life vest. She hadn't spoken since the article hit the front page. Her silence carried weight that was heavier than outrage, heavier than fear. I felt something stir in my chest. It wasn't guilt, exactly. It was more like irritation. She'd returned home just days ago, reassured by my promises that everything was under control. Now I was forcing her into exile.

She didn't deserve this. She'd played her part flawlessly: charming, elegant, always tireless in her devotion to appearances. The perfectly polished political wife, standing as a pillar of philanthropic grace. And here I was, dragging her through back roads toward a private airfield under a false name. But sentiment was a liability now, and it was one I couldn't afford.

I maneuvered through D.C. traffic with precision, my eyes flicking between mirrors and intersections. The terminal was quiet this time of day. The pilot had been well-compensated for his discretion. My travel plan was flawless. Once airborne, we'd refuel in the Azores before continuing to our final destination. By morning, we'd be beyond the reach of federal prosecutors and grand jury subpoenas.

"Daddy, why are you driving so fast?" Madison asked from the back seat, her voice small and uncertain.

I glanced at her through the rearview mirror, forcing the corners of my mouth upward. "Just excited for the trip, sweetheart. Paris waits for no one."

She smiled, and I felt my stomach twist.

We moved beyond the city limits, the skyline receding in the rearview like a life being shed. The streets thinned, replaced by the wide, quiet roads that led to the airfield. I exhaled slowly as we turned onto the unmarked drive. I checked to make sure there were no police cars or unmarked federal vehicles. Our head start worked.

"We're going to be fine," I said, more to myself than to Beth. "It's a minor political flare-up. I'll let the attorneys posture and file motions. Lay low until the press turns their attention elsewhere."

Beth didn't look at me. She stared straight ahead, her tone flat. "They mentioned murder, Richard."

"Allegations," I said, clenching my jaw. "No proof and nothing solid. You know how these things work. Nothing will stick."

The security gate at the airfield opened without hesitation. The SUV rolled forward, tires crunching gravel. The private terminal was a low, discreet building with tinted windows and minimal signage. Beyond it, the sleek form of my Gulfstream G650 waited on the tarmac, stairs already lowered, engines beginning their preliminary checks. The pilot stood at the bottom of the stairs, clipboard in hand, a perfect picture of routine private aviation service, as if this were just another congressional trip.

"We're almost there," I said, parking near the terminal.

Preston rolled his eyes. "This is stupid. I have a game tomorrow."

"You'll have better stories to tell than basketball scores," I replied, climbing out and looking around the airfield. Seeing that it was still clear, the nagging tension between my shoulder blades began to ease.

I motioned for Beth to escort the children toward the plane while I retrieved my briefcase from the trunk. Its contents brought me some much-needed relief along with the fact that in a couple of more minutes, we'd be airborne. In three hours, we'd be over international waters, and by tomorrow, this would be someone else's problem.

Beth and the children had nearly reached the stairs when I noticed something odd. The pilot's stance had changed, becoming stiffer, less natural. Then I saw why.

A tall, broad-shouldered man emerged from behind the Gulfstream's nose, moving with the quiet authority of someone who'd spent his life hunting dangerous men. His stride was unhurried but deliberate, the kind that made people instinctively step aside. Beside him, a younger woman moved in sync, her posture sharp, her eyes sweeping the tarmac with calculated precision. The two looked alike, and I could tell they were cut from the same cloth genetically and professionally.

Behind them, ten figures in tactical gear appeared from the shadows of the terminal, the words "U.S. MARSHALS" emblazoned across their jackets. My legs froze. The briefcase in my hand suddenly felt like lead. Beth stopped beside me, one arm curling protectively around Madison and Preston. She didn't ask questions. There was no need.

"Senator Winbush," the man called out. His voice didn't rise, but it carried clean across the tarmac. It was the tone of someone who never had to repeat himself.

In that moment, I recognized him: Curtis Duncan, the bounty hunter.

"There's been a misunderstanding," I replied, injecting the kind of practiced authority that once commanded Senate chambers and network cameras. "I'm taking my family on vacation. This is harassment of a sitting United States senator."

Curtis didn't stop. He continued toward me at a steady pace, his face unreadable. The woman with him remained in position like a second shadow, eyes moving with surgical precision, missing nothing.

"Vacation with emergency passports and two million in cash?" Curtis asked, stopping just ten feet away. "That's one hell of a spontaneous trip, Senator."

I had no idea how the hell he knew that. It was as if he'd had a camera inside my damn house. My grip tightened around the briefcase handle. "I demand to know the meaning of this intrusion. I'll have your badge for this."

"You're not in a position to make demands," he said coolly.

He nodded toward the terminal. Another figure stepped into view, this one in a tailored suit with a badge gleaming from his belt. The weight of the moment settled heavier with every footstep.

"Senator Richard Winbush," the man called out.

"Ray," I said, "tell these people who I am."

"We have a federal warrant for your arrest on charges of conspiracy against the United States, corruption, money laundering, and the murder of Jonathan Boykins."

"This is absurd," I said, stumbling back a step. "This is a political hit job orchestrated by my opponents. My attorneys will—"

"Your attorney was taken into custody an hour ago," Bradford cut in, unfolding a document. "Along with your chief of staff and your financial advisor. They're already talking, Senator."

Behind me, Beth started to cry, silent at first, mascara running down her cheeks. Madison clung to her arm, eyes wide with confusion. Preston stood still, his expression blank, his understanding dawning slowly but surely.

The ground beneath me felt like it was shifting. The polished image I'd spent years perfecting, a respected lawmaker, family man, a true patriot, crumbled to reveal what I truly was: cornered and exposed. My hand moved toward my jacket pocket, where the familiar weight of the Glock pressed against my ribs.

Curtis's stance changed. A subtle shift in posture told me he was ready. "I wouldn't," he said, voice low but steady. "Not in front of your kids."

The words interrupted the panic in my head. Madison was watching me, her eyes wide, full of fear for the man who she no longer recognized as the one who read bed-time stories and clapped at recitals. She was looking at a stranger, a man contemplating violence and with nothing left. My hand fell away from my jacket.

Deputy Bradford stepped forward, handcuffs glinting in the morning sun. "Richard Winbush, you have the right to remain silent. Anything you say can and will be used against you in a court of law."

As the cold metal closed around my wrists, I looked toward my family. Beth had pulled both children against her, her eyes no longer meeting mine. In that moment, I realized I'd lost more than my freedom. I'd lost the illusion they'd lived under for years.

"Take care of them," I said hoarsely as Bradford guided me toward a waiting SUV. "They didn't know anything."

Curtis watched as I was placed in the vehicle, my once broad shoulders now slumped in defeat. The curtain had fallen on my performance as the righteous public servant.

"Your family will be looked after," Bradford assured me, closing the door on my new reality.

Chapter 43

U.S. Marshal Deputy
Raynard Bradford

The blue lights were still fading from my peripheral vision when I stepped away from the convoy. The job was done, the senator secured, and yet my pulse hadn't settled. It never did after a takedown like this. Not when the name in cuffs carried this much weight.

I didn't look back at Winbush. I didn't need to. I already knew the expression he had on— that hollow, stunned stare, like the rules had suddenly changed on him mid-game. Like he didn't understand how a man with power, pedigree, and a private jet could end up in shackles. That's the look of a king realizing the crown was borrowed. I had more important things to handle.

"Duncan," I called out as I made my way over.

Curtis turned, calm as ever, like he hadn't just helped dismantle a billion-dollar web of corruption. He moved like a man who'd done what needed to be done and made peace with whatever came next.

I stuck my hand out. "Appreciate you, brother. For everything."

He gripped my hand tight. "You already know. It's mutual."

I gave a nod, and one of my guys stepped up with two black duffel bags, both heavy and full of government gratitude.

"Million dollars. As agreed," I told him. "Feds wanted to wire it, but I figured you'd want to touch what you earned."

Curtis took the bags, weighed them like he was checking for more than just money. "Tell the bureau their gratitude weighs just right."

Then, without warning, he pulled me into a hug, quick but solid, like brothers who didn't have to explain anything to each other. He clapped me on the back, and for a second, I remembered why we ever trusted him in the first place.

"We're square now, Ray," he said. "That misunderstanding between us, it's buried."

I stepped back and shrugged. "Wasn't no misunderstanding far as I'm concerned."

His sister Lauryn stepped up, making her presence known.

"You know half that money's mine, right?" she said, eyes flashing.

Curtis smirked. "What you mean, half?"

She bumped him on the arm, grinning. "You heard me. You wouldn't even be breathing if it weren't for me."

He laughed, shaking his head like a man who knew when to quit while he was behind.

My team started loading up the vehicles. I glanced back at the SUV where Winbush sat, staring out the window like his whole world had turned to smoke. Which, to be fair, it had.

"What happens to his family?" Curtis asked.

I followed his eyes to Beth Winbush. She was holding their kids close, her eyes locked on one of my female deputies explaining what came next. The woman looked shattered. Not guilty. Just . . . lost.

"Not our jurisdiction," I said. "Unless they were involved, they're just collateral. Caught in the fallout."

Lauryn moved beside Curtis, her tone quieter. "Sometimes the guilty ain't the only ones who pay."

She wasn't wrong, and I had a bad feeling we weren't done yet. Not by a long shot.

They say a man's ambition can be his salvation or his curse, and for Senator Richard Winbush, it was both. He had moved through the corridors of Washington like he owned every damn square inch, wrapped in custom suits and campaign smiles that could make devils nod in approval. He talked a good game, but underneath the surface, the man was slick with greed—the kind of greed that didn't just touch people. It devoured them.

His reach stretched far beyond the Hill. It reached down into places men like him never stepped foot in— the dirt roads and humid corruption of Haiti. That's the thing about power: it rarely gets its own hands dirty. It hires men like Johnny Boy to do the dirty work and then hires someone else to silence them when they become a liability.

I wasn't supposed to know much, only enough to put cuffs on the bad guys and bring 'em in. They never told me how deep the rot went, but I could smell it. After fifteen years in this game, your gut becomes your bible, and mine had been screaming since the night Johnny Boy died.

Curtis Duncan had called me himself. Said he had Johnny alive and ready for transport.

"Handled clean," he said. "No resistance. He knows the deal."

I remember that call clear as day. I remember how calm Curtis sounded: calm, but tired. He wasn't green. He'd been in the dirt long enough to know how fragile justice could be. And that night, I heard it in his voice. He was trying to do right by it.

Then, before I even made it to the alley, it happened.

Pop. One round to the back of the skull, clean, quick, and precise.

When I got there, Johnny was laid out like a butchered deer. My partner Jesse crouched beside the body, looking at the mess.

"Sniper," he said quietly. "Professional job."

"Who the hell signs a hit like this in the middle of a transfer?" I asked.

Jesse looked up. "Someone real confident they won't be touched."

They wanted to pin it on Curtis, saying he set Johnny Boy up, claiming he went rogue and couldn't be trusted. I watched the press release come through like it was routine: *Internal investigation ongoing, suspended pending review.*

They wanted him gone, and fast, but I didn't buy it, not for a second. That's when I started digging. It began with the security-rotation logs. On the surface, they were boring, just rows of names and timestamps, a bureaucratic paper trail meant to track who came and went. But buried in all that mundane detail, one name kept surfacing in places it shouldn't have: Vinton Kane.

At first, I didn't know who the hell he was. The name didn't show up on any internal memos or staffing rosters. No digital footprint, LinkedIn, Facebook, nothing. That was the first red flag. These days, ghosts only exist when someone wants them to. So, I dug deeper, and what I found made my skin crawl.

Kane was ex–Special Forces, off-book most of his career. In the black-ops community, they called him The Harvester, a name whispered more than spoken, usually followed by silence. His specialty, making murders look like suicides, disappearances, or natural causes. The man didn't just eliminate targets. He erased them.

His name wasn't where you'd expect it, either. It was buried in the clearance list, squeezed between catering staff and janitors, as if someone wanted it seen but not noticed. Hidden in plain sight. That's how professionals do it.

The deeper I went, the uglier it got. The money trail was a maze of offshore accounts and dummy corporations. It started with a wire transfer, just under reporting thresholds, funneled into a shell company in the Caymans. From there, the money moved through a string of equally shady fronts, each one designed to scrub the trail clean. But timing doesn't lie. Every transfer lined up with one of Kane's known or suspected deployments.

The final destination was a political action committee called Patriots for American Energy. It sounded wholesome enough with red, white, and blue branding and a flag-waving mission statement. But beyond the surface, it was a piggy bank for laundering dirty money. The kind of PAC that gave Winbush just enough distance to claim innocence, even while he signed off on the deals. And right at the center was Senator Richard Winbush, the puppet master.

I didn't need a warrant to feel the truth in my gut: Kane didn't just happen to be nearby when Johnny Boy got clipped. He was sent. Someone greenlit it, and that someone wore thousand-dollar suits and smiled for cameras like he gave a damn about the American people. He needed Johnny Boy dead. He needed Curtis framed. That way, Winbush could sweep in, claim the mine, and ride off into the sunset on a wave of campaign donations and cushy corporate board seats. It was ruthless, and it almost worked.

Now that Winbush was behind bars, you'd think I'd feel satisfied. I didn't. Because while the mastermind was in custody, the hitman was still out there. Johnny Boy's killer hadn't vanished; he'd just gone dark. And until I found Vinton Kane and dragged him into the light, this case wasn't over.

Epilogue

Curtis

I gripped the steering wheel with loose hands, the rhythm of the road beneath my tires matching the steady thrum of anticipation in my chest. Beside me, Lauryn sat with her head tilted against the window, her eyelids heavy but refusing to close, neither of us wanting to miss this moment, this final passage through a city that had nearly broken us both.

I glanced at my sister, the morning light brushing across her profile, softening the sharp lines of the warrior I'd come to depend on. The last seventy-two hours had stripped us bare: tense standoffs in hollowed warehouses, and a final reckoning in the marble halls of power where Senator Winbush's polished image shattered beneath the weight of everything we'd uncovered. Now, with him in federal custody and my name officially cleared, the adrenaline had drained from my system, leaving behind a strange, unsteady lightness, like the silence after a storm, too fragile to trust.

"Feels strange, doesn't it?" I said, my voice barely louder than the purr of the engine. "Like waking up from a nightmare but finding out you brought something back with you."

Lauryn shifted in her seat, her eyes drifting from the passing scenery to my face. "You mean the part where we nearly died, or the part where we took down one of the most powerful men in Washington?"

"Both." I stretched my fingers on the wheel, feeling the ghost of soreness from where I'd gripped my weapon during that final confrontation. "When I trained to do this shit, they never mentioned the aftermath. The quiet after the storm."

A smirk tugged at Lauryn's lips. "I'm pretty sure the idea of the aftermath was just cleaning your weapon and prepping for the next mission."

"True enough," I said.

I glanced over at Lauryn again, her eyes distant, reflecting a maze of memories that mirrored my own. We were both carrying the weight of what we'd uncovered. The corruption that reached the highest levels of government, Gede Gang soldiers exposed as pawns in a far more dangerous game, and the allies we never expected—along with enemies we never saw coming. It all sat like scattered puzzle pieces, waiting to be sorted. But neither of us had the complete picture yet. Not really.

When I flicked the turn signal and veered off the direct route to the airport, Lauryn's posture shifted. Her attention snapped to the present.

"Scenic route?" she asked, her voice laced with that familiar mix of curiosity and suspicion, an art form only a sibling could master after decades in the same trench.

I kept my eyes on the road, but a small smile played at the corners of my lips. "Just one stop to make before we leave."

"This stop have a name?" Lauryn raised an eyebrow, straightening in her seat as recognition dawned in her eyes. The teasing note in her voice suggested she already knew the answer.

"Won't take long," I replied, deliberately avoiding the question as I navigated toward a quieter residential area where historic brownstones stood in neat rows, their facades glowing amber in the strengthening morning light.

"Sure it won't," Lauryn said, her tone carrying a knowing weight that made my ears warm despite myself.

I pulled the car to a gentle stop along the curb in front of a particularly well-maintained brownstone with a small pot of persistent autumn flowers flanking the steps. The neighborhood held the dignified hush of early morning—curtains still drawn, the occasional light indicating someone's early rise to meet the day.

"Wait here," I said, turning off the engine and pocketing the keys.

Lauryn made a show of checking her watch. "Clock's ticking, big brother. Our plane won't wait, even for you."

I shot her a look that was half annoyance, half affection. "Five minutes."

"I'll set a timer," she replied with exaggerated seriousness, then softened. "Take what time you need. Just . . . not too much of it, okay?"

I gave a nod and stepped into the crisp air. Every footstep I took toward the brownstone's entrance felt heavy, as if my body had finally decided to tally up every hit, bruise, every sleepless night from the past few days. At the door, my knuckles paused for a moment, and I took a breath or two. I knocked softly but with intention.

The silence that followed was deafening and long enough for doubt to creep in. I began to think that maybe I was too early and she wasn't home. Or maybe this wasn't the moment for goodbyes after all. My mind was all over the place until I heard movement behind the door, then the slide of a chain. The door opened, and there she was.

Mya stood in the doorway dressed in a crisp white blouse and tailored slacks. Her press credentials hung from a lanyard around her neck. She looked every bit the journalist on a mission, ready to take on whatever the world threw her way—as if exposing billion-dollar corruption and surviving abduction was just another Tuesday at *The Washington Post*.

"Curtis," she said, sounding both surprised and relieved. Her face transformed from professional readiness to genuine warmth, the mask of an investigative journalist slipping to reveal the childhood friend beneath.

"Sorry to drop by unannounced," I said, suddenly feeling more like the kid who used to tug her pigtails in Ms. Riley's second-grade class than the man who just helped take down a sitting U.S. senator.

Mya stepped outside, pulling the door shut behind her. The morning sun caught her profile, casting soft light on cheekbones that looked sharper than I remembered.

"After everything that happened, you think I mind?" she asked.

"I wanted to thank you." My voice dipped into a deeper, more serious tone. "For sticking your neck out, risking your job, your name . . . your life, even. Most people would've walked away."

She didn't flinch. "I wasn't gonna let them bury you. Not when I knew the truth was within reach." She paused with a hint of a smile. "Besides, exposing corruption at the highest level? That's exactly why I became a journalist."

"Still . . ." I reached out, fingertips lightly touching her arm. "You didn't just chase a story. You stood up . . . for me."

"For us," she corrected softly. "Some truths matter more than the fallout. And yeah, I'd fight for any source. But I won't lie. The fact that it was you? That changed things."

Her words settled between us, quiet but undeniable.

"I'm heading out today," I said after a few seconds. "Back home. The dust has settled, and D.C. ain't my kind of town anyway."

For a moment, her expression changed. It was just a flash, but I caught it: a look of regret, or maybe it was just that complicated instant that comes when you realize that a chapter closes.

"I figured that's why you stopped by," she replied. "You've always been good at walking away once the mission's done."

"Maybe you'll come down to Waycross sometime," I offered, half teasing. "Write a feel-good feature on small-town charm."

She laughed. "You know I'm from there too, right? That makes me a local, not a tourist."

"Coulda fooled me," I said, smiling. "You talk like you're allergic to humidity and family reunions."

"Maybe I just need a tour guide," she said, her voice softening again. "Somebody who knows the good catfish spots and still remembers how I like my pickles sliced."

We stood there a moment longer with the world buzzing faintly in the distance: sirens and traffic. But here, on her porch, it felt like time had paused just for us.

I stepped closer, drawn in by something quiet and inevitable. Her scent, vanilla and amber, wrapped around me, familiar and new all at once. My hand rose, fingertips brushing her cheek.

"There's something I should've done the minute I saw you again," I whispered. "Something I should have done before you ever left Waycross."

Mya's eyes widened, but she didn't pull away. Instead, she tilted her face up toward me, an unspoken permission. "Better late than never, huh?"

The space between us vanished as I leaned in, capturing her mouth in a kiss that spoke of everything we hadn't said, years of history folded into a single breath. It wasn't rushed or uncertain. It was a knowing kind of kiss, born from childhood ties, missed chances, and the raw truth that only comes after walking through hell and making it out on the other side.

Her lips were soft, hesitant for just a second, then she leaned into me, matching the pressure with her own, like maybe she'd been waiting too. My hand slid from her cheek to the back of her neck, fingers carressing gently. For that moment, it was just us finally standing in the same place, wanting the same thing, at the same damn time.

The sharp blare of a car horn cracked the moment wide open, clean and sudden like a bullet through still glass. We broke apart just as I turned to see Lauryn leaning out the passenger window of the SUV, hair swinging as she raised an unimpressed brow. Her expression was a perfect mix of amusement and annoyance.

"Unless you plan on missing our flight and explaining to Ma why we're not home for Sunday dinner, we need to roll, big brother," she called, tapping her wrist dramatically even though she didn't have on a watch, in true Lauryn fashion.

I turned back to Mya, whose lips were slightly parted, a flush spreading across her cheekbones. She looked like every reason I didn't want to leave.

"I have to . . ." I started.

"Go," she said, finishing the sentence for me. Her hand slipped into mine, fingers tightening just once before letting go. "I know."

That simple understanding, that she knew me well enough to read me without resentment, made something twist in my chest. I grabbed her hand again, pressing it firmly between both of mine, grounding myself in her warmth for a just a few moments longer.

"This conversation ain't over," I promised.

"It better not be. Now, go before your sister leaves you on the curb and tells your mama you got caught up in D.C. drama . . . again," she teased with a smile.

I gave a quiet laugh, reluctant but real, then stepped back. Each step I took toward the SUV felt like the pavement itself was trying to pull me in the opposite direction back to her. When I slid into the driver's seat, Lauryn didn't even try to hide her smirk.

"Took you long enough," she said, buckling in like we were late for a mission. "I was starting to think I'd be flying solo and telling Ma you decided to stay in D.C. permanently."

I started the engine, glancing in the rearview mirror where I could just make out Mya still standing on her steps, watching us.

"Got what I needed," I said quietly.

"Mm-hmm," Lauryn hummed, her skepticism more playful than pointed. "Just so you know, Ma's gonna take one look at your face and know exactly what happened.

That woman's got a sixth sense for all her children's business."

"Wouldn't have it any other way," I said, easing away from the curb and merging into the slow churn of morning traffic.

As we made our way toward the airport, the city stretched and stirred to life around us. But for the first time in a long time, I felt something settle inside me. Not adrenaline or pressure. I'd finally found peace. It was quiet and steady, like a weight I hadn't even realized I'd been carrying had finally slid off my shoulders. Whatever waited for us back in Georgia, whether it was a new case or the unfinished business between me and Mya, I was ready for it.

My phone buzzed in the cup holder. I glanced down and saw the name: *Deputy Raynard Bradford.*

I grabbed it and answered. "Bradford."

His voice came through steady, no nonsense. "Just wanted to say thank you, Curtis. What you did, getting that evidence, helping take down Winbush. It was above and beyond."

I nodded to myself. "Just did what needed doing."

There was a pause, the kind that hinted he had more to discuss.

"You got a minute?"

"Depends," I said, glancing at the side mirror. "Am I still on vacation?"

Bradford gave a short laugh. "Afraid not. I've got another job for you."

Lauryn looked over, catching the shift in my tone. "What kind of job?"

"Name's Vinton Kane," Bradford continued. "Ex-military and contracted muscle. He's the one Winbush hired to kill Johnny Boy. And he's vanished off the map."

My jaw tightened.

"Feds want him alive," Bradford said. "I want him found."

I let the silence hang for a second, then finally said. "Send me everything you've got. I'll find him."

The line went dead. I dropped the phone back into the cup holder and exhaled slowly, eyes fixed on the road ahead. So much for a clean break and whatever quiet future I'd just started letting myself imagine with Mya. We'd barely scratched the surface of what could be, and now it had to wait. Again.

"Let me guess," Lauryn said, side-eyeing me. "That wasn't Ma asking if we wanted fried or baked chicken for Sunday dinner."

"Nope." I sighed, the gears already turning. "Bradford's got a new target. Name's Vinton Kane. He's the one who killed Johnny Boy."

Lauryn sat up straighter, her eyes narrowing. "The one who pulled the trigger?"

I nodded. "Yeah. And he's gone ghost."

She didn't hesitate. "Then I'm going with you."

"Lauryn . . ."

"No. Don't even try it." She turned fully toward me, fire rising behind her words. "You're not doing this alone, Curtis. Not after everything we've been through. You needed me then, and you need me now. I've got your back, just like always."

I kept my eyes on the road, jaw tight. She was right, and I knew it, but that didn't mean I wanted her anywhere near another damn bullet. Still, she was a Duncan, and she was my sister.

"Fine," I said, the word coming out like gravel. "But you follow my lead. This one's gonna get messy."

Lauryn cracked a smile and sat back, folding her arms with satisfaction. "Wouldn't have it any other way."

"Ma's gonna be pissed," I warned.

And with that, we drove off, two siblings, scarred but unbroken, ready to hunt a ghost.

The End